LOGAN'S WORD

A LOGAN FAMILY WESTERN - BOOK 1

DONALD L ROBERTSON

CM Publishing

COPYRIGHT

LOGAN'S WORD

Copyright © 2016 Donald L. Robertson
CM Publishing

Books@DonaldLRobertson.com

ISBN print: 978-0-9909139-0-0
ISBN ebook: 978-0-9909139-1-7

❀ Created with Vellum

PROLOGUE

October 19, 1864

Young Lieutenant Rory Nance lay dying in the fertile Shenandoah Valley. Moments before he had sat astride his cavalry mount, a striking figure—lieutenant in the United States Cavalry. Now he looked up at the men and horses of the Sixth Michigan Volunteer Cavalry as they milled about him. The river valley breeze cleared the air and pushed the stinging smell of gun smoke and blood from the battle scene. Dead and dying men, both blue and gray, and horses littered the normally tranquil forest floor with the carnage of war.

His best friend and troop commander, Major Josh Logan—Logan's tall body and wide shoulders weak from loss of blood—lifted Rory and laid him against the saddle of his dead horse. "You saved my life, Rory," Josh said as he kneeled alongside his friend.

"That almost makes us even," Rory whispered and grinned up at Josh, his even white teeth stained with blood. He gripped Josh's hand, and his eyes squeezed tight from pain. "That Rebel captain did me in, Josh. I think he surely did. Did I get him?"

Josh looked down on his good friend. "You got him, Rory."

They had survived this war together. Now, as the end was near-ing, he was watching his friend's life leak out onto the earth. "Rory, I've been almighty proud to be your friend."

Rory looked up. "Josh, I need you to do something for me."

"Anything."

"This war is almost over, and you're planning to head out and start your horse ranch in Colorado. Could you make a detour to Texas for me? I know it's out of your way, but my folks would feel some better hearing about this from you instead of the war department." A spasm of coughing racked his body, and frothy pink blood issued from his mouth and nose.

Josh could hear the sucking sound from the saber wound in Rory's chest. Josh answered without hesitation, "I give you my word, Rory."

Rory relaxed, leaned back against the saddle, and smiled. "We've had a good run, haven't we?" He was overcome with another spasm of coughing, and his voice grew weaker. "Thanks, Josh. Now ... I'd like to rest." Rory's grip on Major Joshua Logan's hand gradually relaxed. He took two more shallow breaths, and the hope of Texas Ranger Bill Nance and the big brother of Mary Louise Nance died in the beautiful Shenandoah Valley.

Josh continued to grip Rory's hand. He felt a hand on his shoulder. "Major, sir, Lieutenant Nance is dead for sure," Sergeant Pat O'Reilly said. "'Tis a sad thing, his dying. But you need to see to yourself. Your leg and your side are bleeding. It's now that we must attend to you."

"Alright, Sergeant," Josh said as he lay next to Rory, bracing his back against the dead horse.

"Did I hear you give your word you'll go to Texas?"

"Yes, you did, Pat."

"Sir, if you're planning to go to Colorado after this fighting is finished, that'll be quite a distance out of your way."

"Makes no difference, Pat. I gave my word to Rory, and I aim to keep it."

1

August 25, 1867

Joshua Matthew Logan reined the big gray Morgan to a stop, removed his US Cavalry hat, pushed back the black hair that had fallen into his eyes, and wiped sweat from his wide forehead. The scar across his forehead was becoming less pronounced as time passed. He'd been fortunate his opponent was dying when he made this last slash with the saber; otherwise Josh would have remained on the battlefield permanently. Below his pronounced cheekbones, where his hat offered less protection, his face was baked the color of a dry creek bed, the crevices filled with miles of Texas dust.

Slapping the hat back on his head, he kicked his right foot out of the stirrup, swung his long leg over the saddle, and, with a grace not usually seen in such a big man, stepped softly to the ground.

He pulled the water bag from the saddle and walked over to the shade, if you could call it shade, of a big mesquite tree. Shadows were starting to lengthen as the day was drawing to a close. He'd have to make camp soon. The big gray followed, pushing at the water bag.

"Chancy," he said as he rubbed the gray between the ears, "we've been together too long. I'm talking to you and you're bossing me. Now somehow that just don't seem right."

He slowly poured water into his hat and let the horse drink.

"That's enough for now," Josh said.

He took a small sip from the water bag, hung it over the worn saddle, and reached inside his saddlebags. He pulled out some beef jerky and a few oats for the gray. Josh closed the saddlebags and eased his rifle, a .44-caliber 1866 Winchester Yellow Boy, from its scabbard and walked slowly back to the tree.

The rifle had been a gift from a grateful gentleman, Mr. Nelson King. Josh wasn't of a mind to take the Winchester, as much as he liked it, but Mr. King wouldn't accept his refusal. So here he was, with the very best lever-action rifle the world had ever seen.

He gave the oats to his horse, squatted and leaned against the trunk of the tree, careful not to be jabbed by its daggerlike thorns. Josh laid the Winchester next to him, in easy reach should he need it quickly. Texas, in 1867, was only as safe as a man was careful.

Chewing slowly on the beef jerky, he shifted the Colt revolver hanging by his left hip into a more comfortable position and contemplated Chancy.

He and Chancy had seen the bear together. Josh had been there with all of the Logan clan—Pa, Ma, and his brothers and sister—when the horse had been born out of solid Morgan stock. That had been eight long years ago. He had been seventeen, almost three years before the war started. Even then people had been talking about independence and secession, and how folks in Tennessee had better get ready to stand up for their beliefs.

The gray's ears twisted forward, his gaze riveted on the western end of the mesquite thicket. Josh quietly reached for his rifle, stood and moved to his right, keeping the big tree between him and possible trouble.

Two riders were walking their horses slowly through the trees. He stepped out from behind the mesquite. His movement gave away his position, and for the first time the two riders saw him and his horse. They stopped, then turned and rode slowly toward him.

"Howdy," the smaller of the two men said. His twinkling eyes quickly sized up Josh and his horse. "Nice horse."

"He'll do," Josh replied. His rifle was draped casually in the crook of his right arm. It could be brought to bear instantly.

"You seem a mite cautious with that rifle, mister," the other man said. He was the bigger of the two riders, broad-shouldered and husky, with forearms jutting out of his rolled-up, dirty shirt-sleeves like fence posts.

Josh smiled icily. "Where I come from, if you're not a mite cautious, you could be a mite dead."

"Where do you come from?" the smaller man asked.

"Well, I might be more apt to speak of it if I knew who I was speaking to."

Twinkling eyes glanced at his partner, then back at Josh. He seemed to make up his mind, then grinned. "We ride for the Circle W. I'm Scott Penny, and this house-on-a-horse is Bull Westin. Bull's not much of a talker; guess I make up for both of us.

"We've been trailing some strays. Been some Indian activity hereabouts, and we mean to work those cattle closer to the ranch. Indians do like a young heifer or two if they're easy to come by.

"In fact, we were planning on making camp just a ways from here. It's getting late and we need to be moving on. You're welcome to join us if you like. Those Indians prefer easy pickin's, if you know what I mean."

Josh considered for a moment. Spending another night alone on the Texas prairie didn't bother him, even with the threat of Indians. He'd spent many a night alone in a dry camp over the past few years, but if he went with them, it would give him a chance to find out where this Circle W outfit was and maybe locate the Rocking N.

"My name's Logan, boys, Josh Logan, and I'd be much obliged for some company tonight. All the conversation I've had here lately has been with my horse. Course, that's not all bad. He don't talk back."

Josh Logan slid the Winchester Yellow Boy back into the scabbard and swung up into the saddle. He looked at Bull and said, "Reckon I've been traveling by myself so long that I might be getting just a mite cautious."

Bull looked sullenly at Josh for a moment before jerking his horse around into a walk. "It happens," he said gruffly.

There would be a full moon tonight, Josh noticed. The pale white orb rose early above the Texas prairie, looking balefully upon the three riders as they slowly followed the cattle trail. This was going to be a real Comanche moon tonight, bright enough to ride pell-mell across the prairie without fear of unseen gopher holes lying in wait to break a horse's leg or a man's neck, bright enough to take a white man's cattle, bright enough to take a white man's scalp.

"You're not from these parts," Scott Penny observed as they neared a small creek.

It was already getting dark under the thick canopy of pecan trees. The moonlight could hardly penetrate the overhead foliage.

"Nope," Josh replied as he examined the shadows beneath the trees. This was Pecan Bayou, he thought. His friend Rory Nance had spoken many times, during the war, of hunting along the Pecan and the Jim Ned. Jim Ned Creek should be another seven or eight miles west.

Scott Penny and Bull Westin dismounted in the pecan grove.

"We'll camp here tonight," Scott said. "There's water in the creek and plenty of grass for the horses."

"Fine," Josh said as he surveyed the area.

The cut bank of the creek was about fifteen yards away. The creek bottom was rocky and the whole area was covered with old dry pecan leaves and hulls. It was fairly clear of underbrush beneath the trees, but the outer edges of the creek were lined with thick brambles and broomweed.

No one, not even the stealthiest Comanche, could slip quietly through these leaves. The campsite would be well hidden from any observers outside the pecan grove. It would be almost impossible to see into the depths of the grove through the bramble perimeter.

"You picked a good campsite," Josh told Scott.

"Thanks," Scott said grinning at Josh through the deepening darkness.

Josh turned his horse so his back wouldn't be toward the other two men and dismounted, an act that didn't go unnoticed. He rapidly stripped his bedroll and saddlebags from Chancy, then laid the Winchester on the saddlebags and removed the saddle and blanket. After rubbing the horse down and watering him, he staked him out with sufficient rope to feed. He spread his bedroll and sat down, leaning back against his saddle.

Not far down the creek, turkeys could be heard yelping as they walked toward their roost. In a few moments, the crashing and clucking began as they flew up into the big pecan trees, hitting limbs and jockeying for position high above the ground, also above any marauding coyotes or bobcats. They continued to cluck and fuss as they settled down for the night.

"At least we don't have to worry about Indians coming from down the creek," Scott said, listening to the clamor of the turkeys.

"Maybe," Josh said. He picked up the Winchester and worked the lever, throwing out the round in the chamber and driving in a fresh one. Picking up the ejected round, he examined it and slid it back into the rifle's magazine, confirming the magazine was full and there was a round in the chamber. He lowered the hammer on the rifle and laid it aside. Drawing the Model 1860 .44 Colt

Army, he checked all the loads carefully before finally sliding it back into the holster. With both weapons checked, he relaxed against the saddle.

"You expectin' trouble?" Bull asked.

"I never expect trouble. But if it comes looking for me, I aim to be ready," Josh replied.

"You never said where you're from."

"Bull, I assume that's what everybody calls you, you're right. I didn't. Not that it's any of your business; I'm from Tennessee— northern Tennessee."

Bull glared at Josh through the deepening darkness. "I need a smoke," Bull said. He pulled out his tobacco sack and matches.

"You've got a choice," Josh said. "You can go down into the creek bottom, where the light won't be seen, or you can chew it, but don't light it. I crossed Indian sign about a mile back from where we met. They were Comanches and traveling light, probably spoilin' for a fight."

"He's right, Bull," Scott said. "You never know where those Comanches could be. We sure don't want to wake up with our hair hanging on some Indian's lance."

"We're back here in this thicket," Bull said. He rolled the cigarette, put it in his mouth, took out a match, and started to strike the match on his gun-belt buckle.

"Ain't nobody goin' to see us. Anyway, no Yankee drifter is tellin' me when I can or can't have a smo—"

A sickening hollow thud sounded as Josh's rifle butt struck Bull just above the jawbone. He hadn't seen nor had he sensed the speed with which Josh Logan picked up his Winchester by the barrel and backhanded Bull with the stock. The unlit match and cigarette fell silently to the ground.

"Mister, you could kill a man hitting him like that," Scott said.

"He could have killed us if he'd lit that match. I'll not abide stupidity. Specially if it might get me killed."

"Well, I sure wouldn't want to be in your boots. He's gonna be madder than a wet hen when he wakes up."

Josh looked at the crumpled and bleeding figure at his feet. "He won't have far to look. I'll be right here." He turned slightly so he was facing Scott. "If you've a mind to deal yourself into this hand, now's the time."

"No siree bob. That was all his doing. I reckon you might have saved my hair tonight, and I've no call to be put out about that."

"In that case," Josh asked as he returned to his bedroll and sat down. "I wonder if you might answer some questions for me?"

"Well, sure, I'll try. I do a lot of talking, but I don't usually have a lot of answers."

"How long have you been working for the Circle W?"

"It's been a little over a month. Just drifted in from Fredericksburg way. Had an itch to move north—maybe on up to Colorado Territory. Understand there's some gold showing up in those mountains west of Colorado City. So anyway, I needed a little stake since I lost most of my money in a card game down in Brownwood, and I heard the Circle W was hiring. So I—"

"Whoa, slow down, Scott. I didn't ask for your life's history; I just need a little information."

"Uh, yeah, that's been my problem. Pa always said that if words were an axe, I could clear a section of land in a day's time. Anyway, I been working one month at the Circle W. That's where I met Bull Westin. He's been riding for them quite a while."

"Scott, have you heard of the Rocking N?"

"The Rocking N? Yeah, I have. Why?"

Josh ignored Scott's question. "What can you tell me about them?"

"I don't know much," Scott said. "Seems Mr. Nance, he came out here from around San Antone 'bout '45 or '46. From what I hear, he was tougher than an old boar coon, what with all that rangerin' he did.

"He brought his wife and kids. Didn't have but two, a boy and a girl. Plus he pushed up, so the story goes, about a thousand head of those rangy longhorns he choused out of the brush south of San Antone. Supposedly he was big friends with Sam Houston, though I don't know that for a fact, being's I've just been around here for a short while."

Josh leaned back against his saddle, suppressing a grin. For being around such a short while, Scott Penny had certainly picked up a lot of information, some of it more accurate than Scott was aware.

The night had cooled into a comfortable evening. A light breeze was blowing, rustling the leaves on the pecan trees and carrying away the afternoon heat. Nearby an armadillo shuffled through the pecan leaves, searching for grubs and ants. A family of coyotes serenaded the moon as it shone over the hills to the east. The solitude spoke to him, as it had spoken to many of his warrior ancestors on the Scottish moors so many years before.

Through the brambles and sagebrush he could see the prairie surrounding the grove, bright in the light of the moon, peaceful for now. Hopefully it would stay that way. Josh had no desire to confront those Comanche braves. It was obvious from their tracks that they were traveling light and looking for blood. It was his aim to make sure it wasn't his. For that reason, he had moved quickly when Bull started to light that cigarette.

Josh had known from the minute he first saw Bull there would be trouble. Bull reminded him of another man, a sergeant who ran roughshod over his men and intended to do the same with the new shavetail second lieutenant who had taken over the command. The sergeant was a big barrel-chested man, like Bull, with shoulders wide from hard work and knuckles scarred from many a brawl. When he challenged Logan to join him behind the camp and shed his blouse, he was surprised to see the youngster turn, without a word, and stride toward the rear of the camp.

Josh thought about what Pa had told them all, on many occasions, that to go looking for a fight was a fool's errand, for you would surely find one; but if a fight came to you, you'd best get on with it, for it wouldn't go away.

Pa backed this up by teaching all the boys how to fight with their hands, arms, feet, and head, something he'd learned from a Frenchman he'd met down New Orleans way when he was with Andy Jackson. Then the boys practiced among themselves until tempers would flare and Pa would step in.

The sergeant didn't know that. All he could see was a big rawboned youth, barely on the high side of twenty, easy pickings for a barroom brawler like himself. By the time he realized he'd bitten off more than he could chew, it was too late. His face carried the scars of his mistake until a Minié ball from a Reb's musket snuffed his life out six months later.

Josh knew he wasn't through with Bull. The man would have to try him now or later. It was a thing that would have to be finished. Bull had been dealt a blow not only to his head, but also to his pride. No man could continue to live in this country, this wild, prideful land, without defending his honor.

"So how far is the Rocking N from here?" Josh asked.

"Well, sir," Scott responded with a nod, "it depends on who you ask. My boss says it's about a half day's ride from here. But according to Mr. Nance, you're on Rocking N range right now."

2

Josh woke to the turkeys' yelping as they greeted the West Texas morning. He came awake quickly, scanned the area in the dim early morning light, picked up his rifle, and stood. As soon as he moved, Scott Penny woke and looked around.

"I could sure use a cup of ranch house coffee right now, as bad as it is," Scott said.

Josh went to his horse, saddled him, and slid the Winchester into its scabbard. As quietly as possible, he walked Chancy down to the creek for water. While the gray drank, he filled the water bag and his canteen, then went back up to the camp. Bull was awake, sitting where he had fallen.

Blood had clotted on Bull's left cheek just below the hairline. His left eye was black and swollen almost completely closed.

Scott Penny was saddling his horse and chewing slowly on a piece of venison jerky. He turned to Josh with a wink. "Bull here's not feelin' too shiny."

Bull turned his head so that he could fix Logan with his right eye. "You're gonna pay for this one," he said, rubbing his right fist in his left hand. His shoulder muscles bulged under his dirty shirt.

"Anytime you're ready, Bull," Josh said. He waited for a moment, then deliberately turned his back on Bull. "Scott, how far a ride is it to the Rocking N ranch house?"

"'Bout a half day's ride south by west will put you on their doorstep."

"Then I'll be leaving you boys. Watch out for the Comanches. I've a feelin' they're not too far away."

Josh heard the rush of feet in the pecan leaves behind him. He spun to his left, filling his hand with the Colt. Bull was caught in mid-stride.

Josh could see the bloodlust in Bull's eyes. The man wanted to hurt him. He'd seen brawlers like Bull; they waited until a man's back was turned, then attacked. Josh waited for the man to make a decision. Bull didn't appear to be a fast thinker. He was probably weighing his chances. He didn't want to, but if Bull kept coming, he'd kill him; but the man had frozen as still as a block of ice.

He looked calmly at Bull over the muzzle of the Colt. "You have an almighty urge to die, mister. But this isn't the time nor the place. I'll tell you this much; you ever try to jump me like that again, and I'll hole you where you stand. Now drop your gun, real easy, and go hunker down by that tree."

Bull dropped his gun, turned around, moved over to the pecan tree, and sat down. Josh watched the man. He'd been humiliated twice. Josh realized Scott was a talker. He'd have the whole story about Bull spread across the prairie in no time. Bull would become a laughingstock. Well, he'd brought it on himself.

Josh raised a hand to Scott, eased down into the creek bed, and mounted the horse. He could feel the big gray's muscles quiver as he settled into the saddle. What more could a man ask than to be on horseback in a free, wild land like this Texas. He eased Chancy up to the crest of the mesquite-covered hillside just high enough to see over the top. He was only a half mile from the pecan grove where they had camped. He hadn't seen any movement as he rode out of the grove, but a man kept his hair by being careful.

The hill was a plateau that ran west as far as he could see. Mesquite and prickly pear cactus covered the rocky plateau. Occasionally an island of scrub oak provided a haven for deer, javelina, or marauding Comanches.

A family of white-tailed deer browsed contentedly. The two fawns still wore their spotted coats. They wouldn't be around if Indians were holed up nearby. The doe's head shot up as Josh rode over the crest. She watched him for a few moments as he drew nearer, then with a flick of her tail admonishing the fawns to follow, she trotted out of sight.

Only a few yards in from the edge of the hill, Logan saw the Comanche sign. Ten or twelve braves had passed by here last night. The horse droppings were crusting over, but still soft. All the horses were unshod, which meant they hadn't raided anywhere yet. At least, they hadn't captured any horses, and that was a Comanche's passion—horses; horses and killing.

It was interesting, Josh thought, how city folks believed Indians wouldn't fight at night. Night was the ally of the Comanche. When the summer night winds blew across the prairie under a full moon, he rode with blood in his eye and lust in his heart. The Comanche was the best light cavalry who ever sat a horse.

Josh sat relaxed but alert in his saddle as he rode southwest. Survival in this country meant spotting the other fellow first, and that was just what he aimed to do. He had covered thousands of miles on the back of this horse in this same manner, both of them alert for danger. They had been together through some happy and some terrifying times.

Now he had a mission to complete for a friend; a friend who whetted his curiosity with his talk of Texas, of the land

and of the people; a friend who had talked of Stephen Austin, Sam Houston, and even a lieutenant colonel in the United States Cavalry stationed in Texas, Robert E. Lee; a friend who spoke of his younger sister and his concern for her in this harsh but beautiful land; a friend who had brought to him the magic of this land; a friend who died on the point of an enemy's saber.

Chancy had carried Josh into that battle, and now he carried him to the family of Rory Nance.

THE VALLEY WAS at least five miles long, with hills rising from the northern and southern edges. In the bottom, near the southern side, a wide creek flowed southeast. It was covered with heavily laden pecan trees. Even from this distance, he could hear the racket of the red fox squirrels fussing over the green pecans.

The ranch house was on a shelf about fifty feet above the creek bed, well above the high-water mark. It backed up against a small hill that rose out of the valley floor. The two-story lime-stone house was solidly built. Josh admired the way the stone bunkhouse and the ranch house provided good fields of fire for each other. The barn and corrals, across from the house, were well maintained. It looked like Bill Nance believed in taking care of his property.

"Come on, Chancy," Josh said. "We'd best get on with it. The quicker we finish here, the sooner we can be on our way to Colorado."

The big gray horse nodded as if it understood as they started down the hill. It had been a long and tiring trip since they had left Ma and Pa back in the Tennessee hills. The horse sensed they were near a resting place.

Josh pulled up at the hitching rail in front of the rock fence that surrounded the house. The ranch seemed deserted. He had seen no one as he rode up, yet there was no indication of damage or of a fight.

Maybe everyone had left the ranch for the fort because of the Indian reports. He immediately dismissed that thought. From what Rory had told him about Mr. Nance, a report of Indians wouldn't faze him, even a little bit.

Chancy's ears twisted around trying to pinpoint a sound too faint for human ears. Josh also felt it. He didn't know where this ability came from, maybe from some old Scot ancestor, but he knew he had it, and he'd learned to trust it—too many times during the war it had saved his bacon. Rory had always said he was like a cat with nine lives, but Josh knew it was this uncanny ability to know when he was being watched that had saved him.

This time his sixth sense had been slow. Now he was sitting in the open with his Colt snubbed down and his rifle in the scabbard. If whoever was watching was a tad unfriendly, he was going to be in deep trouble.

He heard the sharp metallic click from behind as a hammer reached its full-cocked position. The horse heard it, too. Josh could feel the horse's muscles tense beneath him. They had been in trouble together many times before, and each felt the other's tension.

"*Buenas tardes, señor.* Please do not make a sudden move, for I am an old *vaquero,* and I tend to nervousness. If you move suddenly, you might cause me to jump, and if I jump, I might accidentally touch the trigger on this old and worn Sharps, and it might blow a big hole in your back—right between your shoulder blades. So if I were you, I would sit very still."

"Mister, that borders on being one of the most unfriendly greetings I've ever had," Josh said as he concentrated on sitting perfectly still. "I can tell you, that hitchin' post will move before I do."

"*Bueno hombre*, that's some smart thinking."

"Miss Nance," the *vaquero* called, "you want I should take this *hombre* away from here?"

Josh was thinking how he didn't particularly like the thought of being taken anywhere. In fact, he was starting to get mad—real mad. He had come here to help, to pay a debt, and now he was being treated like a thief. He didn't like it at all.

"Now listen, mister. I've ridden a long way for a good friend. I don't reckon a gun in my back is the reception I'd get if Rory were here."

The ranch house door burst open as an attractive young woman carrying a big Colt .44 dashed breathlessly up to his horse.

"Do you know Rory?" she asked. "His last letter was almost two years ago."

Josh looked down at the young blonde with sky blue eyes. He realized she didn't know about her brother.

3

"Yes, ma'am, I knew Rory," Josh said. "But I could talk a heap better if that Sharps wasn't dead center on my back."

"Oh, I'm sorry," she said. "Juan, please lower your rifle."

"*Señorita*, we don't know this man. It's obvious he's not from around here. I recommend we be very cautious of him," Juan said as he reluctantly lowered the rifle.

Josh heard the hammer click as it was lowered to the safe position. He relaxed and turned around to look steadily at the man who, for a few moments, controlled his life. His appraisal was met, and returned, with an equally level stare. Josh decided that from what he could tell so far, Mr. Nance knew how to pick men.

"Ma'am, I'm Joshua Matthew Logan. I rode with your brother under General Grant's command."

"Mr. Logan, I must apologize once again—I haven't introduced myself. I'm Mary Louise Nance, and the cautious man with the rifle is Juan Alvarez, a truly dear friend."

Josh stepped down from the horse. He noticed the elderly Alvarez had visibly relaxed when Josh introduced himself.

Alvarez must be a close friend to the Nance family to be privy to Rory's letters.

Juan stepped forward and extended his hand. "*Señor* Rory is a good friend, and I know you are his good friend. Welcome to the Rocking N."

Mary Louise said, "Please come in, Mr. Logan, and tell us all about Rory. Oh, I'm forgetting my manners again. You must be tired and hungry after such a long journey. You can clean up and we'll get you something to eat. Papa should be back by then, and I'm just dying to hear about Rory."

"Well, ma'am, that's mighty nice of you. But first I'd like to take care of my horse. Then I'd truly be pleased to wash off this trail dust and sit down to a home-cooked meal."

"*Señor* Logan"—Alvarez stepped forward and grasped Chancy's bridle—"I'd be honored if you would allow me to take care of this fine animal."

Josh started to tell him to be careful, for the big gray was finicky about who handled him, but Chancy nuzzled the older man as if he'd known him forever.

"*Señor* Alvarez, I was goin' to tell you to be careful, but it looks like you've made a friend. Would you put him off by himself, since he's a stud horse."

"I like horses, *Señor,* and most of them like me, and yes, I will keep him away from our other horses. *Por favor, Señor*, call me Juan."

"Juan it is, then," Josh said. "I answer to Josh or Logan. Thanks." He turned to Mary Louise and said, "Ma'am, I'd be much obliged if you could forget the mister. I'm not much for titles. Just call me Josh."

"Why, Mister—uh, Josh—thank you. Won't you please come in now?"

Josh followed her into the house. Rory had talked about his sister a great deal. Logan had never been much with the ladies. When he was younger, he was always too busy working, hunting or fishing, always finding a reason to be with his pa or his brothers in the Tennessee forests. As he grew, he came to realize that he wasn't a handsome man, as men go. He was too big, too awkward around women. The saber cut across his forehead didn't help any either, but mostly, he just never knew what to say.

Before he was barely grown, the war came along, and for almost five years it occupied his every waking hour. Now here he was, in the home of this beautiful young woman, about to break her heart with the news of her brother's death.

"Teresa," Mary called to the kitchen.

A large Mexican woman came into the living room from the kitchen. Her jet-black hair, shot with traces of gray, was pulled back and pinned at the back of her head. She held a dish she was busily drying. A wide smile lit her face as she saw Josh.

"I have ears, Mary," she said. "I know this is our little Rory's friend. We'll have another place for dinner. Now I'll heat some *agua*, for I see Mr. Logan needs a bath—*badly*."

"Thank you, ma'am," Josh said as Teresa walked back to the kitchen.

"Where's Mr. Nance and the rest of your ranch hands?" he asked as Mary led him to a small room adjoining the kitchen. A dresser and a chair were against one wall, with a real honest-to-goodness mirror above the dresser. In the middle of the room sat a big bathtub.

"This is our bathroom," Mary announced proudly. "Father put this in right after Rory left."

She had a right to be proud, Josh thought. There were few homes that had the space to have one room devoted only to taking baths. In fact, there were doggone few homes that even had bathtubs. Why, the only baths he ever had at home were in a washtub when he was young, and later in the river when he grew too big.

"Mighty nice, ma'am."

"I wish you'd stop calling me ma'am, Josh."

"Mary," Josh asked, "where's Mr. Nance?"

"Oh yes," she said, "you asked me that a while ago. Father took some horses down to Brownwood. He should be back for supper. Brownwood's about a half day's ride."

"Here's the hot water," Teresa announced as she marched in from the kitchen. "Supper will be ready soon, so don't dawdle. Come on, Mary, *Señor* Nance should be back soon, and *Señor* Logan can tell us all about Rory then."

"Thank you, ma'am," Josh said as Teresa ushered Mary out of the room, closing the door behind her.

JOSH FELT LIKE A NEW MAN. The hot water had washed away the trail dust and tension. Now his muscles were relaxed as he dressed. He was pulling on his boots when he heard the horses riding up in the yard. The moment he'd been dreading was close at hand. He'd ridden hundreds of miles to do this for a friend. He must have rehearsed what he was going to say a thousand times.

It wasn't like this was new to him. He'd had a lot of practice with all the letters he'd written to loved ones of men killed in his company. He had even told a few fathers and wives in person, but never had it been someone this close. He took a deep breath and opened the door.

Bill Nance was talking to his daughter as Josh opened the bathroom door. Nance turned and strode toward Josh, his hand extended.

"Welcome to the Rocking N—what there is left of it," he said ruefully. "I'm Bill Nance. The few letters we received from Rory sure spoke highly of you. We're mighty proud to have you here."

Josh took the extended hand. "I'm pleased to meet you, Mr. Nance. Rory talked about you all the time."

"Call me Bill," Nance said. "Now let's eat. You can tell us all about Rory and what he was up to when you last saw him. We figured he would probably have made it home by now. But there's many a mile between Virginia and Texas."

Josh could see that Bill Nance knew something had happened to his son, but this was a strong man. He couldn't have survived and accomplished all that he had without great inner strength. That was what it took to settle this great country. Without men like Bill Nance, everyone would still be back in Europe, talking about coming to the new world. This country had been built by men of strength and action, men like Bill Nance.

Rory had told Josh, as they sat around camp on those lonely nights, how his father had traveled to New Orleans when he was only nineteen. There he had spent a couple of years accumulating a handsome stake.

Bill Nance had met Stephen F. Austin in New Orleans, and Austin wove his magic as he talked about Texas. He told Nance he'd been awarded a large land grant by the Mexican government and was looking for a few brave men to come to Texas and settle there. He told him about the wild land. There were buffalo that moved south during the winter. They were so thick a man could walk across their backs for miles and never put boot to dirt.

In southwest Texas, along the Rio Grande near Reynosa, Mexico, there were wild cattle for the taking, cattle that had been brought to Texas by Colonel Jose de Escandon when he attempted to settle the north country in 1749. He established several towns along the southern side of the Rio Grande, but those Mexican ranchers on the north side, in Texas, were continually harassed, killed, and finally driven out by the Comanches and Apaches, leaving their cattle behind.

Austin had given this adventurous young man a Texas transfusion. He would never again be the same. Austin, a man of vision, had seen beneath the surface and recognized the fierce determination that drove Bill Nance. He needed men like him in his new Texas. He also saw something else. He saw the integrity that lived in the heart of this man.

Josh thought it wasn't hard to picture Bill Nance as Austin must have seen him. The tall man who sat before him now was older. His hair was white. His face was a dark brown map of his adventures, baked by the many years in the Texas sun. But there still burned, behind those hard blue eyes, that same fierce determination that Austin must have recognized when, in 1822, he had persuaded Bill Nance to come with him back to Texas.

"Josh," Nance said, "Teresa's fixed a mighty fine meal. Let's go on in and have a seat. Everybody's anxious to hear about Rory."

Josh walked into the kitchen, where everyone waited. Teresa fussed around getting all the food on the table while Nance seated Mary. Josh sat next to Nance, facing Mary across the table. Juan was there with a couple of cowhands Josh hadn't met. He figured they must have driven the horses to Brownwood with Bill Nance. That was still a mighty small crew for a ranch this size.

"Josh, those two boys at the end of the table are Frank Milman and Lee Stanton," Bill Nance said. "Lee's first name is Leander, but don't call him that. He's not very fond of the name."

The cowboys nodded and Lee said, "Mr. Nance, you know I'm partial to Lee. My mother liked Leander; I never could figure why."

As everybody pitched in, Bill Nance said sharply, "Well, Josh, I guess you'd better git to it."

Mary looked questioningly from her father to Josh. There was something in her father's voice. The constant clamor, so common to a ranch house kitchen at dinnertime, suddenly ceased. An ominous quiet settled over the people assembled at the table as they all turned expectantly to Josh.

Josh looked closely at Mary. Her dark eyebrows lifted questioningly as she looked from him to her father and back.

"Bill, I left Rory near Cedar Creek, Virginia, in the Shenandoah Valley. It was the Battle of Cedar Creek. Don't know if you heard about it or not. We were assigned to escort General Sheridan back to his headquarters. He'd been in Washington, meeting with Secretary of War Edwin M. Stanton. General Early's troops attacked our lines the morning of October 19, 1864. When General Sheridan received the message, we rushed back to find our lines retreating and in turmoil. The general turned the troops around and attacked. We were detailed to find and attack Early's cavalry."

Josh looked around the table. The cowhands sat quietly listening. Those boys probably fought on the Confederate side. Josh wondered what they must think, sitting at this table, eating with a Yankee they would have gladly gunned down only a short time ago, and still might if they got half a chance.

He looked again at Mary. He could see the concern on her face, but it was obvious she hadn't yet considered the possibility that Rory might be dead.

"We had them on the run," Josh continued, "but those boys were real fighters. We cornered almost a troop in a bend of Cedar Creek. They decided to fight it out, probably figured it would be impossible to make it across the river alive. I'll give it to them. They had guts. They turned, formed a skirmish line, and charged right back at us. Why, that was some of the hardest fighting I'd been in throughout the whole war. Both sides emptied their handguns. It was man to man, saber to saber. We had them outnumbered, but they fought like demons."

Josh took a deep breath. He knew he had to tell this, but it was like being back there. He could hear the screams of men and horses, the crash of steel on steel, and feel his lungs and eyes burning from the stench of blood and gunpowder.

He could see Rory with his Colt Army in his left hand, swinging his saber with his right. Rory was on his left, fighting like a man possessed. A Reb sergeant took the full force of Rory's saber at the base of his neck. It almost cut him in half. Rory jerked the blade out and thrust it through the side of another Reb about to cut down one of his men.

The fighting was thick and fast. Horses and men were down,

screaming from gunshot and saber wounds. Josh had been shot in his left leg. It didn't feel like it was broken, but it was bleeding like crazy. He remembered hoping the bullet hadn't hit his horse. Several Rebs had Josh busy. He shot one in the face, the bullet striking just below a scar under his right eye. Josh felt the searing pain of a glancing blow along his ribs. He forced himself to turn in the saddle, for he was growing weak from loss of blood, and with his last ounce of strength, thrust his saber clean through the wide-eyed young Confederate cavalryman who had dealt the blow.

"Bill," Josh said, "I sure hate to upset the womenfolk with this. There's some left, and it surely gets worse."

"Go ahead, Josh," Bill Nance said sadly. "This is family, and it begs to be said."

"Well, I was in pretty bad shape. I'd taken a bullet in the leg and had my ribs sliced open. I was losing a lot of blood and getting mighty weak. When I stuck the last Reb, his horse reared. I was so weak my saber was jerked clean out of my hand. My revolvers were empty, and there was this big Reb captain bearing down on me at full gallop. I reckoned I was a sure goner. All I could do was hang on to Chancy as the Reb bore down on me. I knew my time was surely up. Then Rory appeared out of the smoke. The last I'd seen him, he'd had his hands full. Now, there he was cutting between me and that big Reb captain. Neither of them slowed. Both horses went down when they hit."

Josh turned and looked squarely at Bill Nance. "Bill, your son saved my life. Rory's blade hit that captain straight through the heart, but he took the Reb's thrust in the upper chest."

Mary was sobbing uncontrollably into her apron as Teresa, with tears slowly coursing down her cheeks, tried to comfort the girl. Bill Nance was having a hard time. His big brown hands were quivering, and his jaw muscles were knotted, but his eyes were clear. Juan sat quietly, a deep sadness etched across his wrinkled old face.

"That was the last of the fighting," Josh continued. "I fell off my horse and dragged myself over to Rory. He was still alive, but in bad shape. I lifted him as best I could and rested him against his dead horse. 'Josh, I ain't got long,' Rory told me. 'I know you been talkin' about goin' to Colorado. But maybe you could make a little detour down through Texas. You can't take me back, but you can take a message to my folks. Tell them I was buried in the Shenandoah Valley alongside some mighty brave men, both blue and gray. But tell 'em my heart's in Texas ...' He never finished. For he died right then."

Josh sat back and took a deep breath. He had lost a good friend in the Cedar Creek fight, but these folks had lost family.

Mary suddenly pushed her chair back from the table. Her eyes were red and her face streaked from tears. She glared at her father. "If it hadn't been for you and Sam Houston, Rory might be alive today. All you talked about since I can remember was Texas joining and preserving the Union. Well, I don't give a tinker's damn about the Union. I just want my brother back."

Then she turned back to Josh and fixed him with an icy stare. "And you, Mr. Joshua Matthew Logan, you caused my brother's death. If you hadn't been his friend, and he hadn't looked up to you so, he might be sitting here at this table instead of you!" With tears streaming down her face, Mary ran to her room.

"Excuse me, *Señor* Nance," Teresa said. "I must go to her. She's very upset. You know she worshipped her brother. But she doesn't mean what she said. *Señor* Josh, I'm so sorry. Thank you for coming."

Bill Nance looked around the table. Frank and Lee stared at their plates, embarrassed by Mary's outburst, and Juan sat gazing out the window at the darkening hillside.

"You boys go ahead and finish supper," Bill said. "No sense letting good food go to waste. We have a busy day ahead of us tomorrow. I'm going to step outside. Josh, would you join me? You too, Juan, when you finish."

"I am finished now, *Señor*. It will do me good to be outside."

Josh followed Nance out the door. It was another cloudless night. The moon was bright enough to make out the hilltop overlooking the ranch where he'd been just hours before. They walked to the rock fence surrounding the house, checked for rattlesnakes, and sat down. Josh figured that from Mary's response, he might as well plan on riding out in the morning. It was a shame she felt like that, but a man would have better luck reasoning with a bobcat as trying to reason with a woman when she had her mind set. He'd just pack up and head on for Colorado in the morning.

"Josh, what are your plans now that you've delivered Rory's message?" Bill Nance asked.

"Bill, I'm riding up into Colorado Territory. There's some land out there that an uncle purchased. My older brother, Callum, is headed directly from Tennessee. He and I left home together and parted in Nashville. He'll be by himself until I get there. I'd like to be there before the first snow flies. There's a massive amount of work that must be done to get the ranch going before winter sets in. I'm planning on crossing Chancy with the Spanish mustang breed. I'm thinking the endurance of the Spanish, plus the speed of the Morgan should produce quite a horse. Chancy and I've been together since before I left home for the war, and I thought after we got to Colorado, I'd just let him relax and enjoy himself. He brought me through some tough scrapes, and I reckon he's almost like family."

"He is an excellent horse, *Señor*," Juan said. "I know a little about horseflesh, and I have seen few like him. He should make you plenty of fine horses."

"Josh," Nance said, "for the past year we've been having some problems. The Indians have always been a problem, but you expect that out here. About a year ago, we started missing cattle. That was around the time that the Circle W ranch moved in. Now I can't prove anything, but they've been increasing their herd size pretty fast. The owner, Jake Ruffcarn, has tried to buy me out a couple of times. This ranch is not for sale. Now that he's brought in some gunhands, I reckon I've got a good idea what he'll try next. But he won't get this ranch—not while I'm still alive."

"Yeah, I've met a couple of his men," Josh said. "One of 'em, a guy by the name of Bull, was a mite unfriendly."

"If you had a run-in with Bull Westin, you'd best watch your back. The man is a brawler and a back-shooter. If someone doesn't shoot him first, he'll eventually stretch a rope."

Bill Nance took out his pipe and tobacco. He sat quietly in the moonlight while he packed the tobacco into his pipe. He didn't light it, but put it into the corner of his mouth. "Josh, like a lot of people, we had it kinda rough during the war, what with me siding with Sam Houston, then Rory going off to fight for the North. Now I'm not complaining. Lots of folks had it much worse than us. We made it through fine. But since the war's been over, we have a new kind of trash moving into Texas. They're speculators and carpetbaggers.

"They're here to rape the state, get rich quick, and get out. I hate to say it, but it looks like the army's backing them up. I figure that this Jake Ruffcarn is one of them. You know if it looks like a snake, crawls like a snake, and bites like a snake, it's pretty easy to figure out—it must be a snake."

Josh sat quietly on the rock wall, listening to Nance. He hadn't planned on staying long, maybe just a few days to let the horse rest up, but this was Rory's family. Even if his sister wished Josh were dead, they still needed help. The fact they had only two cowhands working the ranch indicated that most folks around here didn't cotton to what they saw as Yankee sympathizers.

Well, he'd just hear Bill Nance out. Maybe there was some way he might help without staying too long. There was the fort where Nance had taken the horses. He might just ride up there and have a little discussion with the colonel. Anyway, Nance hadn't asked him to stay yet.

"Josh, I guess what I'm saying is I need some help. Juan and I have been around some, and we can sure take care of ourselves. But we only have two fellers workin' for us. They're good cowhands, but they ain't gunfighters. The closest help, not counting the fort, is Duke Jackson down at the Gap. He opened his operation about three or four years ago. But he's about a day's ride and he has his own ranch to take care of, specially since it's that Comanche time of year.

"I'm surprised they haven't hit us yet. It boils down to the fact that we're up against the Indians and Ruffcarn. So, if you could see your way clear, I'd be much obliged if you'd hang around for a while. At least until things settle down."

There it was. If he didn't get moving pretty soon, the snow would catch him long before he could get to Colorado, and Callum would be stuck doing all the work alone, but these folks were Rory's family, and they were in a tough situation. The only thing was, Mary sure didn't want him around here. She'd made that pretty clear.

"What about Mary? She didn't seem too pleased about me being here, and I reckon my staying won't sit too well either."

"Josh," Bill Nance said, "you've got to understand, she and her brother were real close. After their mother died, Rory took his sister under his wing. He virtually raised her until Teresa came along. I was gone a lot, rangerin' during that time. So now she's hurting real bad. I kinda figured something might have happened to Rory since we hadn't heard from him. Then when you showed up, I knew you wouldn't be by yourself if he was still alive. So I was expectin' it. I don't think it ever entered her mind that he might be killed. He was bigger than life to her. Now she's had a terrible shock. But she's strong; she'll get past this. Why, one of these days, she'll thank you for staying."

Josh thought about it for a moment more. A light breeze drifted up from the south, bringing the faint sour-sweet smell of a skunk. Something must have frightened it. A fox barked on the creek. Josh did like this country. He could understand why, so many years before, Bill Nance could have been entranced by the tales of Austin.

"Okay, Bill, I'll stay for a while, at least till we get this Ruffcarn thing sorted out."

"Good," Nance said. "I've done a lot of rangerin' and fightin' in my time. But Juan and I are getting older. Rory wrote about your campaigns and tactics. I liked what I read. I want you to be foreman. You run the show. Just tell me what you need."

Josh looked at Nance and Alvarez thoughtfully. "I appreciate the confidence. I'll do my best. First thing we need are some more men—good men, not just gunslingers. I'll leave for Camp Wilson tomorrow and look around."

Bill Nance stuck out his hand. "Fine, Josh. Welcome to the Rocking N. I'll tell the boys right now."

"No, don't tell anyone yet, not even Mary," Josh said. "When I ride into Camp Wilson and do a little checking around, it'll be on my own. I'm kinda curious how this colonel finds himself so able to side with Ruffcarn. I'll just sniff around a little. Soldiers love to talk. You never know what they might say over a bottle."

Juan Alvarez placed his hand on Josh's shoulder. "Be careful, amigo. Ruffcarn's men may be at Camp Wilson. This Bull is a dangerous man. Watch your back."

Nance nodded his agreement. "You also want to be on the lookout for Indians. They're out in force. We crossed several trails today on the way back from town. There's nothing a Comanche likes better than a good horse. Believe me, if they see you, they'll chase you till you drop."

A smile played at the corner of Josh's mouth. "Well then, if they see me, I reckon I'd better not run."

4

J osh was at the corral before daylight. He'd decided to leave Chancy at the ranch to let him rest. It had been a rough trip and it wasn't over. Colorado was still a long way off and through some rough Indian country.

He cut out a big rangy roan. The horse looked strong with plenty of staying power. As Josh was tightening the cinch, Nance came walking up.

"Gittin' an early start, ain't you?"

"Yep," Josh said. "I figure on getting into town tomorrow in time to check around before the troopers hit the saloons."

"It's not much of a town," Bill Nance said. "A store, a black-smith, and a couple of saloons are just outside the fort. Camp Wilson's only been around for a couple of months, but there's a good bet it's gonna grow now that there's some protection from the Comanches. The storekeeper and blacksmith are straight shooters.

"The blacksmith also runs a stable. You can put your horse up there. His name is Leonard Bakton, but everybody calls him Tiny. You'll understand why when you see him.

"Jeremiah Diehl is the storekeeper. He also has a boardinghouse. He's one tough old hombre. We rangered together with Captain Jack Hays down San Antone and Laredo way. South of the border, I saw him draw his Colt, shoot three times, and down three of Colonel Najero's lancers. Naturally, he doesn't have much problem with rowdy cowpokes or soldiers. He's kinda on the small side, but you'd never know it in a fight. He and Victoria have a store in Austin. They came out with the soldiers, to open Diehls' Emporium and Boardinghouse next to the Shamrock Saloon.

"Don't know much about the owner of the Shamrock Saloon. Name's Cecil Starit. His games are straight, and he treats the boys right—never seems to take advantage of them when they're drunk. But that's all I know about him. He's been in town a couple of months, like all the other townsfolk. He's friendly, but doesn't talk much."

Josh led the roan out of the corral and swung up into the saddle. The big horse bowed his back, crow-hopped a couple of times, settled down, and stamped his feet impatiently.

"That leaves the King 7 Saloon," Nance continued. He patted the horse a couple of times on the neck. "Watch your back in there. A man by the name of Wesley Pierce owns it. He's another one not a lot is known about. He showed up from back East with everyone else in town, when the fort opened. Big man, kinda dark complected; always wears black. He wears two pearl-handled guns, both tied down. He can use them, too.

"A drifter accused him of cheating. The man had a bullet through his brisket and he hadn't even cleared leather. Pierce is a man to keep your eyes on. Ruffcarn always seems to stop in at the King 7 when he's in town."

The roan stomped his feet again, shaking his head against the bridle.

"Seems anxious to be on his way," Josh said.

"He's a good horse, plenty of wind. He'll work for you all day and never look back."

"I appreciate the use of him. It gives mine a chance to rest up. We've still got a long trip ahead of us when we finish here.

"Tell Teresa thanks for the breakfast. A man forgets how good it is to slide his boots under a real table for a hot meal. I'll see you in a few days."

"One other thing, Josh," the old ranger said, "keep an eye on the creek beds. The Comanches like to lay up along the creek during the day. I wouldn't want to lose my new foreman the first day on the job."

Josh raised a hand as he turned the roan out of the ranch yard. The sun was just beginning to climb over the hills behind him. He watched the bright yellow beams quickly descend from the red clay and gray boulders on the hillsides to the golden grasses that waved in the valley.

The light green of the long-leaved mesquites flowed down the hills to give way to the deeper greens of the oak and pecan trees along the Jim Ned. It was no wonder Bill Nance was willing to fight for this valley. This was home for him. He'd raised a family here, had buried his wife here. Josh understood what having a home-place meant.

Josh reached the hilltop and let the roan out into a lope. The horse needed to burn off a little of the wild edge before he settled down to the day's travel. After a few minutes, he slowed him to a fast walk. The roan moved along, smoothly covering the distance —not as smooth nor as fast as Chancy. That Morgan was a fine horse. Josh, while keeping a sharp eye on his surroundings, thought back to the day the colt had entered the world, fighting and kicking.

That little colt was up on his shaky legs almost immediately. Those big eyes took in his new world with brash confidence as he wandered around the stall, investigating everything; then he turned around, raced back, and butted the flanks of his ma for his first meal. Right there Pa said, "Josh, this colt's your'n for life. You take good care of him, and I've a feelin' he'll take care of you more'n you know."

They moved through the mesquite on the hilltop, far enough back from the crest to prevent their silhouette from catching any unfriendly eye. Continuing to keep a constant lookout, his mind wandered again back to Tennessee.

Grandpa Logan had always admired good horseflesh. He would have been tickled with the enthusiasm of the colt. Josh remembered that old man as if it were yesterday: a tall man, with wide shoulders, though a little stooped with age. He could still feel those huge hands that lifted his four-year-old body with ease, and the security he felt when he was with his grandfather. He loved his grandfather's stories told around the fireplace at night after his mother and father had finished reading to them.

His grandfather had gone west, from North Carolina, with Daniel Boone. They had opened the Wilderness Road to Kentucky. It hadn't been without cost. Many had died from disease, some from mishaps that befall men in the wilderness: a slip of the axe, a broken leg while out hunting or scouting alone, and Cherokee arrows. Josh could still remember hearing about Daniel Boone and his famous rifle.

The rifle was a long-barreled flintlock. Unlike the British muskets, the barrel had grooves cut inside it that spiraled toward the muzzle. The spiraled grooves bit into the .32-caliber lead ball, forcing it to spin as it traveled down the barrel. This provided much greater stability to the bullet and gave it great accuracy out to two hundred yards or more, much to the dismay of Boone's enemies. Daniel Boone, it was said by some, could shoot a tick off a bear at two hundred yards. Thus the name for his rifle, Ticklicker.

When his grandfather saw the Cumberland Mountains of Tennessee, he knew he was home. Daniel persuaded him to continue, to what later became Boonesboro. The next spring, however, he returned to Tennessee. On Short Mountain, in the eastern Cumberlands, he built his cabin.

Grandpa Logan brought his new bride, against the wishes of her well-to-do parents, from North Carolina. Together, they made their home. Josh's Pa, his aunt, and all of his uncles had been born in the cabins built on that land. The Indians burned them to the ground twice. The family rebuilt their home each time, and there they stayed. Yes, Josh understood the meaning of a home-place and the need to defend it.

Josh reined the roan over to the hillside. He eased him into a thicket of scrub oak, just close enough to see beyond the crest of the hill, but camouflaged from view by anyone in or across the valley.

Camp Wilson was still more than a full day's ride to the north. He'd been riding for a couple of hours and figured to give the horse a break. He didn't want the Comanches nor the Circle W bunch to suddenly appear over the hill while he was out of the saddle.

Everything was quiet. Down the creek a pack of coyotes were playing near their den. He could see the half-grown pups jumping high in the tall grass, probably chasing a mouse. The two adults lay in the short green grass under the trees, taking advantage of the breeze that labored to cool the late summer morning.

Josh's gaze was attracted up the creek by a flock of turkeys that came dashing out from under the trees. They had been calmly chasing grasshoppers, a staple in their diet. Now they ran quickly into the tall grass and broomweeds on the valley floor. He could occasionally see a bronze-colored back or red head of a gobbler as they ran through the grass.

He turned in the saddle and opened his saddlebags. He pulled out his binoculars, two extra Colts, and a bandolier filled with .44-caliber rimfire cartridges for the Winchester. He draped the bandolier over the saddle horn, checked the loads in the two

Colt revolvers, and slid them under his gun belt. The Winchester Yellow Boy held seventeen rounds. There were five rounds in each revolver. That gave him some pretty impressive firepower. It also didn't take into account the two boxes, of fifty rounds each, for the Winchester or the extra loaded cylinders for the revolvers in the saddlebags. He didn't want a fight, but Pa had taught him to be ready if one came his way.

Josh checked the thicket along the creek with the binoculars. The turkeys had been in the edge of the pecan trees, chasing grasshoppers. They wouldn't have left that quickly unless something spooked them. He waited. He'd seen this game played many a time. The one who moved first usually lost. Probably whoever or whatever had scared them still had no idea he was on the hill. If it were Indians, they would wait till everything quieted down before they moved. The Comanches would be watching the hillsides like hawks. If he moved now, he would be spotted. Movement in the war could bring instant death. Here, it might not be as quick, but you would be just as dead. He waited.

Thirty minutes passed. The coyotes had seen the turkeys. They had watched tensely for a while, all play forgotten. Now the adult coyotes stretched and lay back down. The young ones went back to their previous game. Forty-five minutes went by. The roan was getting restless, and Josh had just about decided the turkeys had been spooked by an animal, maybe an armadillo rooting around in the leaves.

Josh eased the binoculars up and checked the valley—nothing. He took one last look at the coyotes, then swung the binoculars back—there they sat.

He counted twelve Indians. They must have been in the dry creek bed, hidden by the high banks. Most had a bow, though he could see a couple of rifles. They were all mounted on splendid horses. Each horse was painted in black Comanche warpaint. One of the warriors was pointing directly at him. He was over seven hundred yards away in an oak thicket with just his head over the crest of the hill.

Now they all seemed to be focused on him. How the heck could they have spotted him? He glanced at the sun's location and realized they must have caught the flash from the sun's reflection when he turned the binoculars back from the coyotes—what a greenhorn mistake.

"Well, horse, if we move, they see us; if we don't, they ride up here to check out the flash. Either way, we're in for a fight. So let's not keep 'em waiting."

He had spotted a ravine just deep enough to protect him and the horse. It was about four hundred yards farther across the mesa. There was little cover around it for about fifty yards, just some scattered mesquite. It would give him a good field of fire, protect his horse, and put the Comanches in the open.

He swung the horse toward the ravine. Instantly he could hear the whooping of the Comanches as they saw the movement. They recognized a single horseman, an easy prey.

Josh galloped up to the ravine, leaped off his horse, and led him down into the bottom of the draw. He tied him to an exposed tree root, grabbed his saddlebags, and climbed quickly back to the edge of the ravine. He had just laid out the bandolier, extra revolvers, and extra cylinders when the Comanches came charging up over the hilltop.

He resisted the temptation to fire. Josh knew the Winchester's capability and his own. When the Indians galloped over the crest, they were about three hundred yards away. He might have been able to drop one at that distance, but if he did, he would be giving away his advantage. A killing shot at that range would alert them. They would split up, circle him, and attack from several directions. He wanted them together and close. If he could get them into the clearing, he stood a good chance of at least wounding and maybe killing three or four. That would give the others something to think about.

They had spread out, almost in a skirmish line. It was breath-taking to watch as they dodged through the trees and prickly pear patches at full gallop. They were yelling and whooping as they came, confident that they had run their prey to ground. Josh had been on both sides of this type of attack during the war; he calmly waited as they rapidly closed the distance.

A shot was fired, cracking harmlessly above his head. He marked the Indian who fired and calmly chose him for his first target.

They broke into the clearing, their black war paint glistening in the morning sun. Josh waited one more moment, centered the front sight, and squeezed the trigger. Dust leaped off the chest of the Indian who had fired the first shot as he was catapulted from his horse.

With a quick thrust of his left hand, he levered another round into the Yellow Boy's chamber, aimed, and fired. The Comanche on the far end of the skirmish line rolled off his horse. Josh swung to the opposite end of the line, quickly centered the sight on a huge brave, fired, and swung to another, knowing instinctively his bullet had found its mark.

He felt his hat fly off as an arrow swept it from his head. The Indians were now within forty yards; time for one more shot with the rifle. He picked out the nearest brave and, firing too quickly, missed. Josh filled his hands with the big Colt .44s.

They were close. He could hit them with a rock. At this range, after years of practice with the revolvers, he was deadly. The Indians had started turning their horses to parallel the ravine. Several were sitting erect, firing their bows as they swept past. Others were completely hidden on the opposite side of their horses, firing under their horses' necks while riding at a full gallop. Somewhere in the recesses of his mind, he couldn't help but admire this superb display of horsemanship.

Josh watched coolly, his mind detached, as the Colts barked their message of death with deadly accuracy. Arrows flew all around him. He felt a tug and burning in his right arm, but he didn't stop. He was bare-headed, a tall determined man, fighting against what most folks would consider insurmountable odds. He calmly fired the Colts.

As they swept past, now out of range of the revolvers, Josh picked up the Winchester once again. Those men meant to kill him in a most painful manner. He couldn't let them get away. The rifle spoke twice. One Indian fell. Another Comanche jerked, grasped his horse's mane, and managed to stay mounted.

They were gone. Where moments before there was bedlam, now there was only an eerie, dust-covered stillness. Josh quickly filled the rifle with six more rounds; then he replaced the cylinders of the two revolvers.

Now he had a moment to survey the battlefield. From just inside the line of trees to within twenty feet of his position, he counted five Indians. He knew he had hit at least two more.

Quickly he eased down into the ravine and checked the roan. He would be in real trouble out here without a horse. The roan was nervous and glad to see him.

"How you doin', horse?" Josh asked. He moved up close and rubbed him on the neck. "Just thought I'd make sure you're okay."

He pulled out two arrows that had stuck in the saddle. Neither had penetrated the tough leather of the saddle. There was a shallow gash along the roan's right flank where an arrow had sliced a little too close. Other than that, he was fine. Satisfied with his inspection, he moved back up to his firing position.

Josh scanned the hill for any movement that might indicate the remaining Indians were preparing for another attack. There was none, but he didn't kid himself. They hadn't gone.

There were too many of their brothers lying on the hill for them to leave. The Comanches weren't ones to press a losing attack, but they would do everything in their power to give their brothers a proper burial. Comanche braves feared few things, but they did fear their angry brothers coming back from the dead and haunting them.

One of the braves he'd shot with the revolvers moved. Josh could see him clearly. He was no more than thirty feet away. Josh remembered that one in particular. He'd been hidden behind his horse, shooting his bow from under the horse's neck. All Josh could see, when he fired, was his face and right shoulder.

Well, he couldn't just leave him to die. It was one thing to kill a man in battle, but quite another to let him lie there and bleed to death. Josh checked the hill once again, stood, and walked toward the Indian. The Comanche heard Josh, rolled over, and watched him approach.

Josh had never seen a fiercer countenance. His face was painted almost completely black except around his eyes. They were circled in white, starkly contrasting with the rest of his face and the red blood covering the left side of his head. His hair was slicked back with buffalo dung and tied to one side of his head. It was his eyes that caught Josh's attention. They were blue. This was a white man under the dirt and sun-browned skin.

"You understand English?" Josh asked, the Winchester leveled at the man's chest.

Probably no more than twenty-five years old, he calmly appraised Josh. "Yes."

5

"You're a white man," Josh said.

The Indian made a wiggling motion with his index finger. "I am Snake People—Komantcia," he stated proudly.

"Where did you learn to speak English?"

"From priest who stayed with us two winters."

"What happened to him?" Josh asked.

"Priest go back to mission in Mexico.

The Indian couldn't take his eyes off the Winchester. He was obviously mystified at it firing so many times without reloading. Josh moved closer to examine the head wound. The wound had bled a lot, as head wounds were apt to do, but it looked like he'd only been grazed; at the worst, a possible concussion. He would live.

The question now was what to do with him. It was obvious the Indian would try to kill him the first chance he had. He might have been white once, but he was all Comanche now.

"You killed many warriors," the Comanche said. "How is it your rifle can shoot so many times without stopping?"

Josh kept a keen lookout. He didn't want those other Comanches to surprise him while he talked to this one. "It's a Winchester. It fires many times without reloading."

"How many?"

"Many," Josh said. He could feel the animosity this man felt for him. Two days, two enemies—the way things were going, by the end of the week he'd have half of Texas after him.

The Indians came riding slowly through the mesquites. They had caught the riderless horses and were leading them as they walked their horses toward Josh. When they reached the first fallen brave, two of them dismounted, picked him up, and tied him over his horse. The remaining braves kept watchful eyes on Josh.

The wounded Indian stood. The bleeding had slowed, but was still coursing down the side of his face. He was a tall man. The muscles rippled across his scarred and tattooed chest as he fought to maintain his balance.

Josh had no idea what they were going to do. Besides their bows, several of them carried lances, with feathers and scalps dangling from them. Carefully, keeping a close watch on all of them, he slung the Winchester into the crook of his right arm. He could bring the rifle into action instantly from that position.

They all eyed the rifle in wonder and desire. Each would have traded all of their horses and wives to own it.

"What's your name?" Josh asked.

The Indian pulled himself to his full height. "I am Eyes of Hawk. I spotted you on the hillside. It is for my far way of seeing that my father named me."

The other Indians had gathered the remaining dead. Now they waited for Eyes of Hawk.

"I will go," Eyes of Hawk said. "But first you must say your name."

"I'm Joshua Logan. Understand this. I didn't ask for this fight.

You brought it to me. I'll neither hunt nor attack your people. But if you try to harm me or my friends, though you may take my life, I *will* take yours."

Eyes of Hawk watched Josh intently; then he turned and strode to the waiting Comanches. He swung up onto his horse and grasped his long plains lance from the brave leading his horse. Slowly he walked his horse up to Josh.

Josh stood his ground. He didn't think the Indian would try anything now, but he'd best be ready.

Eyes of Hawk drew up his horse in front of Logan. He looked down at him with an indiscernible stare. "I will leave for now. Today, with your golden rifle, you have fought well. I see that you are a warrior. We are also great warriors, and this is our land. We will meet again, Joshua Logan. Then the winds of fate will determine which of us will survive."

The Indian wheeled his horse around. He and the remaining braves rode north with their dead and wounded in tow.

Josh watched them until they were out of sight. He glanced toward the sun. The fight had been short, but the palaver had taken some time. It was past noon and he wanted to reach the fort by noon tomorrow.

He figured on having a big steak at Diehl's boardinghouse after he'd looked around town. Maybe he could find out how the townspeople felt about Ruffcarn and his crowd.

Josh also wanted to know about the army colonel. It sounded like he was favoring Ruffcarn. Josh could think of no reason why the colonel would choose to favor anyone, especially Ruffcarn. He was a United States Army colonel favoring a Southern rancher over a man who had believed in the Union and had a son fighting for it. *I definitely want an answer.* It also seemed like Ruffcarn and Pierce, the owner of the King 7 Saloon, were almighty friendly, according to Mr. Nance. There were some mighty interesting puzzles to unravel around these parts.

Josh walked back to the ravine. It was eerily quiet now; a mockingbird copied a cardinal's song in a nearby mesquite tree, while a covey of half-grown bobwhite quail fluttered under a mound of prickly pear, taking a dust bath. The light summer breeze softly rustled the leaves of the trees. It was hard to imagine the dying that had happened just a short while earlier. That was the way of all battles; the land quickly returned to normal.

He replaced the fired cylinders in his revolvers, dropped the two boxes of .44s into the saddlebags, and tossed the bags over his shoulder as he walked slowly back to the horse.

The roan was ready to leave the ravine when Josh led him out. The horse was edgy from the shooting and the smell of blood, some of which was his from the gash on his hip. Josh was equally anxious to leave the hilltop.

"Relax, boy," he said as he slipped his boot into the stirrup. He swung up into the saddle, leaned over, and patted the roan on the neck. The horse swung his head up and down. Josh wondered just how much these horses could understand. He had always had the ability to calm nerves in stressful situations, not only of animals but also people.

Since he had left home for the war, it seemed he'd constantly been involved in death. It was never something he searched after, but it always seemed to find him. Some men, back East, put their feet under the same table every evening, the table laden with fare prepared by a loving wife. Those men never knew the danger and violence of the war or the westward trek.

Which life was better? Maybe neither. Each man traveled his own road. He had his own battles to fight. The man back East might not be involved in a life-or-death struggle, but he was nonetheless struggling for survival, survival in a forest of deceit sometimes more deadly than a Comanche's war lance.

No, thanks, Josh thought. *I'll stick to the dangers and problems I know best.*

He turned the horse back up the ridgeline. This day had

started well, but had gone downhill fast. Josh knew there could be more trouble waiting for him in town. A full-scale land grab was developing, with Ruffcarn at the helm. Logan wanted to get into town, get a feel for what was going on, and get out—with no trouble. It looked like there would be plenty of trouble to go around without him starting something in town.

6

The following day, Josh pulled up outside Camp Wilson late in the afternoon. The town, if you could call it that, was typical of many that quickly sprang up around forts and died just as quickly when the forts were abandoned.

It sat about fifty yards north of the fort. There were only four buildings on main street, with a few shanties west of town. Diehl's store and rooming house faced the King 7 Saloon across the street. Bakton's blacksmith and stable was next to the King 7 and looked across the street into the Shamrock Saloon. The dirt street was empty except for several horses tied up at the King 7 and Shamrock Saloon. The army crowd was just beginning to drift into town from the fort.

Josh adjusted the Colt .44 and loosened the Winchester in its scabbard. He always adhered to Pa's admonition not to look for, but to be ready for trouble. He nudged the roan with his spurs. The tired horse didn't need much urging. It had been here before and knew that rest, water, and feed waited for it at the stables. He walked the horse up to the blacksmith shop and dismounted.

A mountain of a man came walking out. Logan was big, but this man towered over him.

"Howdy, mister, name's Leonard Bakton, but most folks just call me Tiny," the big man said. "You looking for a place to put up your horse?"

"Yep, he's had a rough couple of days. I'd appreciate you giving him a good rubdown and a few oats. He's also got a shallow cut on his right flank. I'd be much obliged if you'd take a look at it."

Tiny walked around the horse, rubbing his big hand along the horse's back as he checked the cut.

"You know Bill Nance?" Tiny asked nonchalantly as he checked the cut, his hand casually running over the brand.

Josh grinned at Tiny. "Reckon I do. I'm Josh Logan—friend of his son, Rory. I spent the other night at Bill's place. Been riding quite a ways. He was good enough to loan me a horse whilst mine caught a breather."

"I figured as much," Tiny said. "Josh Logan, huh? Ain't you the feller who put a hitch in Bull Westin's get-along?"

"We had a little disagreement."

"Not the way Scott Penny tells it. Why, he said you durned near knocked Bull's head off. I sure woulda liked to have seen that.

"But you'd best be careful around town. I expect you're planning on spending the night. Couldn't do better than Mrs. Diehl's cooking either. Why, her biscuits float right off the table. If'n she's feeling in a particular fine spirit, she might even whip up some bear sign. Cowboys ride for miles just to put their feet under Mrs. Diehl's table and get a taste of that bear sign.

"But anyway, Ruffcarn usually comes into town on Wednesdays. Tomorrow, being Wednesday, I expect he'll be here. Bull usually rides with him. From what Scott Penny says, Bull has a real mad on. Understand he's been talking around that if he ever sees you again, he'll break you in two. Though, from what I see, he'd best come set for a full day's work."

"Talk's cheap," Josh said. He pulled the Winchester from its scabbard and untied his saddlebags. "But thanks for the warning. I do plan to spend the night. Take good care of the horse. Whatever the cost, he earned it. I'll be over at the store and boardinghouse. I look forward to tasting some of Mrs. Diehl's cooking."

"None better in the state, except maybe Teresa's out at Nance's place."

Josh had to agree with Tiny. Good food was truly appreciated when a man spent most of his time eating his own cooking. Dust puffed from under his boots as he walked toward Diehls' Emporium and Boardinghouse. The main street, if it could be called a street, would be a quagmire with any rain at all. The buildings had a boardwalk running in front of them. They would at least prevent a man from sinking to his boot tops into the mud. He opened the door to Diehl's store and walked in.

Jeremiah Diehl was behind the counter, putting canned goods on the shelves. His back was to the door. He was a physically small man, slightly stooped from age. His starched long sleeves were held tight with garters around his upper arms. His clothes were sparkling clean, and his thick white hair was neatly combed straight back.

"Be with you in a moment," he called in a deep voice, surprising for a man his size. Turning slightly so he could see Josh, he spoke around his pipe. "New in town, huh?"

"I'm Josh Logan. Bill Nance told me you were a man to be trusted. I need a room and maybe some answers, if you could help?"

With the mention of Bill Nance, Diehl turned around. His neatly trimmed handlebar mustache had gone to gray, as had his small goatee. The big Colt .44 in his belt looked out of place. He noticed Josh's glance at the Colt.

"Never know when you might need to kill a snake. Name's Jeremiah Diehl. A recommend from Bill Nance carries a lotta weight with me, young fella. So besides the room, what else can I do for you?"

"Well, sir, I brought bad news to the Nance family. Rory and I rode together in the war. He was killed as the war was winding down. But I would surely like to keep that quiet. I told Bill and Mary Louise last night."

"Whew, I hate to hear that. That was one fine boy. Bill Nance set great store by him. I reckon Mary took it mighty bad. She and Rory were real close. Many's the time when he looked after his sister whilst Bill and I were off rangerin'."

"She sure did. But Mr. Nance said she'd get over it. She struck me as a strong woman. Mr. Diehl, that's not why I'm here. Mr. Nance hired me as his foreman. According to him, Jake Ruffcarn has his head set to take over Bill Nance's ranch, legal or not. I need to know all you can tell me about the man."

"An interesting feller. From what Bill Nance tells me, Ruffcarn showed up here about a year ago. Drove in a big herd of cattle and laid claim to the land just north of the Rocking N. I reckon he figgers to own all the country surrounding him before long, including the Rocking N.

"Ruffcarn's a loud man. Strikes me as a bully who's used to gettin' his way. He won't take no for an answer. That's why he's so upset about Bill. I understand he's made several offers for the Rocking N and been told no pretty clearly. He don't cotton to no. Course, was I him, I'd be real careful about pushin' Bill Nance too far. That man is a real catamount when he gets mad."

"Anything else you can tell me about Ruffcarn?" Josh asked.

"Yep. Since he showed up, cattle started disappearing. Now I'm not saying it's him. Could be rustlers moved in or even some of his men. But it does look suspicious. Ruffcarn's also got several toughs working for him. You want to keep an eye out for them. Course, I hear you already met one of them." A smile played across Jeremiah Diehl's face as he took out a match to relight his pipe.

"What can you tell me about Scott Penny?" Josh asked, trying to sidestep mention of the Bull Westin incident.

"Penny strikes me as a good man. He quit, or was fired, from the Circle W, depending on who you talk to. You know how cowhands are. They love to talk. Seems while you were riding out of camp, Westin decided to put a hole in your back with that big .52-caliber Sharps he shoots. Penny stopped him; put his Colt to Bull's neck, from what I hear. They rode back to the ranch and Penny quit. He's stayin' here right now. Says he's headed for the Colorado gold country. But I think he wants to see what happens between Bill Nance and Ruffcarn."

"I reckon I owe him. You know where he is now?" Josh asked.

Jeremiah Diehl snapped the match across the butt of his .44 and held the flame above his pipe bowl. After taking several draws to get it lit, he took a satisfying pull and said, "Pretty sure he wandered over to the Shamrock Saloon. He's won a little and lost a little. I reckon he's aimin' to win some back. Not much else to do around here if you're not working."

"Thanks," Josh said. "Mind if I leave my rifle and gear with you for now? I'll be back for a room later."

"Don't mind at all. I've been hankerin' to see one of those newfangled rifles for a long time. Now's my chance." Diehl took the rifle and gear. "I might mention, you smell strong of gunpowder. Do a little shooting on your way in?"

"Yeah, I had some Comanche trouble a ways south of here. You might pass the word to the post if you get a chance. I'll be talking to the colonel later."

Josh walked out the front door of Diehl's store and turned right for the Shamrock Saloon.

Starit's saloon was fairly typical. The swinging doors allowed a man to see over them for a view of either the inside or outside. A bar ran down one side, with several tables in the open space on the opposite side of the room. Scott Penny sat at one of the tables, playing solitaire. Cecil Starit, the owner, bartender, and swamper, was behind the bar, wiping down the large mirror that ran the full length of the bar.

"What'll it be, stranger?" Starit asked as Josh walked in, removing his hat and placing it on the bar next to him.

"I could do with a sarsaparilla if you've got one handy," Logan replied.

"Sarsaparilla it is, then," Starit said. He put the drink on the bar and went back to cleaning glasses. Logan turned his back to the bar. "Scott, I hear you're now unemployed."

"That I am, and better for it," Scott said.

"Mr. Diehl told me what happened with Bull. I'm much obliged."

Scott ran his fingers through his hair and scratched the back of his neck. "Well, I sure couldn't let Bull back-shoot you. That big old .52-caliber Sharps would've made a nasty hole. He eased it down mighty gingerly when he felt the muzzle of my Colt against the back of his neck.

"I never liked him anyway. I can't stand bullies, and he shapes up to be one. Although I imagine he still might have a headache." Scott was grinning with the last statement.

"Nonetheless, I owe you. Mr. Starit, set Scott up with another glass of the same."

"You betcha; be glad to do it if you'll call me Cecil," Starit said. He picked up a bottle, carried it over to Scott's table, and poured him another glass.

"Thanks, Cecil. Call me Josh.

"Mind if I join you?" Josh asked Scott.

"Shoot, no. Come on over and take a load off," Scott replied.

Logan put his hat on his head, picked up his sarsaparilla with his right hand, and walked over to Scott's table. He moved his chair around so that he could watch the front and back door of the saloon, a move that was not missed by Cecil Starit nor Scott Penny.

Having a seat, Josh asked Cecil Starit, "When do you expect the troopers to start showing up?"

Cecil looked up at the clock. "The boys should be arriving any moment now. Usually it's five or so when they do start wandering in. A good crowd it is that we normally have. Most of them come here, although there are a few who stop at the King 7, though it boggles me mind why they would, the way Bartholf waters down the whiskey."

Scott took a sip of his whiskey. "Cecil's a straight arrow, Josh. He don't water down the whiskey, he don't allow no cardsharps in, and he don't take advantage of a cowboy with a load on. You can trust him. But he also don't allow no drunk cowboy to bust up his place. He's almighty proud of that mirror, and I'd hate to think what he might do to the man who broke it."

"Aye, proud I am. I had the freighters haul this here beauty all the way from New Orleans by way of Houston. It was bullets I was a sweatin' waiting for it to arrive. But here it is, more beautiful than I could have imagined," Cecil said with an admiring smile and a swipe with a cleaning rag.

Josh smiled and said, "It is that, Cecil, something to be proud of."

Josh turned to Scott and asked, "So what are your plans now? You planning on hanging around or taking off for other parts?"

"I thought I'd hang around for a while, just to see what happens between Ruffcarn and Nance. I'd sure like to see Ruffcarn get his comeuppance. But I'm thinkin' about headin' for Colorado in a while. Understand they've found some gold out there."

"How would you like to make a little money before you head west?" Josh asked.

"I've nothing against making money. What do you have in mind?"

"Scott, Mr. Nance made me foreman of the Rocking N. I'm looking for a few good men. But I'm not going to kid you, a fight is brewing. There could be, and probably will be, some shooting. We've got rustling going on, and that's going to stop. As you know, we also have the Comanche problem. So you'd be earning your money."

"Foreman. I'd love to see Ruffcarn's face when he hears that. You bet I'll take the job. Cecil here has about cleaned me out. And if I stay at the Diehl place much longer, what with all that good cooking, I won't be able to find a horse that can carry me. Anyway, Colorado ain't goin' anywhere."

"Good. Figure on leaving tomorrow. Why don't you check with Tiny Bakton and line up a wagon for tomorrow afternoon. We'll pick up supplies for a couple of weeks, including ammunition. I left a list with Mr. Diehl. You can also pick up whatever personal provisions you need and put it on the Nance tab."

"Guess I'd better get busy," Scott Penny said as he pushed his chair back and got to his feet. "It feels good to be working for a decent outfit again."

"You need any money to tide you over?"

"Nope, I'm set. After I get the wagon set up, I'm heading to Mrs. Diehl's. I sure don't want to miss out on supper. I'll see you there. Just watch your back, *amigo*; you never know when some of that Ruffcarn crew might wander in."

"You do the same," Josh said. He watched Scott Penny push open the swinging doors and disappear around the corner of the saloon.

Josh pushed back from the table, got up, put his hat back on, and strolled over to the bar. Cecil Starit had his back to him, cleaning a glass. Cecil wasn't a tall man, about five feet eight, but he was broad. He reminded Josh of his uncle back in Tennessee. Uncle Floyd was a younger brother of Pa. Pa always said that he got the name Floyd because of the night he was born. It was a cold and rainy October night. Creeks were out of their banks and the valleys were looking at some major flooding. Grandma said a good strong Scottish name for this man-child was Floyd, for the flooding: Floyd David Logan.

Cecil turned around. "Couldn't help but hear that you be the new foreman for Bill Nance."

"That's right, as of night before last. But it would be mighty kind of you if you kept that quiet until I cut it loose."

"Aye, I'll do that. Bill Nance is a man of good character and a fine judge of men. You need anything, you let me know. I think a lot of your boss."

"Thanks," Josh said. He looked up into the mirror to see several dusty troopers march into the Shamrock Saloon. He pulled his hat lower, just enough to make recognition difficult.

"Cecil, get out some of that good Irish whiskey you've got stashed behind that bar for your best Irish customers," ordered the leading first sergeant.

He was followed by several other sergeants and corporals. Two obviously green recruits, just out from the East, brought up the rear. They all swaggered up to the bar and watched Starit slip a sealed bottle from behind the bar and begin to pour.

"Aye, a sad day it is when we have to look for protection from the savages by the likes of this motley crew," Starit said. He shook his head solemnly as he passed down the line. He reached the two young recruits, looked them over, and turned back to the first sergeant. "Pat, is it so now that you're taking babes into President Grant's army? Shouldn't I be getting out a sugar-teat, or will a couple of glasses of milk do?"

Josh smiled at the good-natured banter as he leaned over the bar. It was something that he'd missed since leaving the army.

The first sergeant and the other noncoms roared with laughter as the two recruits spluttered and turned red, not knowing whether to laugh or fight, although from the looks of this Irish bartender, they sure didn't want any part of him.

"Now, Cecil, 'tis a man's drink for them. These boys are doing a man's job, so don't be down-talking the president's finest, or we'll be taking our business to the King 7."

Now it was Starit's turn to roar. It was well known that there was no love lost between the King 7's owner, Wesley Pierce, and the big first sergeant, Patrick Devane O'Reilly.

Logan had immediately recognized the first sergeant when he entered the saloon. They had been through most of the war together. In fact, the three of them—Josh, Rory, and Pat O'Reilly —had become close friends. They had bonded as men do, during time of war, who respect and depend on each other to stay alive.

First Sergeant Pat O'Reilly had given the unknown cavalry trooper the once-over when he came in, but he failed to recognize his good friend. Josh, with his hat pulled low, looked like any other ex-trooper drifting from one job to another.

O'REILLY HAD A GOAL. One more day would see his enlistment up. Over the years, he had saved his money. Because of the training of his mother and father, he was a frugal man and had started making small investments at a young age. After the death of his parents, he'd taken on the added responsibility of caring for his young sister.

Now he was about to begin enjoying the fruits of his planning and sacrifice. He was going west to California. O'Reilly planned to build a lovely home for himself and his younger sister.

They were the last of the O'Reilly line. She had just finished proper schooling back East, thanks to the success of his investments. She'd be arriving on the stage tomorrow. On the same day, his enlistment would be up, and they would be off to California. *Ah*, thought Pat, *'tis a lovely plan.* He was snatched from his reverie.

JOSH WAS LEANING over the bar with his cavalry hat pulled low over his face. O'Reilly hadn't changed much—a little older. "Starit, you let this western cavalry trash into your clean saloon?"

All sound stopped.

The troopers turned toward Josh. O'Reilly looked at him first in anger, then quizzically, as if there was something vaguely familiar about this saddle bum.

"Mister, it's surprised I am that you'd be speaking of the good cavalry such as you are. 'Tis obvious from your clothes you were once one of us," O'Reilly said.

The cavalry troopers moved away from the bar and began to make a circle around Josh.

He continued to face the bar with his head down and his hat pulled low. "Well, I see it never changes. You sergeants always need your boys to fight your battles for you."

"Stand back, boys. It seems I must administer a lesson to this out-of-work saddle bum. It's time he learned he can't be making statements like that of President Grant's finest, whether he's in or out of the service."

O'Reilly reached out, grabbed Josh by the sleeve, and spun him around. As he did, Josh swept off his hat and flourished it with a grin. "O'Reilly, you always did have a hot Irish temper."

"Major Joshua Logan, as I live and breathe," Pat said as he burst out laughing.

"No longer major, just Josh. By golly, First Sergeant, it's good to see you. I figured that after you were transferred to the west, I'd not see you again. You're looking mighty fine. Although I see you're still drinking that rotgut Irish whiskey."

O'Reilly had Logan by both shoulders and was grinning from ear to ear. "Tomorrow, Josh, it'll no longer be first sergeant. I'm retiring and it's out to California I'll be. The plan is to build a fine home to gaze out upon the likes of the Pacific Ocean. Grand it will be, truly grand."

Josh thought for a moment as he looked at Pat. O'Reilly had

been a good friend to Rory. He deserved the opportunity to help his dead friend's family.

"You're getting out tomorrow, you say? How would you like to give the family of an old friend a hand and get paid for it to boot?"

7

"What do you have in mind?" First Sergeant O'Reilly asked.

Josh nodded toward a table. "Why don't we grab a table. This might take a while."

"Laddies, I'll be joining my good friend over at the table for a bit. We've some catching up to do," O'Reilly told the troopers as he moved to the table and sat down.

Josh sat, put his hat on the table, and said, "Pat, you've been here long enough to know there's a fight brewing between the Circle W and the Rocking N."

"Aye, I've heard some about it. Seems Ruffcarn could be making a move on this fella Nance. Don't like Ruffcarn and his crew, but I don't really ken Nance or the lads a-working for him."

Josh smiled ruefully. "Doesn't the name Nance ring a bell for you?"

O'Reilly rubbed his chin as he thought; then his face lit with recognition. "As I live and breathe. Are you saying this Nance is one and the same as Rory's father?"

"Absolutely. He built his ranch in this country. He fought the Comanches and Apaches. He lost his wife here and raised Rory and Mary Louise, Rory's sister. Now this Ruffcarn moves in, and it looks like he's intent on taking over this country, including the Rocking N.

"Pat, Mr. Nance has hired me as foreman, and I sure could use some help. I'll be straight up. I'm sure there's going to be some shooting and probably some killing. I'd prefer not, but I think it's in the cards. Mr. Nance and his daughter need help now. So what do you think about postponing your California trip for a while?"

O'Reilly sipped on his drink and thought for only a moment. "I'm with you. But I'll tell you, there be some complications. I said I was going to California, but I didn't tell you who with. My wee sister, Fianna Caitlin O'Reilly, is going with me. She's been back East in school and is raring to come West. Not only is that the truth, but she'll be arriving on tomorrow's stage."

Now it was Logan's turn to sit back and think for a moment. Having O'Reilly's sister here could complicate things. He didn't want to put her life in jeopardy. On the other hand, he could sure use O'Reilly's help. "That complicates things a mite. I don't want to delay your and your sister's California trip. But Mr. Nance and I could use the help of a man like you. You think she would mind staying at the Diehls' place for a while? I feel sure she'd be safe there. Jeremiah Diehl is a tough hombre and he'd protect her no questions asked. The ranch would pick up the tab."

"Josh, you've never met a finer girl than me sister. She's smart as a whip, but lordy, she's strongheaded. I know for sure she'd be mad as a wet cat if I didn't help the family of a good friend."

Josh relaxed a little. Finding O'Reilly here was a great boon. The man had been in many skirmishes. He was a man to be depended on. He also was an excellent tactician. This was going to be a tough fight, but with O'Reilly and Penny on the payroll, he'd be free to scout around and find out where the cattle were disappearing to and what was happening with this land grab.

They sat and talked until, looking up, Josh saw that darkness had settled on the town. He also realized how tired he was. He'd better get back to the Diehls', get something to eat, if anything was left, and get to bed. He needed rest, and this might be his last chance for a while. "Pat, what time does the stage come in tomorrow?"

"Supposed to be around noon, if it's on time. They're carrying an extra guard with the Comanches on the prowl. Hopefully she'll arrive on time."

"Okay, I'll meet you at the stage tomorrow. I'm gonna grab a bite and hit the sack. It's been a long day."

The two men stood and shook hands. Josh walked by the bar and tossed a three-dollar gold piece onto the counter.

"Cecil, how about a round for President Grant's finest," he said as he walked out the door.

First Sergeant Pat O'Reilly watched him as he strode out the door. "Buckos, there goes the best cavalry officer who ever straddled a horse. Cecil, fill your glass, for I have a toast."

Cecil Starit filled the glasses all around, then poured one for himself.

Josh stood outside for a moment against the saloon front, letting his eyes adjust to the night. He could hear O'Reilly in the saloon.

"Here's to Major Joshua Logan," Sergeant O'Reilly said, "the best cavalry officer, the best fighter, and the best friend could a man ever have. Drink up, me lads, for ye have seen the best."

Josh smiled and turned left, heading for the Diehls' store and boardinghouse. The howls of coyotes came from just outside town. It was always funny how two or three coyotes could sound like twice that many.

His mind slipped back to more serious matters as he stepped into the Diehls' Emporium and Boardinghouse. Ruffcarn would be in town tomorrow. That would give him a chance to talk to him and see what the man was like. There would also be the chance to size up some of his crew. Hopefully he would have a better feel for how to attack this problem.

Attack, he thought. That might be exactly what he would have to do. First he wanted to check the lay of the land and figure out where Mr. Nance's rustled cattle were being kept, if they hadn't already been moved out of the country. He didn't really think that had happened yet. They might have tried to move them to Brownwood or Fort Worth, but Mr. Nance would have heard of that. They were probably still in the area, somewhere. As hot and dry as it had been, they would definitely be close to water. That would help.

"Well, it's about time you got back here, young man," Mrs. Diehl said. "If you're planning on eatin' here, you'd best be on time."

"Howdy, ma'am. Josh Logan's my name. Sorry I'm late. Got to talking with a friend I haven't seen for a couple of years and completely forgot about the time. Sure didn't mean to miss your dinner, what with all the fine compliments I've heard about your cooking."

"You just come and sit yourself down here at the table. So happens I saved some leftovers for you, you being a good friend of Rory." Mrs. Diehl poured a cup of coffee for Josh as she bustled about the kitchen and said, "Mr. Diehl told me about his death. I'm so sorry to hear about that fine young man. Bill and Mary Louise set great store by him. They must be devastated."

"Yes, ma'am, Mary Louise especially."

"I know. That girl worshipped her brother. Why, he took care of her almost by himself at times, when Bill was out rangerin'. But she's a strong Texas girl. She'll get past it. Now you go ahead and eat, then git up to bed. You look plumb tuckered out."

"Mrs. Diehl, you have no idea. I sure appreciate you keeping this steak and biscuits for me. They're delicious."

"Eat up now. Here's a piece of peach pie. It'll go fine with another cup of coffee," she said, pouring his coffee with one hand and putting the pie on the table with the other.

"Victoria, the man will founder on all that food," Mr. Diehl said as he came down the stairs. "You have another cup of coffee handy?" he asked as he sat down and winked at Josh.

"Jeremiah, you know where the coffee is," Mrs. Diehl said with one hand on her ample hip. "I know you married me for my cooking, but you know I don't fetch and carry for any man."

"Honey, I married you for your good looks. Why, you were the prettiest girl in Texas, and still are."

As Mrs. Diehl poured him a cup of coffee, she placed her hand on his shoulder. "Jeremiah, you were always a smooth talker. But that's not why I married you." She walked back to the stove with a smile on her face.

Josh missed this type of banter. This reminded him of his ma and pa. They cared for each other and didn't mind letting the kids know it. He planned one day to settle down, hopefully in Colorado. He could visualize his own ranch, with a wife by his side to work and build something of value for their children. Josh knew the most valuable assets he could give his children were what his parents had given to him and his brothers and sister. He hoped he had become the man they wanted him to be. They taught them that their word was their bond; never lie. Wasn't anything much worse than a liar. They taught them to stand up for themselves and for those who were weaker. When you're in the right, never back down. They taught them many other positive things that he would always be in their debt for.

"Mr. Diehl, I've got a little problem," Josh said. He was eating the peach pie, and it was mighty fine. "Don't know if you know First Sergeant O'Reilly. He's a good friend and was also a good friend of Rory. He's getting out of the army tomorrow, and I've hired him to work for the Rocking N."

"Why, I do know him, Josh. He's a fine man. I think you made a good decision. Didn't know he knew Rory. That's a surprise."

"Yes, sir, it was a surprise all around. I was surprised to see him, and he was surprised that Bill Nance is Rory's father. But yes, he is a good man. That's not my problem. He and his sister planned to travel to California when he retired. She's arriving on the stage tomorrow from back East. He says she'll be completely behind him helping out a friend. But she's going to need a place to stay, and I was wondering ..."

"Wonder no more, young man." Mrs. Diehl spoke up. "She'll have a place to stay here with us as long as she likes. I can't wait to have another woman in this house. She'll be so refreshing. I can also find out about everything that's going on back East."

"Thanks again, ma'am. She could also need some protection while she's here. Once the shooting starts, and I feel certain it will, she could be in danger."

Mr. Diehl leaned forward on the table. "Josh, we'll keep a lookout for her. I promise you, she'll be safe here."

"Thank you both. That takes a real load off. I know that Pat O'Reilly will be mighty pleased, too. I want you to know I appreciate your help. But now, as good as all this food was, especially that peach pie, I'd better get to bed before I fall asleep right here at the table."

"Son, you go right upstairs, second door on the right. You relax and sleep well. Nobody'll bother you. We'll see you in the morning," Mr. Diehl said.

Josh made it upstairs into his room. He saw his rifle and gear sitting by the bed. He checked the loads in his revolver, dropped it back into the holster, unfastened his gun belt, and hung it on the iron headboard. He slipped off his boots and collapsed onto the bed. It had been a long tough day. He needed to do some planning for tomorrow before going to slee...

8

S unlight streamed through the window, tracked across the bed, and struck Logan's closed eyes. A moment passed, his eyes opened, then, astonished at sleeping so late, he rolled out of bed.

"Don't think I've ever slept this late," he said to himself, disgusted with his late start. He could hear Mrs. Diehl talking downstairs as she poured coffee and dished up breakfast. He grabbed the pitcher on the dresser and dumped some water into the basin. Josh yanked his shirt off and splashed water onto his face. He looked at his image in the mirror. *You're one beat-up-looking character.* He reached to his forehead and traced the scar with his index finger, shrugged, and combed back his thick black hair with his hands. He reached into his saddlebags, yanked out a clean shirt, and slipped it on over his head.

Josh pulled on his boots, and, swinging his gun belt around his waist, he buckled it tight, pulled out his .44 Colt, and checked the loads. All looked good, so he grabbed his gear and the Winchester and headed downstairs.

Diehl, Tiny Bakton, and Scott Penny were all gathered around the table. Not much talking was going on because they were attacking the food Mrs. Diehl had set out before them. Not stopping, they looked up and nodded to Josh.

"Good morning, Josh. I trust you slept well? We thought it best to let you sleep, since you looked pretty tired last evening," Mrs. Diehl said and gave him a smile.

"Yes, ma'am, I sure did. Last night has to be the best sleep I've had in a coon's age. Sorry if I'm late again."

"Well, you just have a seat at the table. I fixed plenty this morning. Especially knowing Tiny was going to be here."

Tiny Bakton's fork, loaded with venison sausage and egg, stopped in mid-travel. "Mrs. Diehl, you know how much I love your cooking—and I heard you might have fixed some bear sign this morning."

Mrs. Diehl smiled as she picked up a tray from the counter. Under the kitchen towel cover rested a large stack of doughnuts. She knew men would travel from miles around just to get the fresh pastry. She placed them on the table. "Enjoy your treats, boys." She turned to Josh and poured him coffee as he reached for the bear sign, along with Tiny, Mr. Diehl, and Scott.

Mrs. Diehl brought Josh some eggs and sausage. "You men have everything you need. I've some sewing I must get done. You know where everything is, just help yourself."

Multiple "yes, ma'ams" and "thank you, ma'ams" followed her out of the kitchen.

As Tiny reached for his second doughnut, Diehl turned to Josh. "If you don't mind my asking, what are your plans for today?"

Josh had been mulling over his plans. "Mr. Diehl, I don't mind your asking at all. Later today, Scott will be renting a wagon from Tiny. He'll then be over to your store. We've got a pretty big order. Plus, we need to stock up on some additional ammunition. I'm expecting we'll be needin' it. First Sergeant O'Reilly will get his discharge today. After his sister gets into town and they've had time to visit, he and Scott will head out to the ranch. I'll be taking my time and scouting out the country on the way back to the ranch."

Diehl said, "Josh, you know Jake Ruffcarn and his crowd should be showing up today? They usually get here around noon or before."

"I do. I'll be meeting with Ruffcarn today to see if I can get a feel for what he's planning to do. Don't imagine I'll get much, other than a measure of the man. That's important."

Scott spoke up. "Josh, you can expect Bull Westin to be with Ruffcarn, and I know Bull has a big mad on."

"Scott, I realize I'm not finished with Bull. But I can't let that interfere with our plans. We need to find out what's happened to our cattle, where they are, and who's responsible. When we find out, we'll rectify the situation. You'd best be on your toes, too. Ruffcarn can't be too happy with you."

Scott grinned, picked up his chair, and turned it around so he could lean on the back. He crossed his arms over the back of the chair and said, "I reckon he might have a bee in his bonnet. But I'm just small potatoes. He's after the Rocking N. He's going to be madder than a wet hen when he finds out Mr. Nance has hired himself a foreman—and that foreman is you. If you're planning on confrontin' him, I reckon I should be around, just to keep everybody else honest."

Josh knew Scott was right. It wouldn't hurt to have some backup around when he was dealing with Ruffcarn or Bull. "Thanks, Scott. Yeah, why don't you hang around until I get a few things taken care of before you leave town."

Tiny hadn't said much, but he'd made a big dent in the bear sign. He stood up. "I'd best be gettin' on back to the stables. Got some blacksmithin' to do. Mr. Logan, I'd say you've got a tough row to hoe. That bunch is plumb mean, so if'n I was you, I'd be careful who I turned my back on."

Josh nodded. "Good advice. I'll do that. I'll also be down later today to settle up with you and pick up my horse. If you'd put some oats aside for me, I'd be much obliged. It'll be a few days before I get back to the ranch."

"Yes, sir, I'll be glad to. Mrs. Diehl, always great food, and that bear sign was a heavenly thing. I'm puttin' a fifty-cent piece on the table," Tiny called.

"Thank you, Tiny; have a good day," came from upstairs.

"Tiny, I'll go with you and get the wagon so I can get it loaded," Scott said as he also stepped away from the table.

The two men walked out together, Leonard Bakton ducking to walk through the door, dwarfing Scott Penny. Scott had his hat pushed back on his head and one last doughnut in his hand.

"Josh, could you hang around a moment?" Diehl asked.

Josh waited patiently. It took a few moments; then Diehl said, "I spent a few years rangerin' and I'm pretty good at sizing up men. You'd best be aware of a couple of men. Wesley Pierce and Grizzard Bankes are two dangerous hombres. Bankes is a gunfighter. He ain't the sharpest knife in the drawer, but he's fast. Killed a man here no more'n two weeks back. The cowhand he shot hadn't even managed to clear his holster when Bankes was shooting. But something to know—Bankes missed his first shot. I figger he depends on speed so much he ends up missing that first one."

Josh nodded. "That'll eventually get him killed. Pa always said, 'It's the first shot that counts, boys,' and that philosophy has saved my life more than once."

Diehl nodded his agreement and continued, "Wesley Pierce— I don't quite have him figured out. He comes across to me as a gambler and a cold hombre. He doesn't work for Ruffcarn. But every dang time Ruffcarn comes into town, he goes straight to the King 7. Pierce owns the King 7. Of all the men around Ruffcarn, including himself, I'm thinkin' Pierce is the smartest and the deadliest. You want to keep a close eye on him. He's easy to recognize. He wears all black, including his hat, and you seldom see him outside the King 7."

"Okay, clear out of my kitchen. I've got cleaning to do and, Mr. Diehl, you've a store to run," Mrs. Diehl said as she swept back into the dining room.

Diehl laughed and said, "Yes, ma'am," as he and Josh moved into the store. Diehl shifted the Colt around where it would be more accessible, and slipped on his store apron.

Josh took his rifle and saddlebags with him. "Mr. Diehl, I'll be needing some additional lead, powder, and four boxes of .44 rimfires for the Winchester, if you've got them."

"Haven't seen any of those around yet, but I did get some .44s a while back for the Henry. Let's see. I'll be; I've got those four boxes right here. Will they work in that Winchester of yours?"

"Yes, sir. The two shoot the same ammunition."

There was a commotion outside, and they saw a group of riders coming in from the south. Josh recognized Bull riding just behind the lead rider, who must be Ruffcarn.

Diehl walked over to the front window. "Josh, Ruffcarn's in the lead. You already know Westin, and the hombre to the right of Westin is Grizzard Bankes. The other three men are some of Ruffcarn's hands. He's got about twenty or so ... and still hiring. Don't know those guys."

The group followed Ruffcarn into the King 7 Saloon. Grizzard Bankes stopped just before entering the saloon and took his hat off, beat dust from his shotgun chaps while looking around, turned, and went inside.

"Bankes is cautious," Josh said.

"He's a gunman. Not the best, but he hasn't lived this long by being careless," observed Diehl.

Josh packed the powder and lead for his .44 Colts into his saddlebags. "Mind if I leave my gear here for now?"

"Nope, set your stuff here behind the counter. Wouldn't want anyone to get itchy fingers where your Winchester's concerned."

Josh turned to walk out the door just as the stage rolled around the corner. The driver pulled the horses to a stop in front of the Diehls' boardinghouse. Diehl walked out behind Josh.

"Morning, Hank. You're running early today," Diehl said.

"Yep, got an early start. I expect to run at least on schedule today. That's if we don't run into any of those blasted Comanches," Hank said.

The shotgun rider up top tossed down two bags, turned, and climbed down to the street.

With the increased Indian trouble, the stage was carrying two shotguns. The second was inside, and he was the first person out of the coach. Josh watched as the man turned and held out his hand. A strong, young, feminine hand grasped his from inside the stage. Fianna stepped lightly to the box that had been placed below the stage door. Just a glimpse of trim ankle could be caught as she stepped down. Her bright green eyes surveyed the false-front buildings, the boardwalk, and the townspeople who had gathered to see the stage. The stage arrival was always an event in Camp Wilson.

Josh had known some extremely attractive ladies, but he couldn't take his eyes from this woman. She was taller than he had expected. Pat O'Reilly wasn't a tall man, so Josh expected his sister to be a small girl. Instead it looked like she was at least five feet six. She stood straight, and the light gray traveling dress that she wore accentuated the curves of her body. She turned her head toward him. Her hair matched the red glow of the morning sun. He felt a shock, as if hit by a bolt of lightning. Her green eyes looked right into him. He thought he saw her take a short, quick breath, and he could swear she had experienced the same feeling.

She quickly broke eye contact and looked around for O'Reilly. Since the stage was early, O'Reilly was still at the fort. Josh stepped quickly forward and removed his hat. "Good morning, ma'am," he said. "I assume you must be Miss Fianna Caitlin O'Reilly?"

"Why yes, I am," she said.

Fianna looked up into his face, and Josh felt his chest tighten. She held his gaze with a confident look. There was nothing brazen about this girl, but she exuded confidence, just like her brother.

Since everyone had stepped away from the stage, Hank pulled it down to Tiny Bakton's livery stable to change horses, leaving the street clear.

"Miss O'Reilly, if I may introduce myself, I'm a friend of your brother, Pat. The stage is earlier than expected, but I'm sure Pat will be along shortly. When we talked yesterday, he was sure excited about seeing you. My name is Joshua Matthew Logan."

Fianna extended her hand to Josh, and when he took it, he felt the soft strength in her hand. This was no milk-toast hand-shake. He could feel, as well as see, her composure. Josh realized he was holding her hand longer than normal. He quickly released it. He could feel himself turning red.

"Fianna Caitlin O'Reilly, sir. A friend of Pat's is definitely a friend of mine." She smiled at him, and he knew he was smitten.

"Let me take your bags in, Miss O'Reilly," Josh said as he picked up her bags from the street.

"Let me take yore bags in, Miss O'Reilly," Bull Westin mimicked. "Now ain't that about the sweetest thing I ever did see."

Usually Josh was completely alert to his surroundings. His sixth sense, at least that was what Ma had called it, had saved him on several occasions. This was the second time in almost that many days it had failed him. Today it was like his vision had narrowed down to where the only thing he could see was Fianna.

Josh placed the bags onto the boardwalk and turned around to see Bull Westin with Jake Ruffcarn, Grizzard Bankes, and two of Ruffcarn's toughs.

"Why, Mr. Logan, ain't you agoin' to introduce me to this fine-lookin' filly?" Bull asked.

"Bull, I knew you for a loudmouthed bully when I met you.

Since then, I've found you out for the back-shooter that you are. Now I see you also have no respect for women. Because Miss O'Reilly is here, I'm going to give you one chance. Turn around, get on your horse, leave this country, and never let me see you again."

"Logan, I'm gonna kill you. I'm gonna do it slow. Your lady friend there is going to get to see what you're made of."

Grizzard Bankes and the two Circle W toughs started moving around to circle Logan.

"Hold it right there, boys." Diehl had Logan's Winchester leveled at Bankes.

"Aye, I think it would be well if you boys relaxed and enjoyed the show," said Cecil Starit. He stood behind them, next to the Shamrock Saloon, the gaping muzzles of his scattergun pointed at their bellies. At that distance the buckshot would spread enough to hit them all.

Ruffcarn said, "Stand easy, boys. This is Bull's show. He can take care of himself."

Josh Logan fixed Bull with a flinty gaze. "Westin, you called this dance; now start the music."

Bull charged Josh.

Josh smoothly stepped out of Bull's path and grabbed his beefy left arm. Using Bull's momentum, Josh spun and threw him headfirst into the hitching post in front of Diehl's store and boardinghouse. Bull's head hit the hitching post with a sickening thud, and he momentarily dropped to his knees. He shook his head, lunged to his feet, and charged. Josh ducked, taking a glancing blow to the left side of his head from a deadly right. He smashed a left jab hard into Bull's mouth and nose. Blood exploded across Bull's face.

Surprised at the sight of his own blood, Bull straightened and threw a looping left. Josh stepped inside the intended blow and drove a savage right into the left side of Bull's head. Bull went to his knees. He looked up at Josh, hate in his eyes, spit out a tooth, and struggled to his feet. Josh blocked a left and stepped into Bull. With all of his weight behind the blow, Josh smashed a left into Bull's mouth and nose again; white cartilage could be seen from Bull's crushed nose. Bull was stunned, swaying. He was almost out on his feet. Pivoting his body to leverage every ounce of his weight into the blow, Josh swung a powerful left, catching Bull just below his right ear.

Josh stepped back. Bull toppled unconscious to the ground, his face an almost unrecognizable mass of blood, bone, and flesh. Josh quickly flexed both hands to ensure nothing was broken, and looked at Ruffcarn, Grizzard Bankes, and the other Circle W riders.

"When he comes to, tell him, for his health, he'd best leave this country. I've no use for a back-shooter. He tried to bushwhack me once. If I run into him again, I'll kill him as quickly as I'd kill a rabid skunk. Now get this piece of slop out of here."

Ruffcarn stepped out to Logan. "Mr. Logan, you're a mighty hard man. But I like hard men—they're the only kind I hire. If you have a moment, maybe we could have a talk—over a drink?"

Josh looked around at the crowd that had gathered in the street. Penny and Starit were covering his back. Jeremiah Diehl leaned against the hitching post just outside his store, Josh's Winchester cradled in the crook of his left arm.

"Yeah, you're just the man I've been looking for," Josh said. "I'll meet you in the Shamrock Saloon in five minutes."

"I was thinking more along the lines of the King 7. Join me there?"

"I reckon not. Mr. Starit here earned my business by covering my back. So I'll see you in the Shamrock." Josh watched Ruffcarn's face turn red, and it looked as if he was going to say something else, but changed his mind. Josh waited for a moment and then turned back to Fianna.

As Josh walked back to Fianna, he continued to flex his

hands. He needed to keep them limber just in case. "Sorry about the interruption. Now, let me help you with your bags."

Fianna was cool, as if she'd been watching a croquet match. She smiled up at Josh. "Why, thank you," she said, and placed her hand on his arm.

9

J osh leaned against Starit's bar. Cecil was behind the bar, wiping glasses as if nothing had happened. Scott Penny sat at a table in the Shamrock, playing a hand of solitaire.

Jake Ruffcarn walked into Starit's establishment, motioning for Grizzard Bankes and the two cowhands to wait at the end of the bar, and strode up to Josh.

Josh looked at Grizzard Bankes and said to Ruffcarn, "You keep a rough crew."

"This is rough country. I'll get right to the point. You look as if you can handle yourself, and I'm always looking for another good hand. I'm hiring, if you're looking. I fired a man yesterday, so I need a replacement." Ruffcarn turned and stared at Scott Penny.

Bankes barked a sound intended to be a laugh. Penny just kept on dealing cards, apparently completely absorbed in his game of solitaire.

"Way I heard it, the man quit. But that's not the point. The point is, you'd better be looking for two men. Because if you keep Bull Westin on, you're signing the man's death warrant. The next time I see him, I'll kill him."

Josh watched Ruffcarn's face turn scarlet. It was obvious he wasn't used to being talked to in such a manner. His knuckles had turned white, gripping the bar.

"Logan, I'm offering you a job."

"I already have a job."

Ruffcarn's eyes narrowed. "Where?"

"I'm the new foreman for the Rocking N."

Ruffcarn's voice dropped low with anger. "You're making a bad choice, Logan. Sometimes men die when they make bad choices."

Josh locked Ruffcarn in a cold gaze. "Ruffcarn, we all die— some sooner than later. So I'll just take that as a piece of friendly advice. Otherwise, I might have to take offense, and I'm almighty tired of being offended today.

"But while we're discussing the vagaries of life, I might mention that there's been an awful lot of cattle just wandering off the Nance place lately. Just so there's no misunderstanding, anyone on Nance property will be treated as a rustler and will be dealt with appropriately."

"You saying I'm a rustler?"

"Reckon you can answer that better than me. But I'll tell you this. I don't like your kind. You bully people. You take what you want with no thought of the other man. When you run across someone you can't bully, you try to break him. Well, you just found a nut that's going to be plenty hard to crack. I don't take to being pushed, and I sure don't take to having my friends run over. So, since you've had your say and I've had mine, why don't you take your cur-dog crew and get out of here."

Ruffcarn stared at Josh. His neck bulged red with rage. Josh could see the man was considering pulling his gun; then Josh watched as the rage left Ruffcarn's face and reason returned. After staring at Josh for a moment more, Ruffcarn wheeled and stomped out of the saloon.

Grizzard Bankes, relaxed and leaning against the bar, looked Josh over, tipped his hat, and smiled. "I reckon I'll be seeing you."

He then turned and ambled out of the Shamrock, his two men following.

"Josh, you sure don't waste any time. Why, it appears to me you've made more enemies in the last two days than I have in my whole lifetime," Scott Penny said, a grin spreading across his freckled face.

At that moment, the saloon doors swung open and an angry, retired, Irish first sergeant marched through the door. "What's this I hear about me bonnie sister being insulted on the streets of this town by that blackguard Bull Westin?"

"That's been took care of, Pat—and plenty well it was." Cecil Starit spoke up from behind the bar. "This here friend of yours, Major Josh Logan, took it upon hisself to pummel Westin to a bloody pulp. He posted Westin out of town. Then he all but called Ruffcarn a rustler. Mighty pleased was I to hear the likes of what I heard. And him just as cool and calm as a summer's evening."

First Sergeant O'Reilly turned to Logan. "It's in your debt I am. If there's ever a thing you need of me, it's yours. 'Tis a sad thing that I couldn't have taken part or at least seen the action.

"But now I have a piece of news. I no longer call the US Cavalry home. Today I'm me own man and ready to go to work for you. The colonel even gave me my favorite horse as a retirement gift."

"Congratulations, Pat. That's little enough for the years of service that you've given this country. You deserve it. It's good to be working with you again.

"Now let's get to planning. I want to find those cattle and get them returned to Mr. Nance. Next, I must find out what Ruffcarn is up to. I know he wants the ranch, but I'd like to know why and how he's planning to do it."

～

RUFFCARN STOMPED into the King 7 Saloon. "Gimme a drink!" he yelled at Bartholf. Bartholf was a huge man. Ruffcarn had known him for many years—not as a friend, but as an enforcer for Pierce. The man's arms were the size of most men's thighs. His white shirt was sorely tested trying to keep those shoulders contained, but today Ruffcarn was enraged over his talk with Logan. He kicked one chair out of the way, stomped across the saloon, and pulled up another at Pierce's table.

Pierce pulled at the bottom of his black vest and smoothed the brim of his black, wide-brimmed felt hat. He watched with unblinking dark eyes as Ruffcarn dropped into his chair.

Bartholf brought a drink over to Ruffcarn, set it down, and walked slowly back to the bar.

"Bring me that blasted bottle," Ruffcarn yelled, slamming the empty glass on the table.

"You've worked yourself into a mighty hefty mad, Ruffcarn," Pierce said. He pulled a small silver knife from his vest pocket, where it was held by a delicate silver chain. With the steady hands of a surgeon, he began to methodically clean his fingernails. "You have a reason, or is this just your day for mad?"

Ruffcarn's head shot up at Pierce's remark. He grabbed the bottle out of the huge hands of Bartholf and poured himself another drink, sloshing some onto the table. "Don't needle me, Pierce. I'm not in the mood for it. I've just come from talking to a dead man. He don't know it yet, but he's already got a plot in his name up on Boot Hill. He's gonna find out he can't shoot his mouth off at Jake Ruffcarn and live to talk about it."

"Jake, before you start talking about a dead man, you'd better make sure he can't shoot something else besides his mouth, or you might end up with dirt in your face," Pierce said and smiled. The smile never moved above his mouth. It showed perfect white teeth below a drooping handlebar mustache. His eyes remained as cold as a Texas blue norther.

"I surmise you must be referring to this Josh Logan. From

what I've heard, you might be rousting out the wrong man. He doesn't appear to be a man who takes too kindly to being pushed."

Ruffcarn glared at Pierce. "He's working for Nance. He's taken a job as his foreman. So how does that grab you—partner?"

"Keep your voice down, Ruffcarn," Pierce snapped. The silver knife stopped for a moment, then slowly started working on the next nail. "We have an agreement, and I expect you to keep it. I don't want anyone to know we're partners, at least not yet. You shoot your mouth off like that again and you'll have more trouble than Josh Logan. You understand me?"

Ruffcarn sat back slightly in his chair. The whiskey was doing its work. He was starting to relax. He realized the mistake he'd made with Pierce. This was definitely not a man to cross.

He'd known Pierce for a long time. They'd been in business before in New Orleans. He couldn't say they were friends; men like Wesley Pierce didn't have friends, but they did work well together, at least as long as they didn't cross each other.

Pierce was slick, but Ruffcarn had always felt he was smarter than Pierce. Maybe that was why Pierce had stuck with him for so long. This deal was shaping up to be the best they'd ever done. His partner was right. For now, they needed to make sure there was no obvious business connection between them.

"Yeah, you're right," Ruffcarn said. "Logan got under my hide like a festered mesquite thorn. Plus, I've been in this forsaken dust bowl for a year, and you just showed when the fort opened."

Pierce closed his silver knife, curled his long fingers toward himself, and examined his fingernails. He slipped the knife back into his vest pocket. "I know you've been out here for a while, but this is going to pay off big for us. So get a grip on yourself, and let's talk. If Logan is working for Nance, that puts a whole new light on things. You're right in that he needs to be stopped, and stopped quickly. Maybe you ought to sic Bull on him."

"Bull? He isn't looking too good after the beating he got from Logan."

Pierce adjusted his vest again before answering. "He doesn't have to look good to squeeze the trigger on that Sharps. Just get him out of town and let him finish off Logan while he's headed back to the ranch. That way it could have just as well been Comanches."

Ruffcarn thought for a moment, then said, "That would work. I was thinking we'd have Bankes brace Logan as he comes out of the saloon today. Bull could be standing by as insurance."

"Jake, why take the chance? Logan could be faster than Bankes. I doubt it, but he could be. In that case, you'd lose Bankes."

"Yes, but—"

"And," Pierce continued, "if Bull kills him away from town, no one is the wiser—no questions and no investigations."

Bull Westin was sitting at a table in a dark corner of the saloon, working on his third drink. The doctor had sewn up his nose, but it would never be the same. Bull's labored breathing could be heard from across the room.

"If you send Bull out as if he's leaving town, he can wait in those scrub oaks south of town. All he has to do is determine which direction Logan is going when he leaves, get ahead of him, find the right spot, and *boom,* your troubles are over." Pierce smiled his icy smile again.

Ruffcarn thought for a moment. Pierce was slick. It would never do to have him for an enemy. This plan had merit. If something happened to Logan on the way back to the Rocking N, it would get blamed on the Comanches. Also, Logan was a Yankee. With the exception of Penny and that Irish bartender, he wouldn't be missed. Penny was just a drifter, so he didn't count at all. As far as Starit, they would have to deal with him sooner or later, but there was no rush.

"That's a good idea, Wesley. When do you think we should do it?"

"Well, Jake, what's that old saying, 'there's no time like the present'?" What say we get it done right now?"

Ruffcarn leaned back and looked over at Bull in the corner. "Bull, if you're feeling up to it, why don't you join us."

Bull Westin stood and shuffled over to the table, dropping into a chair with a groan.

"Have a drink, Bull," Ruffcarn said, leaning over and filling Bull's glass. "How are you feeling?"

"I've sure felt better, Mr. Ruffcarn, I surely have."

"Bull, I'm concerned about you. Logan told me to tell you to get out of this country or he'd kill you." Ruffcarn shook his head in sympathy. "Why, it just doesn't seem fair to beat a man up and, after he's beaten, post him out of the country. It just doesn't seem right."

"I ain't leaving, Mr. Ruffcarn. That is, not unless you say I must."

"I'm sure not going to tell you to leave, Bull. But I'd hate to see Logan gun you down."

"He ain't gonna do that, Mr. Ruffcarn." Bull wiped gingerly at his nose. "Not if I get him first."

Jake Ruffcarn rubbed his chin, contemplating Bull's last statement. "Why, Bull, that might be a good idea. But Logan could be mighty fast with a gun, and though I know you're good with your fists, you may be no match for Logan."

Bull's attempted smile turned into a grimace, showing his broken teeth. "Mr. Ruffcarn, it would pleasure me something fierce to blow a .52-caliber hole through that blue-belly's brainpan."

"That would do us all some good. Why don't you wait outside town, figure which way he's going. Then you can get well ahead of him, and ... well, you know what to do after that. Just make it quite a ways from town. If Logan disappears, they'll blame it on the Comanches."

Bull shoved his chair back and stood. "Reckon I'll just get goin' then, Mr. Ruffcarn."

"You do that, Bull," Jake Ruffcarn said as Bull shuffled out the back door of the saloon.

"That's that. All we have to do is wait."

"We'll see," Pierce said. "We'll just see."

10

L ogan and O'Reilly joined Scott Penny at his table.
"There's two things we need to do fast," Josh said as
he was sitting down. "First, we need to reinforce the
Rocking N. Right now Mr. Nance has only two hands and Juan
Alvarez working for him. He's a retired ranger, and I've a strong
feeling that Alvarez can be a real catamount. So those two men,
even though they've a mite of age on 'em, are powerful protection
for the ranch. But the three of us added to that crew will only
make seven. With the Comanches and Ruffcarn, I figure we need
at least two more men.

"The other thing we need to do is find those rustled cattle. I
know they could already be out of the country, but I've got a
hunch that they're stashed somewhere on, or close to, the ranch.
There's at least three hundred head missing. At ten dollars a
head, that's over three thousand dollars. That's a big loss for the
ranch, and we need to find them and get them back pronto."

Scott Penny leaned back in his chair, balanced on the back
two legs, pushed his hat back, and said, "I might be able to help
on both counts. If they're still there, I know some boys down
Brownwood way who were looking for work a while back. Good

men who ride for the brand. If you like, I could ride down there after we get back to the ranch, and see if they might still be looking."

Josh nodded. "Tell Mr. Nance what you're doing and that I said it was okay, and head on down there. And Scott, we're not looking for gunslingers. We're looking for good cowboys who aren't afraid of a fight. I don't want any professional killers working for the Rocking N, and I know Mr. Nance won't stand for it."

"Boss, these are good boys. They sure as shootin' aren't afraid of a fight, but they know how to work cattle. Now there might be three of them there. Are you up to hiring that many?"

"No more than three. If they're riding together, so much the better. Men work better when they work with friends."

O'Reilly sat quietly, listening to the conversation.

"Boss, I've also got an idea where those cows might be. Now, not sayin' I haven't thrown a wide loop once or twice, but I had nothin' to do with rustlin' Rocking N stock." Scott stopped for a moment.

Josh gave Scott a steady look and said, "I believe you, Scott. If I hadn't already made up my mind about you, we wouldn't be talking right now."

Scott nodded and continued, "There's a place over on Pecan Bayou, nice little flat with good grass and water in the creek. It's way over on the northeast side of the Nance ranch, and with the few hands they have, nobody ever goes up there. I heard some of the boys talking, and I'd bet that's where they've got 'em stashed."

"Okay," Josh said, "here's what we'll do. Pat, here's a list of supplies. You and Scott get a rig from Tiny. Get it loaded up with the supplies and head for the ranch. I'm going to talk to Colonel Sturgis while you and Scott are loading up. Then we'll meet for lunch at the Diehls' and be on our way.

"By the way, Pat, is there anything I should know about the colonel?"

Pat nodded. "A good man he is, Josh. A graduate from the Academy. He made brevet brigadier general in the war. He's a career cavalryman, devoted to his country and his men."

"That surprises me. He's been buying all of his beef and horses from Ruffcarn. I suspected there might be something between the two."

"No chance of that," O'Reilly said. "He's an honest man, a tough man, but an honest one."

"Okay. Thanks, Pat. I'll approach him a little differently than I had planned. Anything else?"

Both O'Reilly and Penny shook their heads no.

"We're burning daylight, so let's get moving," Josh said as he pushed back his chair and stood.

O'Reilly and Penny stood as Josh did, and they started for the door together.

"Thanks, Cecil," Josh said as he strode for the swinging doors.

"Aye, a pleasure it is. You boys keep your peepers open. That Ruffcarn is a bad man and doesn't much like losing," Cecil Starit said as the three walked to the doors.

"Save some of that sweet rye whiskey for me return, there, Cecil. I'll be back before you know it," said O'Reilly as he went through the door.

"Boss," Scott said, nodding toward the south side of town, "looks like Bull took you at your word."

Josh watched Bull Westin ride out of town. "I hope so. I don't like the man, but I prefer to kill no man."

"Aye, that I understand. But it's an open eye you'd best keep. For that man is a back-shooter if ever I saw one and, in me humble opinion, begs for killing," O'Reilly said, then spat into the dirt.

"I'll keep an eye out," Josh said as he started toward the fort headquarters. Scott and Pat walked down to the livery stable to pick up the wagon Tiny was holding for them.

Josh mulled over the plans for the day and for the next few

days or weeks. Hopefully it wouldn't be weeks. Now, late into August, if he didn't leave soon, Callum would be out there by himself. His brother was a good man, but with the two of them working together, they might get all of the building done before the major storms started blowing in. Chancy and he would have to push it to make it there before the cold set in, even if they left now. It was going to be a race against time, to find the cattle and block Ruffcarn's plans to take the Rocking N, but however long it took, he would find those cattle and stop Ruffcarn. Callum would understand.

Josh, out of habit, removed his hat as he walked into the newly built administration building and stepped up to the sergeant's desk.

"Josh Logan to see Colonel Sturgis."

"What's your business with the colonel?" the sergeant asked as he looked the big man over. His gaze momentarily stopped at the cavalry-issue hat, trousers, and boots that Josh wore.

"Who is it, Sergeant?" boomed a voice from the back office.

The sergeant came to his feet and moved to the door of the colonel's office. "Sir, a Mr. Josh Logan to see the colonel."

"Well, don't keep him waiting, man. Send him in."

"Yes, sir," the sergeant replied. "You can see the colonel now."

"Thank you, Sergeant," Josh said as he entered the office.

Colonel Sturgis rose to his feet, stepped around his desk, and extended his hand. "You must be Major Logan. A pleasure to meet you. First Sergeant O'Reilly has told me much about you."

Josh shook the extended hand. "Nice to meet you, Colonel. But it's no longer major, just Josh or Logan."

Josh made a quick appraisal of Colonel Sturgis. The silver leaves on his shoulder boards indicated he was a lieutenant colonel. Sturgis carried command well. His dark, curly hair, mustache, and goatee rode on a confident leader. He didn't look like a man who would deal in shady practices, and O'Reilly liked and trusted him. That carried weight.

"Have a seat," Colonel Sturgis offered as he returned to his chair behind the cluttered desk. "So, Josh, what brings you to Texas? It's certainly a great distance from Michigan."

"Yes, sir, it is. My home is actually Tennessee. I enlisted to serve with the Sixth Michigan Volunteer Cavalry when it was formed in Grand Rapids. Currently I'm on my way to Colorado. Hoping to start my own ranch there."

"Interesting. I heard of a Major Josh Logan with the Sixth Michigan in reference to the Battle of Cedar Creek. Might that be you?"

"I was there; can't speak to what you heard."

"Major Logan, what I heard spoke to your exceptional leadership in thwarting Early's attack."

"Thank you, Colonel. I was only following orders. A lot more men than just me stopped General Early."

"Well, have it your way. I heard your actions were aggressive and exceptional. Now what can I do for you?"

"Colonel, I mentioned I'm headed to Colorado. This, I hope, will be only a short detour. A good friend lost his life while saving mine in the Cedar Creek battle. Before he died, he asked me to take a message to his family. That was my initial reason for being here.

"Have you heard of Bill Nance?" Josh asked.

"I have. He owns the Rocking N ranch south of here. Good operation, from what I hear. I believe he was a ranger for quite a few years."

"That's him. It was his son who was killed at Cedar Creek protecting me."

"He supported the Union?" Colonel Sturgis asked. His eyebrows lifted and his head moved slightly forward.

"He did. Mr. Nance gave his son for it, not to mention the loss of friends. He's asked me to be his foreman until the rustling matter is cleared up."

"Rustling? I've not heard of any major rustling taking place around here. Certainly there's a cow or two taken now and then, specially by the Comanche, but that's all that's reached my ears."

"Colonel, there's wholesale rustling taking place on the Rocking N. I aim to find out who's doing it."

"Any suspicions?"

"Yes, sir, but I'll keep that to myself until I have more to go on. I have another concern. Why is the fort only buying beef and horses from Jake Ruffcarn?"

Josh watched the colonel's face closely for any sign of surprise or deceit. There was none.

"I found that of interest also," the colonel said. "I can't say I like the man, but Ruffcarn has a letter from the colonel in charge of purchasing in the Department of Louisiana & Texas office stating that Ruffcarn is to be the sole provider of beef and horses. I fired off a telegram to headquarters and they confirmed the letter. I'd like to spread the purchases around, especially to someone like Mr. Nance, but my hands are tied."

"Thank you, Colonel," Josh said as he rose to his feet. "Would you mind if I use your telegraph? I'll write it up and have someone bring it. I've got to be pulling out to find those rustled cows."

The colonel stood and walked Josh to the door. "Not at all. Send it up anytime. I'd like to offer you some help, but we're stretched almighty thin with the Indian problem. By the way, I did receive your message about your Comanche encounter. Sounds like you had some good luck surviving that bunch."

"Yes, sir, I was lucky—thanks to Mr. Winchester and Mr. Colt."

The colonel laughed as they walked out of the building. "It's a pleasure meeting you, Major Logan. If I can be of service, let me know."

"Thank you, sir; I'll be seeing you," Josh said. He shook the colonel's hand and headed back to the Diehls'. Looking up to the crystal-blue sky, he noticed thunderheads starting to build off to the distant southwest. Josh had experienced a couple of these summer Texas thunderstorms. They were usually accompanied by heavy rain, wind, and sometimes hail. He had heard that twisters sometimes showed up in them. He and the crew needed to be leaving immediately after lunch. He quickened his step to meet the men, and maybe Fianna, before heading south.

11

"Come on in, Josh," Jeremiah Diehl said.

Everyone was already gathered at the table, and Mrs. Diehl was just sitting down next to her husband.

"We left you a seat next to Fianna," Mrs. Diehl said with a twinkle in her eyes. She smiled and nodded toward the open seat.

"Thank you, ma'am. I've built a sizable appetite, and that fried chicken smells mighty good," Josh said. He pulled out the chair and sat next to Fianna. She turned slightly and, with a brilliant smile, strummed a chord inside him that had never been touched. The corners of her emerald green eyes crinkled slightly with her smile. He felt his pulse quicken. Josh tried to remain nonchalant as he said, "Afternoon, Miss O'Reilly."

"Hello, Josh. Thank you for this morning."

"Wasn't nothing, ma'am. That man needed a lesson in manners."

"Josh, why don't you drop the Miss O'Reilly. You can call me Fianna or Fi if you like." Again, Fianna smiled up at him and placed her hand lightly on his arm.

Josh felt the warmth of her hand on his arm. *How can I feel like this about a woman I've just met—and the sister of my good friend?*

He smiled at her as she lifted her hand from his arm, having left it there just a little longer than necessary.

"This chicken is going to taste doubly good to me," Mr. Diehl said. "A rooster that finds it necessary to start crowing at three o'clock in the morning wears my patience thin. I'll sleep good tonight."

There were a few chuckles around the table. Josh felt relieved that the attention was off him. The girl sitting next to him was literally taking his breath away. He'd heard of things like this happening quickly. He'd never believed it. A man had to maintain a level head and be conscious of his surroundings. He couldn't; he didn't have time to become interested in Fianna. He loved that name. It fit her perfectly, right down to the few scattered freckles that floated across her soft white skin like flecks of butter on top of the fresh milk in Ma's churn.

Wait a minute—he was headed for Colorado, and no woman, especially one as attractive and as educated as Fianna, would have any interest in being with him or starting a ranch in Colorado. She was headed to California, with her brother. How would O'Reilly feel? They had fought side by side through most of the war. They trusted each other. He had to put her out of his mind.

"Now don't be bashful," Mrs. Diehl said. "Dig in. We've plenty more where that came from."

Josh filled his plate, as did Scott, Pat, and Tiny.

"You boys get all the supplies loaded?" Josh asked Pat and Scott.

"Aye, we did," Pat O'Reilly said. "That's a lot of ammunition. Hope we don't need all of it. But as I've always said, better to carry a tad more weight and have an extra bullet when the time comes."

"Yep, you boys near cleaned me out of powder and lead. But I've another load coming in soon," Mr. Diehl said. He reached across for another piece of his favorite rooster. "Gotta eat fast, Tiny's at the table, and he likes fried chicken."

"Mrs. Diehl's fried chicken is about the best I've ever tasted," Tiny said around a mouthful of chicken. "Josh, I've saddled your horse, and he's ready when you are. Also doctored up that scratch —there's no sign of infection. He's as good as new."

"Thanks, Tiny," Josh said. "Scott, you and Pat head to the ranch as soon as we're done with lunch. Looks like there's a storm brewing out to the southwest. You might have a wet camp tonight."

Scott nodded thoughtfully. "There are some well-protected camping spots along the way where we can be out of sight and out of the weather. Should be back to the ranch by noon tomorrow. You'd best keep an eye out for Westin. Wouldn't surprise me none for him to be lying up somewhere, waiting for you."

"Aye, laddie, Westin is a sorry excuse for a man. You should have killed him when you had a chance. Sorry, ma'am." O'Reilly directed the last to Mrs. Diehl. "Don't mean to bring up such at your fine table."

"Sergeant O'Reilly, my husband is a retired ranger. I've seen and heard good and bad, and I know about the likes of Bull Westin. Thank you, but you need not apologize for the truth at this table," Mrs. Diehl said.

"Thank you, ma'am. I do have a worry. I have a concern of me sister. Fianna is a lovely lass who has lived her life back East. I wouldn't want some yahoo from Ruffcarn's bunch bothering her with me not around to protect her."

"Pat, I can take care of myself," Fianna said. "I'm no shrinking violet. I know how to shoot, and I know how to ride. I'll not be bothered by anyone I don't want bothering me. And, I'll have you know, I've taken care of myself for a few years past."

"Now don't be laying those fiery green eyes on your brother, girl. I care about you and that's it."

"She'll be safe with us," Jeremiah Diehl said. "I'm not one to speak of myself, but let me just say, though I am a little older, I'm no stranger to gunplay. You need not worry about your sister.

"Thank you, Mr. Diehl," Pat O'Reilly said. "'Tis happy I am that you'll be keeping a watchful eye out for her. I trust Ruffcarn's bunch not a bit, nor the likes of that Pierce. Mark my word, Pierce is a man who bears watching. He is much too slick, I'm thinking."

"Pat, if you're ready, we've got a long trail to get back to the Rocking N," Scott said. "If we leave now, we might make the ranch by lunch or a little after tomorrow."

"Ready and raring I am, laddie. Come here, girl. Give your old brother a hug to help me on my way. It's sorry I am we can't be headed for the California country. But you know I must help a friend before we go."

Fianna got up from the table and walked around to her brother. "Pat, the fact that you can be counted on is one of the things I love about you. Don't worry about me. We'll go to California, or wherever we're destined to be, when the time comes. I love you, Pat. Now take good care of yourself."

Pat gathered her in his big, burly arms. "It's truly good for these old eyes to see you again, lass. I'll be back soon."

As Scott and Pat walked out the door, Josh stood to leave. "Mr. and Mrs. Diehl, thank you for your hospitality. Be seeing you soon."

Josh walked toward the door where Fianna was standing. He stopped and looked down at her. *She's too good for a Tennessee boy like me.*

Fianna extended her hand to him. "Thank you again for your assistance this morning. Won't you please take care of yourself?"

Josh took her hand. "Yes, ma'am, I—"

Fianna's full, sweet lips spread in a touching smile. "Fianna, please, Josh."

"Yes, Fianna, I sure will. You do the same." He reluctantly released her hand and walked out, turning to his right to head down to the stables.

Mr. Diehl walked back into the store.

∾

"JOSH WILL BE FINE," Mrs. Diehl said to Fianna as she put her arm around her. "I've lived around men my whole life. Occasionally one like Josh comes along. There are few like him. I married mine."

Fianna, her green eyes glistening, smiled at Mrs. Diehl. "Thank you, but we've only just met."

"I know, dear. Sometimes it happens like that. Then it's up to us to decide what must be done. Men are good at many things, and Josh is one of the best; but they're seldom good at knowing a woman's feelings—or even theirs. As I said, there are times when we must lovingly guide them." Turning back to the table, she said, "Now, would you help me with these dishes?"

∾

SCOTT AND PAT had pulled the wagon down to the stables and were tying their horses to the back of the wagon when Josh walked up. "I'll ride with you boys for a ways."

"We can always use another set of eyes," Pat said as he pulled his cavalry-issue .56/.52 Spencer out of the scabbard on his horse. He checked the Spencer to make sure it was fully loaded with one in the barrel, and slid it up next to his seat on the wagon. He also put the Spencer case, with ten loaded magazines for rapid reload, next to him.

"You still shooting that Spencer?" Josh asked.

"Aye, I could have made the switch to the Henry, but I prefer the Spencer's .52 caliber to that puny .44 of the Henry. When it is that I level the Spencer on something or someone, I know they're going down. Unlike that newfangled Winchester ye have. If there's ever a Winchester that packs a wee bit more power, then I shall have one."

Tiny walked out of the stable leading Josh's roan. The horse looked rested and ready to go. Josh slapped the horse on the rump, slid the Winchester into the boot, slipped his foot into the stirrup, and swung up. The roan started to bow his back, thought better of it, and shook his head. Josh felt the roan was equally ready to be off.

"Tiny, we'll see you in a couple of weeks. Okay, boys, let's move out," Josh said.

Pat popped the reins and clucked to the two horses pulling the wagon. They started south.

"'Tis a pretty good ride we have ahead of us," Pat said. "I'm noticing those clouds abuilding down south."

"Yep. We'd best keep the slickers handy. We'll be needing them later today, if I don't miss my guess," Scott said as he headed his horse south alongside the wagon. Josh guided the roan to the driver's side.

Josh touched his finger to his hat, and O'Reilly waved to Fianna as they pulled away from the stables. Fianna smiled and waved.

THEIR ACTIONS WEREN'T MISSED by the crew in the King 7 Saloon.

"Looks like they're on their way," Ruffcarn said to Pierce. "That army sergeant is with them. Wonder how that happened?"

"From what I hear," Pierce said, "he and Logan were friends from the war. I see Penny is also with them. Seems Logan is planning to make a fight of it. This isn't going to be as easy as you first thought."

"What he don't know is that it's going to be a short fight for him. Once Bull takes care of him, the rest will be easy," Ruffcarn said.

"Well, you just leave the O'Reilly girl to me," Pierce replied. "I've got plans for her that don't include anyone else. I saw that high-and-mighty look she had when she stepped off the stage. I can surely take care of that."

Ruffcarn turned from the door and looked at Pierce. He knew how Pierce had handled women in New Orleans. That was a major flaw in his personality. Several women had disappeared after being seen with Pierce, but the New Orleans police had never been able to prove anything. That worried Ruffcarn. Men of the West revered their womenfolk. There wasn't much worse a man could do than to disparage or harm a woman in the West. Why, he'd be hunted down like a varmint, then treated worse.

"Wesley, why don't you just let her be. We don't need that kind of trouble."

Pierce turned his cold eyes on Ruffcarn. "You take care of your own business and keep your nose out of mine. Nobody will know what happened to her. Anyway, if they should find her when I'm through with her, they'll figure it was Indians."

Even with his concerns, Ruffcarn needed Pierce. He also didn't want to rile the King 7 owner. Pierce wasn't a man to anger. Ruffcarn watched the wagon and men out of sight, and returned to the table to finish his drink.

12

J osh led off as they traveled almost due south leaving the town. Though it was early afternoon, the heat of the sun was beginning to dissipate as it disappeared behind the growing cloud bank.

Scott eyed the approaching thunderheads as they pushed and roiled themselves upward, turning darker with the sun behind them. "Don't think we'll make more than ten or twelve miles before that weather catches us."

Pat nodded. "Aye, 'tis likely true. We'll be wet for sure before the day ends—not like we haven't been there before."

The three men kept their eyes moving as they drew farther from the town and fort.

Josh, though he was deep in thought, didn't let that distract him from screening every tree and bush along the trail. Comanches could hide in the open and they'd never be seen until it was too late.

Josh turned slightly in the saddle to face the wagon. "I don't imagine Bull left the country. My bet is he's somewhere ahead, hoping to get a shot at me. I don't think he'll try anything until we split up—that's the way back-shooters work. But still, if he found the right place that would give him good cover and protection, he might give it a try."

"Aye, a brave man he's not. Although I hear he's deadly with that Sharps."

Scott nodded. "I can vouch for that. He loads that .52-caliber monster with 475 grains of powder. I've seen him knock down a buffler at over five hundred yards. I can't stand the man, but he can shoot."

The trio traveled in silence for several miles, listening to thunder rumble from the approaching line of thunderstorms.

Pat moved around on the wagon seat for a more comfortable position. "We're gonna get wet for sure, and it'll be soon. Looks to me like it's gonna be a gully washer. How about stopping for a pot of coffee while we can."

Josh looked across at a flash of lightning. "Good idea. It's early enough where the fire shouldn't be noticed. Smoke will dissipate fast with this wind. Let's pull down into that patch of oaks."

Pat guided the wagon between rocks as they pulled into the stand of pin oaks. The men dismounted, tied their horses, and while Josh remained on lookout, Pat and Scott quickly found some wood that would burn with little smoke. Scott dug a shallow hole for protection from the wind, shaved some tinder and started the fire. The wood caught quickly.

Pat pulled some coffee from the wagon and tossed it into the pot of boiling water, moved it to the edge of the coals, and walked over to Josh. "Those buffalo are quite a sight, aren't they?"

Josh had been watching a small herd of about two hundred move across the prairie several miles ahead. "Yes, they are. Looks like the weather is starting to make them a little nervous. Don't think any animal likes that lightning. I know I sure don't. It's getting a lot closer. Hope we can finish the coffee and get on our way before it hits."

"Coffee's ready," Scott called. "Get it while you can. Looks like the wind is starting to shift from the east to the west. I'd say we're in for a major blow."

"Not the best coffee that's ever passed my lips, but it gets the blood flowing," Pat allowed.

They quickly finished their coffee, dumped the pot onto the fire, and covered the remaining coals with dirt. The three men grabbed their slickers and got them on just as the first gust hit.

"Don't like that green tint in those clouds," Scott observed. "Reckon we could get some hail out of this, and maybe worse. Could be a tornado hiding in that thing."

Lightning slammed into a tree. The horses' eyes were rolling, and the team looked like it was ready to take off. Josh grabbed the roan and calmed it. Pat worked with the team, and Scott handled the remaining two horses. There was a slight hillock deeper into the trees. Josh yelled, "Get the team and horses behind that rise. That'll break some of the wind and give us a little more protection if it should start hailing."

They moved the team and other horses behind the rise just as the main force of the storm hit them. The heavy rain was bad enough. In just minutes, everything was drenched. Then it started hailing. It started out small, the size of sleet; then the large hail came.

"Get under the wagon," Josh yelled.

They scrambled under the wagon, at the same time trying to control the team and their other horses. It was the best they could do. Josh watched helplessly as the hail bounced off the horses' backs. The trees and the hill were blocking most of it, but he could still see them wince when they took a direct hit.

Scott leaned over and yelled, "Wish there was some way we could protect the horses more. They're sure taking a beating."

"Hopefully, this'll not be lasting long," Pat yelled back over the noise of the wind and hail as the hail continued to beat their horses.

As suddenly as it came, it was gone. The wind died down quickly. Leaves stripped from the oaks littered the ground.

Immediately, they were out from under the wagon, checking on the horses.

Josh examined the roan first, stroking the Roman nose and talking to him to calm him down; next he went to the team. "How do your horses look?"

"Mine's fine, excepting a few bruises," Pat said.

"Mine too."

Josh continued to examine the team and found the bay with a cut and bleeding left front fetlock. "Looks like the bay took a pretty bad hit. The fetlock joint is bleeding and he's favoring it."

Josh walked the team around, and the bay continued to favor the leg. "He'll never make it to the ranch. Let's get him unhitched and, Pat, if you don't mind, we'll put your horse in the harness. Reckon we're still close enough to town for you boys to head back and switch out a healthy horse with Tiny. You can spend the night there and start out again *mañana*. It'll put you a day later getting to the ranch, but I don't see how it can be helped."

Scott walked over, checked the bay, and started unhitching him. "Yeah, boss, looks like you're right. I hate to turn around, but I don't see any other answer."

Pat brought up his horse and, after a little persuasion, they got him settled into the harness.

Josh stepped into the saddle. "It appears the rest of the horses have some nasty bruises, but it sure could have been a lot worse."

"A lot worse," Scott said. "I've seen horses and cattle killed from hail. If it's big enough, it'll kill whatever is in the open. Why, I remember down around Uvalde four or five years ago we almost had a herd wiped out. That storm hit early in the morning and we immediately had a stampede. There was one big mossyhorn running like crazy. He was hit in the head with a chunk of ice the size of a bucket—drove him right to his knees. Why—"

"How about you hold up that story until we get back on the

trail, and you can share it with Pat on your way back to town," Josh said with a wink at Pat. "We let Scott get to spinning a yarn, and we're liable to be here for the rest of the day."

Scott grinned and turned to Pat. "We've got plenty of time. I can't imagine letting you miss out on a good story."

Scott's brow wrinkled slightly. "By the way, how you reckon Bull fared in this?"

"Hopefully he's dead," Pat said as he turned and spit. "But he likely found a hole somewhere."

"Let's just keep our eyes open," Josh said as they left the concealment of the oaks.

Pat stopped the team for a moment and turned to Josh with a twinkle in his eye. "Now, Major, you keep your eyes sharp and clear. I've no desire to give Fianna any bad news."

"You keep *your* eyes sharp, and I'll see you at the ranch in a couple of days," Josh said gruffly. He raised a hand, the buckboard turned north to town, and Josh quickly turned south to keep Pat from seeing his face. How the heck did Pat know about his new feelings for Fianna? He wasn't even sure about it himself. Anyway, he was headed for Colorado Territory, and Fianna and Pat were off to California. He wasn't even sure that Fianna had any feelings for him. How could a beautiful woman care for a big galoot like him? Even if she did, nothing could come of it.

He let the roan out into a lope. It felt good to be in the saddle. There were still several hours of daylight left. He'd be able to cover some miles today. The roan felt like he, too, was enjoying stretching his muscles after the storm.

Josh carefully surveyed the plains and arroyos. This country was cut with arroyos. Most were dry, but still had vegetation along their edges. They were sliced out of the hills from heavy rains that coursed down the hillsides. This passing storm had been heavy enough to fill many of them, although the current would die quickly, and the water would evaporate and absorb into the dry ground.

In this part of Texas every drop of water counted. The short grasses that survived in this area were nourished by the storm. Everything looked washed and clean. The pin oaks, the bluestem grasses and even the prickly pear had put on a new face, enjoying the moisture.

Josh scanned the shinnery-covered hills. He slowed the roan to a walk and, while remaining alert to anything out of place, his mind shifted to the Colorado Territory. His uncle had talked about the valley so often, Josh could picture it. He could see the tall nourishing grass, the stream coursing down from the majestic mountains surrounding the valley on three sides. The mountains were covered with tall pines, which would provide the lumber for their ranch. It was all there waiting for him and Callum, but time was drifting away.

Every day here meant a day less to build a house, barn, and corral for the Spanish mustangs he planned to catch with Callum, but his debt to Rory, and now to Bill and Mary Louise, had to be cleared before he could leave. They were in dire straits and he wanted to help them.

He must find out how Ruffcarn planned to take the ranch and why. *Why* was the big question. They were here in the eastern edge of the Comancheria. Since the war started and the men left, the Comanches rode almost unhampered through this country. Though the army was again establishing posts and forts to control the Comanche, they were still a deadly force to reckon with. Land was available farther east that was much less hazardous to ranchers and their stock. So why was Bill's land so important?

Josh enjoyed the slightly cooler wind that had followed the storm. It was a welcome respite from the stifling summer heat. The sky was clearing from the west. The sun, lowering now, slipped between the higher clouds and the horizon and spread across the plains, highlighting the brilliant greens of the washed-clean oaks, and reds and yellows reflecting off the ochre boulders on the hillsides.

The sun's light also struck the barrel of Bull's .52-caliber Sharps on the hillside, where he lay in ambush. Josh saw the bright flash of reflected light and spurred his horse. The last that his mind registered before the bullet slammed into his head was the puff of smoke from the flash.

The slug hit Josh on the right side of his head, just above his hat brim. He was immediately unconscious, but some innate reaction caused him to grab the saddle horn, only for a moment. The roan was running full out as Josh gradually slipped from the saddle. His left boot slipped through the stirrup and hung as the horse continued to race across the prairie.

BULL LEANED BACK AND SMILED. "Gotcha, ya blasted blue-belly." He watched as Josh slumped forward, then slowly slipped from the saddle. When he saw that Josh's foot was caught in his stirrup, Bull's smile turned to laughter.

His eyes lit with an evil gleam as Josh's body bounced across the sand, rocks, and shinnery and disappeared into the Cross Timbers pin oaks. "That Yankee boy is a dead man for sure," he said out loud. "He was dead before he hit the ground." Bull knew he never missed with the Sharps. This was a good day. Revenge was sweet. He stood and leaned back to stretch the back muscles that had stiffened.

When he saw Josh split off and Pat and Scott head the buckboard back to town, he knew his time had come. Bull was familiar with the perfect spot for the ambush, and he shadowed the Yankee cavalryman toward it.

Bull had been caught on an open hillside when the storm hit. If it hadn't been for his hiding on the downwind side of his horse, he felt sure he would've been killed. Even so, he had some major bruises besides those he'd sustained in the losing fight with Josh, and a big lump on the side of his head from the hail. His hat had saved him.

Now he was hurting. He was stiff and sore and needed a drink. He figured Mr. Ruffcarn and Pierce would be pleased to know that Logan would no longer be a problem. There sure wasn't any need for him to try to find Logan. The way that horse was moving, he'd probably never catch up with them. Anyway, Logan would be coyote bait by now.

Bull stepped into his saddle and, with a self-satisfied smirk, chuckled low in his chest. This was a good day's work.

JOSH'S BODY was like a rag. He bounced off the rocks and slammed into a pile of prickly pear. He twisted and turned, unconscious as he smashed against the ground. The roan's left rear hoof hit him in the ribs, but he felt nothing. He hit the shinnery, and his shirt was ripped to rags. The roan raced into the thick pin oaks of the Cross Timbers. The big horse turned to miss a huge oak, and Josh's foot slipped out of the boot that was hung in the stirrup. He rolled across the grass and crumpled against the tree.

Except for his legs, there was almost no place on his body that wasn't bleeding. Blood was still flowing from the bullet wound in his head. His face was covered with cuts, each one bleeding. Prickly pear thorns were stabbed into his back and shoulders, with a pad still stuck to the back of his neck. He felt nothing. He lay broken and still against the tree as the shadows grew and the sun disappeared behind the red hills.

13

Bull rode into Camp Wilson as the waning moon crept above the eastern hills. Pain still surged through his face from Logan's blows, but he felt good. He'd ambushed men before, but Logan was personal. Laughter rolled up from his belly as he relived the sight of Logan's body bouncing across the prairie, smashing into the cactus and shinnery. Carefree for the first time since he'd met the Yankee near the Pecan, he walked his horse boldly down main street to the King 7 Saloon, stepped down and hitched him at the rail. Elation surged through his body as he pushed the saloon's swinging doors open.

He stood there for a moment. All eyes swung toward him. Three troopers at the bar stared at him for a moment before turning back to their drinks. His swollen face and nose still showed the results of his fight with Logan. It would be some time before it healed, and his nose would always be misshapen. Bartholf, wiping glasses behind the bar, glanced up. His eyes dismissed Bull as he went back to his glass cleaning.

Ruffcarn and Pierce were sitting at a table in the corner, away from the bar. Ruffcarn's surprise was written across his face. Pierce's face registered nothing. His eyes held Bull's in a cold stare for a few moments before he went back to his game of solitaire. Ruffcarn nodded to the empty chair at the table, indicating Bull should have a seat.

Bull swaggered across the room, pulled out the chair, and dropped his huge bulk into it. There was a bottle on the table. Ruffcarn turned to Bartholf. "Bring us another glass."

Bartholf dropped the glass in front of Bull. Ruffcarn waited as Bull filled his glass, downed it, and filled another. "What are you doing back here?"

"That no-good Yankee is dead."

Pierce glanced up from his cards. "You killed him?"

"Dead as a stomped rat."

Pierce dealt another card. "Logan appeared to me like a hard man to kill. Are you sure he's dead?"

"Sure as I'm sitting here at this table," Bull said. "Why, that .52-caliber slug knocked him out of his saddle like a sack of flour. Prettiest sight I ever did see. I tell you, I loved every minute.

"I watched that crew split up after the storm. I figured about where he was going, rode on ahead, found a likely spot, and waited. He never even knew he was dead. One second he was riding along, sitting tall and proud, and the next second he was coyote fodder. My, my, my, it was something to see," Bull gloated.

Ruffcarn slapped Bull on the back. "Good job. Have another drink. In fact, have the whole bottle. You earned it," he said as he slid the bottle over in front of Bull.

Pierce wasn't done. "What did you do with the body?"

At this, Bull answered defensively, "I ain't done nothin' with it."

Ruffcarn's smile turned down and his brow wrinkled. "You did check on him? You rode up to him and poked him or did something to make sure he was dead?"

"Didn't have to. I shot him in the head. When he rolled off his horse, his foot got caught in the stirrup. You should have seen him bouncing through those rocks and pears. He was dead before his head ever hit the ground. But he was double dead with that horse running flat out and dragging him like he did. After a while the horse headed into a thicket of pin oaks. Didn't figger there was any need to follow him—Logan was already a long time dead."

Pierce looked at Ruffcarn. "He may not be dead."

Bull slammed his glass back onto the table. "He's dead, I tell you. He's dead. I shot him. I saw him being dragged. There's no way a man could live through that, no matter how tough he is."

Pierce turned back to Bull. "Keep your voice down. You didn't ride up to him. You didn't check him. I don't care what you did or saw. A man like that doesn't die easy. He could still be alive."

Bull shook his head and turned to Ruffcarn. "Mr. Ruffcarn, you're worrying for nothin'. I tell you, I killed him. He ain't gonna be a bother to no one. Why, the coyotes probably already cleaned up any sign of him."

"Alright, Bull, we believe you. Pierce is just being extra cautious. Why don't you take this bottle and get a room from Bartholf. You can rest up tonight, and we'll head to the ranch in the morning."

Bull slid back his chair. He took the bottle and nodded to Pierce. "Mr. Ruffcarn, I swear he's dead." Bull walked off muttering under his breath.

Ruffcarn wanted to believe Bull. This could be great news. Everything would go so much easier if Logan were dead. But he was still concerned that Bull hadn't physically checked Logan. "So what do you think?" Ruffcarn asked Pierce.

"I think varmints are probably feeding on him right now. Bull is a dead shot. Then you add being dragged by his horse, and the odds are high he's dead. But there's always a long shot, and Logan is, or was, a tough *hombre*. But yeah, I think he's dead."

Ruffcarn leaned back with a smile. "That's settled. Now we can get along with our plan. When we have the Rocking N, we can start our search. Then we can go and do anything we want. I'm ready to get out of this Godforsaken country and get back to civilization. Maybe California or New York or maybe even Europe."

"Don't get too anxious. We still have a long way to go and a lot to do to get Nance's ranch. He's a hardhead and will probably never sell it to us. But now, with Logan gone, we can kill them all if we have to. No one will be the wiser. And I've got a date to put a snotty little Irish girl in her place."

"Pierce, her brother is still around and he's ex-army. You'd best be careful with him or we could have all those soldier boys riled at us. At least wait until he leaves. Scott Penny is also still here, and I've got a feeling he can be trouble."

"I'll wait, but not too long. I think those boys are leaving town tomorrow. After that, she's fair game—and, Ruffcarn, don't you try to interfere with me. It wouldn't be smart, or good for you or our business deal."

"Sure, sure. But let's just keep a low profile till we can consummate this deal."

Pierce's black eyes lit up as his lips lifted in a sinister smile. "Good choice of words; I think I'd like this deal consummated sooner than later."

FIANNA WAS WORRIED as she looked around the table. Her brother, Pat, sat across the table from her. Scott sat next to him. Mr. and Mrs. Diehl sat at each end of the table. She scanned each face. She wasn't the only one who was worried.

"Do you think he's okay," she asked anyone who would answer.

Pat reached across the table and patted her hand. "He's fine as the hairs on a frog. There be no tougher man that I know. Just because Bull is back in town means nothing. He was probably hiding, waiting for Josh to leave."

Fianna peered into her brother's eyes. She knew he was only trying to comfort her, for she could see the worry in his eyes.

Mrs. Diehl smiled at her. "He's one of the toughest men I've met. I don't know if anything has happened to him, but I have faith that no matter what, he'll survive."

Scott chimed in, "Tiny set us up with a team for the wagon, so we'll be heading back that way in the morning. I'm sure he's fine, but we can keep a lookout for him. Of course, he didn't have much farther to go before he turned a little more east. But we should be able to confirm he's okay."

Fianna thought for a moment. "I'm going with you."

"No, lass. 'Tis not smart. We have many a mile of Comanche country to pass through before we reach the ranch, and with a wagon. This isn't the time or the place for you to be with us."

"Pat, I'm going!"

Mrs. Diehl reached for her hand. "You must think, my dear. As helpful as you might be, you'll still be a distraction on the trail. Your brother and Scott don't need their attention divided while traveling through Comanche country. I know. There's been many a time I've wanted to go with Mr. Diehl, but common sense won out. They'll be safer without you. Trust me."

Fianna lowered her head. "There's so much I don't understand about this country. But I just want Josh to be safe. Is that asking too much?"

Mrs. Diehl continued to hold Fianna's hand. After a sad, understanding smile, she said, "No, dear, that isn't too much to ask. But there are times we must help our menfolk by staying home so they needn't worry about us while they're about their business. Here, we have the army and, of course, Mr. Diehl."

Jeremiah Diehl smiled at Fianna, then looked at Pat as he said, "You're in good hands here, Fianna."

Fianna raised her head. Her eyes were glistening, but her chin was up as she looked at her brother. "Alright, I'll stay with Mr. and Mrs. Diehl. I'll wait. But, Pat, please, as soon as you can, send me word of Josh."

"Aye, lass, I'll do that, as soon as I can. 'Tis my thinking now that we should all get some rest. We'll begin early in the morning."

"Sounds good to me, although I think I might sleep better if I had a touch of Cecil's medicine," Scott said as he slid his chair back from the table.

"Aye, a wee nip would do me fine also. Mr. Diehl, would you care to join us?"

"Don't mind if I do," Jeremiah Diehl said as he glanced at his wife.

"Go along with you now, and stay out of trouble," Mrs. Diehl said.

∿

THE THREE MEN walked to the Shamrock; the only sound was the scuffling of their boots along the boardwalk. As they entered, Cecil Starit was stacking chairs on the tables, preparing to close.

"Is it Irish nectar you'll be wanting tonight?" Cecil asked as he glanced at the three men entering his saloon.

"Aye, it is, and you might bring the bottle and four glasses, if you're a mind to join us," Pat said as they unstacked the chairs and sat at the table.

"Thanks for the invite. I'd be pleasured." Cecil brought the bottle and four glasses, poured each a shot, and said, "To your health." They each drank; then Pat poured another round.

"Did you see Bull ride back into town?" Cecil asked.

"We did, which has us wondering why he came back. He's a back-shooter, and I know for sure that Josh has him buffaloed," Scott said.

"'Tis not a good sign, I'm thinking—him being back," Pat said. "But I've been knowing Josh Logan for many a year, and hard it is for me to imagine that Bull could've gotten a shot into him."

"Any man can be ambushed," Scott said. "Even the best. I'm thinking that we head out in the morning just as we planned. We've been hired by Josh to do a job for Mr. Nance, so nothing has changed."

"I'm with you, lad. We can leave bright and early and keep an eye out for any possible ambush. If it happened before he was to turn off, we'll find it."

"I think you boys have the right idea," Jeremiah Diehl said. "Heaven knows I hope that Josh is fine, but if he isn't, Bill Nance will need your help even more."

"Then there it is," Pat said. "A final toast to Josh's safety."

14

"Get up, son. You can't be lying there. You've got to be moving. If you lie there, you'll die. No son of mine ever died because he was a quitter."

"Pa?" Josh whispered. "Pa, are you there?"

Josh felt the warmth of the sun slipping through the treetops. He looked toward the warmth, but could only see a diffused red. His eyes were closed. Try as he might, he couldn't open them. He tried to raise his head and was engulfed in a sea of pain. He was being stabbed all over his upper body. It was like needles jabbed into his body, especially in the back of his neck, when he tried to turn his head. He moved his left hand up to his neck. "What the blazes is stabbing me?"

His hand found the prickly pear pad, as spines lanced into his fingers. He jerked his hand away, trying to figure out what it was. Tentatively he reached back again, felt a spine, moved his fingers away from it, and grasped an open space on the pad. He ripped the pad from his neck, leaving a few spines embedded. Now at least he could turn his head, even though the spines torn from the pad still pierced his skin.

"Why can't I see?" He felt around his face, his eyes. They were crusted over with a hard, flaky material. Slowly, painfully, he began to rub and pick flakes away from his eyes. When he felt most of the substance gone, he moistened his fingers with saliva and continued to rub. Gradually his eyelids opened. He looked at his fingers, blood. Some of the encrusted blood remained over his eyelids, but he could see.

What he saw shocked his clouded mind. There was almost no place from his waist up that wasn't covered with blood. He tried to think through the pain. *How did I get here? What happened?* Gradually yesterday's events started coming back. *I remember the sun coming out. The glint on the hillside. I spurred the roan. The last thing I remember was the puff of smoke. I must have been looking right at it.*

Josh hurt all over, but his head felt like it was going to explode. He tentatively touched the right side of his head. He felt a long blood-encrusted gash. It hurt like blazes. *Bull Westin. I knew he was a back-shooter. Should have been more alert.*

His mind couldn't stay focused. He could swear Pa had been here, but he knew that was impossible. Gradually he started assessing his injuries. His left boot was gone and his left leg hurt like the dickens. He flexed it and it seemed to work fine. He moved his right leg—no pain. *At least some part of me doesn't hurt.* His gun—he felt frantically for the Colt. Somehow the leather thong had held his gun in place. He breathed a short sigh—it hurt to breathe. Josh pushed himself up into a sitting position. He passed out.

He was out only a few minutes. As he regained consciousness, he reached into his right pocket and sighed with relief. His Barlow that Pa had given him was still in his pocket. At least he had his knife and Colt. He needed to sit up. Josh took a deep breath and was rewarded with a sharp pain in his right side. *Hope that's not a broken rib. My left boot is gone; my left leg hurts like the dickens. I must have been dragged. Where's the roan?* Josh looked around him as best he could ... no roan. He pulled himself up against the big oak tree and leaned back. Sharp needles stabbed him all over his back. *My gosh. The horse must have dragged me through a mile of prickly pear. I've got to get these things out of me.* Josh passed out again.

When he came to, he started picking out the prickly pear spines that he could reach. His upper body was covered with them. Methodically he worked. Each long barbed spine dug into his flesh and required a distinct yank to get it out. He removed the majority of the long spines from his arms and chest, but the tiny fuzzy barbed spines remained. He was thirsty. He hadn't had any liquid since the coffee the day before. He had to find water. He had to start moving. Josh passed out again.

"Come on, Josh. You'd best be moving. You've got to find water, my boy. You can do it. You're a Logan. Your ma and I are counting on you."

Josh woke up and looked around. He could swear he heard his pa, but no one was around. He knew he had to get moving. If he stayed here, he would die. He might die anyway, but not like this ... not giving up. *I need a walking stick.* He pulled out his Barlow and opened it. A green pin oak limb about six feet long lay within his reach. *Must have blown off in the storm.* He reached out, pulled it to him, and slowly trimmed the branch with his Barlow until it was as clean and smooth as possible. He slipped his knife back into his pocket, and using his newly found staff, braced against the tree and slowly stood. His head throbbed and it was hard to focus. He took his first step and fell. Josh lay there for a moment, pushed off from the ground with his lacerated hands, rose to one knee, grasped the staff with both hands, and took a couple of deep breaths that were cut short by the pain in his right side. He slowly pulled himself to his feet.

He had to get to the ranch, but first he had to find water. It would be easier after the rain, although the water would be soaked up fairly fast in this dry country. He staggered forward, deeper into the trees. There was a slight slope here. If he cut across it, he might find a streambed. He kept moving forward, drifting in and out of delirium. He felt like his father was close, guiding him. He fell again—and again. Each time he got back up.

It was hard walking with only one boot. His sock had quickly been eaten away by the rough ground, and the sole of his left foot was bloody. He kept moving, one foot in front of the other. One more step; he had to find water. He had covered several miles. His head drooped, and he found it hard to keep his eyes open; then he fell, this time over the small creek's embankment. He tumbled down the side, through the brush into the rocky creek, and passed out again. He was within inches of water, but he wasn't moving.

TRAVELS FAR HAD BEEN WATCHING Josh since the previous afternoon. He'd seen Bull shoot. He watched as Josh had been dragged into the timber. He waited until Bull left, then rode after the fallen man. The trail was easy to follow; blood was everywhere. The man would be dead when he found him. He would take his scalp and whatever of value and leave him.

The old Kickapoo had no use for the white man. His people had originally lived in the green land of the north, near the big lakes. Life was good and game was abundant. Then the white men moved in; they had been driven from their land farther and farther south. Now they were in Texas. There was plenty of buffalo and other game, but now they had to also contend with the Comanche.

Travels Far came up to the white man as he lay unconscious next to the tree. He had watched the man through the night and heard him speak through his delirium. Travels Far was a patient man. He could take this man's scalp anytime. He waited. The white man, as if in a trance, rubbed his blood-encrusted eyes. He fumbled around, searching in his half-blinded state, and found a limb. With his knife, he trimmed the limb into an acceptable walking stick; then he rested. After his short rest, he gathered himself and, using the walking stick in one hand while bracing himself against the tree with his other, he pulled himself erect and moved off in a staggering shuffle. The Kickapoo was fascinated that this man, as seriously hurt as he was, had gotten to his feet, and even though he constantly fell, he continued to move forward. The Kickapoo respected strength and bravery. This would be interesting to see how long the white man could keep going. Ah, he fell again. He lay there not moving.

Travels Far, no more than seven or eight feet behind Josh, sat his horse quietly, watching the white man. He wouldn't get up this time, and if he wasn't dead, the Kickapoo would kill him. Again he watched, amazed, as the man pushed himself up and started staggering forward again. He could see the massive head wound on the right side of Josh's head. Blood was still seeping down over his ear and his neck, yet he continued to move forward. As he followed Josh, he began to think, *This white man doesn't deserve to die like this.* It would take a huge spirit to keep a man moving with the injuries he had. As the distance covered by Josh mounted, Travels Far made a decision. He would take this white man to his village. There the women could work with him. The man would probably die, but the Kickapoo people would not take his life.

Travels Far followed slowly behind the man. Each time he fell, he would rise again and move forward. He was now leaving a bloody footprint from his left foot. The sole of his foot was raw, but he kept moving forward. The Kickapoo wondered if the man would notice the creek he was approaching. The creek had pecan trees and pin oaks along the outer bank. Near the bank was a line of brush. The white man kept moving. He stopped momentarily at the brush line, pushed on through, and stepped over the edge. He fell, rolling into the creek bed, where he lay still. Water was only inches from his face. Travels Far could hear him talking to himself.

"I CAN MAKE IT, Pa. I won't let you down," Josh mumbled. He moved his arm to get up and struck the water. He fumbled desperately forward and dropped his face into the water. It was fresh and cool. It tasted good as it trickled over his swollen tongue and down his parched throat. He splashed water over his head, cleaned his eyes and tried to cleanse his head of some of the blood—it was still bleeding. He lay quiet for a moment, then drank more water. How far had he come? *If I only knew more about this country. But somehow I'm going to make it out of here. I know it.* Josh wanted to roll over onto his back and relax those back muscles, but his back was covered with the prickly pear spines, and it felt like a thousand needles when he attempted to lie on his back.

He drank more water. He had no means to carry water. *I must drink as much as I can before I start out again.* He lay a moment more, then struggled to his feet, fell back to his knees, vomited most of the water he drank, and passed out.

TRAVELS FAR RODE his mustang into the creek bed, sat for a moment watching Josh, then slipped off his horse. He examined the white man closely. His body was bleeding and bruised; his left foot was raw; his left knee was swollen so much it was tight inside his pants leg. Shaking his head, he wondered, in disbelief, how the man could even stand on this knee. He looked over the white man's hands. They were raw and bloody. They had taken tremendous punishment while he was being dragged. Travels Far examined Josh's head wound. *This white man was lucky. If the*

bullet had been the thickness of buckskin leather closer, he would be dead. Travels Far carefully moved his hand over Josh's upper body. It was covered with prickly pear thorns, not only the big thorns, but the small fuzzy needles that worked their way into the flesh with every movement. They must come out or they would sour and smell and might even cause the man to die—if he didn't die from his head wound or from injuries inside his body.

The old Kickapoo slipped his arms under Josh's arms and clinched his hands together on his chest. He lifted Josh with one smooth motion and carried him to the mustang. The horse rolled his eyes at the white-man smell but stood his ground as Travels Far spoke to him softly. With one motion, he powered Josh across the mustang's withers. Josh lay on his stomach with his head to the left side of the horse and his legs hanging on the opposite side. Travels Far leaped onto the back of his horse, spoke to him again, and nudged him with his heels. The horse went up the opposite bank, carrying the Indian and the white man.

15

After saying their goodbyes, Scott and Pat had gotten an early start. Tiny had the wagon hitched with a new team and both their horses saddled when they reached the stables.

"Good luck finding Josh," Tiny said as the two men were tying on their saddlebags. "Sure hope he's okay."

Pat's brow was wrinkled with worry. Concern for his friend had kept him awake much of the night. He climbed onto the wagon seat and grasped the reins in his big hands. "We'll be keeping an eye out for sure. Josh is a tough *hombre*. I'm hoping it's nothing we'll be finding. That'll mean the lad is at least alive."

Scott nodded. "I reckon we'll find something. Bull Westin wouldn't dare to come back into town if he thought there was a chance of running into Josh. Josh posted him out of town, and Westin knows that their next meeting will be his last. I hate to say it, but I think Josh was bushwhacked, and we'll probably find him."

Tiny shook his head. "I sure hope you're wrong, Scott. I surely do."

The hot summer sun was sliding up toward midmorning

when they pulled up at the point where Josh had split off and they'd headed back to town. Not even noon and the sun was already intense. Scott yanked off his kerchief and wiped his face. "If Josh ain't dead, I sure hope he still has his hat. Without your hat in this country, it don't take long for this heat to kill you."

"He'll be needing water, too, laddie. Let's just move along his trail and see if we can spot anything."

Scott moved ahead of the team as he tracked Josh. It was easy after the rain. His tracks were deep, as the hooves of his horse had sunk into the muddy ground of yesterday. Today the ground had already dried, and the horses stirred little puffs of dust as they walked. "Looks like Josh let the roan out a little to let him stretch his muscles," he said as he registered the distance between the horse's tracks. After a while, he could see where Josh had pulled him back to a walk. The roan was a big horse and, even at a walk, he covered a lot of country. "We'll be reaching the point where Josh would have been turning southeast soon. If we don't find anything before then, we'll have to head south to get to the ranch."

"We'll be going a bit farther yet," Pat said. With Scott doing the tracking, he kept a watch for any possible ambush site. They were in Indian country, and it never paid to relax out here. He had been in the cavalry for what felt like his whole life. Whether it was Indians or Johnny Rebs, a man had to be on his toes all the time.

"Hold it up," Scott said as he stepped from the saddle. He could see where the roan had leaped forward from a walk. He examined the ground and shinnery patches. There it was: a spot of blood. "Why don't you climb down and take a look at this."

Pat stepped down from the wagon and walked over to where Scott was kneeling. "Shades of the devil," Pat exclaimed. He reached down and picked up the coagulated blood. "He should've killed the bushwhacker when he had the chance."

Scott walked a little farther. "It gets worse. Look at this."

Pat walked over to Scott—there was sign that made his flesh crawl. "It's looking like his foot caught in the stirrup. That crow-bait roan must've took off running and dragging Josh. Lord have mercy, look at the blood." Every few steps there was another impression in the ground or blood on the prickly pear where Josh's body had been ravaged. "Well, as much as I don't like this, at least maybe we can find him."

Scott climbed back onto his horse to follow the gruesome trail; Pat trailed behind in the wagon. The roan was heading for a bunch of pin oaks.

Scott noticed another set of horse's tracks. These were unshod. "Looks like Josh has more trouble. There's an Indian following him." When they entered the tree line, Scott found Josh's boot where it had finally slipped off his foot. He saw where the horse's momentum had slung Josh against the old oak's trunk. Blood had pooled here. Josh must have been here for a long time. He saw where Josh had pushed himself against the tree trunk. Scott got off his horse and picked up a prickly pear pad covered with blood. He carried it back to Pat. "Look at this."

Pat just shook his head. "Aye, 'tis hard to imagine the pain this boy must be in. But I know him, and the lad is no quitter. As long as there's an ounce of strength in his body, he'll be fighting. Though I'm mightily concerned about the Indian."

They followed Josh, noting where he would fall and get up, fall and get up. What was interesting was that the Indian's horse had been moving very slowly. It looked like he had been walking right behind Josh. When they came to the creek, the brush was bloody, and the sign told the story. Josh hadn't even noticed the creek before he fell.

Scott dismounted, and Pat followed him down into the creek. It wasn't running, but shallow pools of water from yesterday's rain stood in the creek bed. Reading the sign, Scott saw where Josh had drank from the creek, vomited, and passed out again. They could see where the Indian had picked him up—no small feat—and evidently laid him over the horse, and leaped up behind him. The horse's tracks led up the other side of the creek bed. Scott mounted up, and Pat waited as Scott continued to follow the Indian's tracks until they disappeared on the rocky ground east of the trees. Scott cast about trying to find the tracks. He gradually increased his circle, but there was no more sign of the Indian. He had just disappeared.

Scott rode back to the creek bank, where Pat was brewing some coffee. "What do you think?"

"I'm thinking Josh is either in really big trouble or a very lucky man." He held up his hand as Scott started to say something. "Have some coffee, lad. You asked me; now let me explain." Pat and Scott squatted by the almost smokeless fire and drank their coffee. Pat continued, "This Injun could have killed him at any time. 'Twould have been easy with Josh's condition. But he didn't. He followed him for a long distance. Indians respect courage. And this one saw great courage in Josh's determination to continue. He might be taking him to heal the lad, if that's even possible. Of course, it's wrong I've been before. But I'm thinking I'm right this time." Pat sipped his coffee as he stared into the fire.

"Yep, sure could be," Scott said. "Although he just might be taking Josh to his camp to have a little fun. You're right about one thing. They do respect courage. But they also prolong the death of brave men. The Injun believes it makes him stronger. But having said that, I sure hope you're right."

"Aye. We'd best be going, if it's the ranch we'll be reaching tomorrow."

While Pat scattered the fire, pouring the remaining coffee over it, then kicking dirt over the sticks, Scott took the saddle horses down to the creek to drink, and brought water up to the team. After they had a chance to drink, Scott brought the saddle horses up the embankment and tied his horse to the wagon. "How about I drive the wagon for a while?"

The Irishman handed over the reins. "I'm beholden to you. My rear was getting almighty tired of that wagon seat." They turned out of the timber and headed for the ranch.

RUFFCARN HADN'T SLEPT WELL. It wasn't that the bed was uncomfortable; he'd slept in a lot worse. He just couldn't shut down his mind. His partnership in New Orleans with Pierce had proved to be massively profitable. The guns they'd sold to the South established friendships that they both needed and also brought in huge profits. They had branched out into real estate and had done well. It was like they were money magnets. Their connection with that United States Army major, now a colonel, was a stroke of genius. Yes, they had to split their gunrunning profits with the colonel, but he could provide all of the gunpowder and weapons they could sell. It had turned out to be a profitable relationship.

Regrettably, the wife of a prominent landowner had disappeared. There had been others, but none this highly placed or as popular. She'd been well known in New Orleans society. Unfortunately, she liked gambling and gamblers. The last person she'd been seen with was Pierce. In their investigation, the police turned up three other women who had disappeared under questionable circumstances. Two of them had last been seen with Pierce, and one with him. Ruffcarn had never harmed a woman in his life. He'd not harmed her, but his name came up in the investigation because he'd seen her last, and he was a partner with Pierce.

Sometimes, he wished he'd never met Pierce, but then they had been extremely successful together, and this time they stood to make a fortune. Shaking his head, he climbed out of bed, poured some water into the basin, and washed his face. There was a knock on his door.

"Yeah."

It was Bankes. "Boss, you said you wanted to leave by six. It's five now, and Bartholf is rustling up some eggs."

"I'll be down shortly. Is Pierce down yet?"

"Yep, he just walked in."

"Get Bull and you two make sure all the boys are ready. We'll head for the ranch as soon as we eat."

"Sure thing."

Ruffcarn heard Bankes's steps echoing down the hall as he headed downstairs to the bar. *I'll be glad to get back to civilization. And it'll be much more relaxing when I no longer have to deal with Pierce.* Ruffcarn knew he was smarter than Pierce, but the man disturbed him. Pierce was like a coiled rattlesnake; a man didn't want to be close to him when he was mad. He slipped his wrinkled shirt on, belted on his gun, and pulled his boots on. He grabbed his hat as he went out the door.

Downstairs, Pierce was seated at his table, eating eggs, bacon, and biscuits that Bartholf had made. He was dressed as usual, black shined boots, black pants, starched white shirt with black garters around his biceps, black vest, black tie, and black hat. His black jacket was hung over the back of his chair. His cold dark eyes focused on Ruffcarn as he walked up to the table.

Ruffcarn pulled up a chair, scraped some eggs and bacon from the platter on the table, and reached for the plate of biscuits. "Bartholf's not a half-bad cook."

Pierce nodded. "The soldier boy and Scott already left this morning. Be interesting to know what they find."

Ruffcarn nodded. He'd like to confirm that Logan was dead. "We'll just have to wait to know for sure. But I've never seen Bull miss."

"Always a first time. But I doubt that he did. You pulling out this morning?"

"Yeah, we're heading back to the ranch. I want to make sure Nance's ranch continues to lose cattle. We've got a big flat over on the Pecan that'll take a couple thousand head. Those Rockin' N cowboys will never find them there. We'll get them rebranded and sell them to the army. With our contract, we can wipe Nance out. But we need to increase the pressure on him. How's our contact in Austin doing on voiding Nance's ownership of the ranch?"

Pierce's brow wrinkled slightly. "Having some problems there. Nance has a lot of friends in the capital. If we talk to the wrong people, he could get wind of it and sour the deal. We want to make sure this slides through without a hitch—push too hard and our whole plan goes up in smoke."

Ruffcarn picked up a piece of bacon and slid it into his mouth. "You think you'll need to go to Austin? That might speed things up. A little pressure on the right person might make a difference."

"Maybe, but not right now. Give it another couple of weeks. If this works, we'll have his ranch and can start our search. It shouldn't take too long to find what we're looking for. Once we do, we'll be riding high. You just keep rustling his cattle. You might ride over and make him another offer. If we could buy the ranch outright, then that would save the hassle of going through Austin."

"Wesley, that old man's not going to sell and you know it. The only way we're going to get it is through your connection in Austin—or kill him."

"Look, it won't hurt to try once more. If he says no, nothing's lost. With Logan out of the picture, he just might say yes—so give it one more try."

Ruffcarn had finished his breakfast. He stood, grabbed his hat, and motioned to Bankes, Bull, and the other cowhands.

"Sure, I'll do it. That'll give us a chance to find out about Logan, and who knows, he might sell."

Ruffcarn led his crew out the door.

PIERCE AND BARTHOLF were the only two remaining in the King 7 Saloon. Bartholf picked up the dishes from the tables and took them out to the kitchen. He came back and started wiping down the tables. "You think Nance will sell out?"

Pierce rubbed his forehead for a moment. "No, I doubt seriously that he will. But if he does, it saves us a lot of time, and it keeps Ruffcarn occupied."

Without looking up from the table he was cleaning, Bartholf said, "You're going to have to kill Ruffcarn before this is over. You know that, don't you?"

"Maybe, when he outlives his usefulness. I almost hate to. We've been partners for a lot of profitable years."

"He's weak. He don't mind beating on someone, or having another man do his killing, but he doesn't have the stomach to outright kill a man, or a woman. You can't depend on a man like that."

Pierce took a sip of his coffee. "You could be right. I'll have to keep that in mind. For now, I've a feisty girl on my mind, and I'm going to have to make her acquaintance." He smiled a smile that would freeze water, and pushed back from the table. He got up, slipped on his coat, adjusted his six-gun, and walked out the swinging doors of the saloon. His boots glistened as the morning sun struck them. They echoed ominously on the boardwalk.

16

J osh's face and upper body were swollen almost beyond recognition. He had been in the Kickapoo village since yesterday. During that time, Travels Far's wife, Nadie, along with several other women of the village, had worked on his abused body. They began by using the hide-scraping blades to scrape the fine prickly pear stickers from his neck, arms, and hands, and his back and chest. It was slow, tedious, and painful work.

Fortunately for Josh, he'd fallen into a deep sleep and was oblivious to what was happening. After getting all of the small spears from his body, Nadie made a paste from chokecherry berries and the peeled crushed pads of the prickly pear. She washed him thoroughly, then coated all of his upper body and arms with the paste. She cleansed his head, peeled a prickly pear pad, and tied it around his head wound. She and her helpers then watched and waited.

∿

JOSH OPENED HIS EYES. He was in a hut. He could see the intricate weaving of the boughs that provided the support for the wickiup. There were no windows. He was alone. He reached for his gun. It was gone. A buckskin shirt, along with his washed pants, was laid out near him. He tried to sit up and fell back. He hurt all over. There was some kind of paste spread over his upper body. It soothed the stinging and burning from the cactus spines. Josh could see the red, inflamed spots under the paste. He had no idea how it had happened. He remembered the puff of smoke—that was the last he remembered. He needed clothes and his gun.

The buffalo skin covering the opening in the lodge was pulled back, and an Indian woman started in. When she saw he was awake, she stepped back outside, and he could hear talking. The skin was again pulled back. An older Indian strode into the lodge. Though he was obviously an older man, his muscular body was apparent since he wore nothing but a breechcloth and buckskin leggings. The man walked to Josh's side and squatted beside him. He stared at Josh for a few minutes. Josh held his eyes and waited. His head throbbed like a blacksmith was inside banging on his skull with a sledge, and when he tried to take a deep breath, sharp pain stabbed him from his ribs.

"You strong man," the Indian said.

"You speak English."

"I learn from trapper as a boy, many years ago near big lakes in far north country."

"You've helped me. You have my thanks," Josh managed to say, although all his body wanted to do was go back to sleep.

The Indian nodded. "It is good. You lucky to be alive. You were shot. Then dragged by horse. Horse ran off."

Josh nodded and again tried to rise, but the Indian lightly pressed him back down. "You rest more. I come back later."

~

WHEN HE AWOKE AGAIN, he had a huge thirst. There was a gourd of water within reach. He drank the water. He could feel his senses returning. He stretched both arms; the pain was lessening. His head hurt and his ribs bothered him, but the stinging and burning was much less. The stuff that had been spread all over his arms and body was gone. *I just might live. But I've got to get back to the ranch. I have no idea how long I've been out. No telling what has happened.*

An Indian woman was sitting near the door, stretching what appeared to be a deer hide that had the hair scraped off. She watched him with a steady gaze. He saw his pants lying next to his bed. He reached out, grasped them and slowly pulled them on. The old woman watched for a moment more, then went back to stretching the hide. *I've got to stand up.* He pushed up with his hands, then slowly stood. His right side hurt and his head throbbed with a dull ache. He could feel scabs on his face. Considering what the old Indian had told him, he was lucky to be feeling any pain at all. He was surprised how the stinging and burning from the prickly pear thorns were almost gone. *Don't know what they put on me, but it sure seems to have worked.*

He touched his head and felt the wrapping around it. When he started to remove the bandage, the woman stopped, laid the deerskin down, and walked over to him. She motioned for him to sit. After he was sitting, she slowly started removing the head dressing. Once it was totally removed, she used a cloth and water to remove what was left of the prickly pear pad. When she had finished cleaning, she went outside and brought back a bowl of what looked like stew. He didn't care what it was; he was starving. He reached into the bowl and picked out a piece of meat. It was venison ... delicious. After finishing that bowl, he again stood. There was a buckskin shirt and moccasins next to where his pants had been. She motioned to him that these were his.

"Thank you," Josh said as he signaled his thanks in universal sign language. He slipped the buckskin shirt on over his head and stepped into the moccasins. The shirt fit perfectly and the moccasins felt good on his feet. He took a couple of steps and pain shot through his left knee. *Is there anywhere on my body that didn't get hurt?* He took another step and his right leg and knee felt fine. He smiled. *I guess there's at least one spot.*

Josh walked over to the buffalo hide, pulled it back, and stepped outside. All activity in the village stopped. Even the kids stopped playing and stared at him. Several of the younger braves eyed him with resentment. He felt sure that his being here didn't please the majority of the village. He stood outside the lodge for a moment, surveying the village. It was not large. He could only see nine lodges among the pecan trees. There were no more than fifteen men visible. There could be more out hunting. There were women and children, so this was no war party. Still, it was obvious that the white man wasn't popular here. He spotted the horses grazing in an elbow of the creek. With the brush around the creek, it made a natural corral on three sides.

The women and children watched him for a moment longer, then went about their business. The old Indian had been squatting, talking with three other men. When he saw Josh come out of the lodge, he stood and headed over to him. "You are feeling better?"

"Still a mite stiff, but I think I'm gonna make it ... thanks to you. My name is Josh Logan. Can you tell me what happened?"

"I am Travels Far of the Kickapoo Nation. Yes, I can tell you everything, for I saw it all. But first, come, sit, and we will have a pipe."

Josh moved to the firepit with Travels Far. The other men of the camp joined them, and the women and children gathered outside the circle. They all looked forward to Travels Far's stories. Travels Far introduced Josh to each of the men, as they sat around the pit. A ceremony existed for preparing the pipe, and Travels Far methodically went through each step. The final step was lighting the pipe. He took a long pull, passed it to Josh and began to talk. "He never saw me. He had been watching you for at least the day. He moved ahead of you and found his spot to shoot from. He was a big man."

Josh coughed slightly as he inhaled the smoke from the pipe. He didn't smoke, and it burned in his lungs, but this was important, and he owed these people his life. The other Kickapoo nodded and chuckled as he coughed, but weren't offended.

Travels Far continued with his story. He told of Josh being shot and dragged, his boot finally coming off, and his being slung against the oak. Additionally, he pantomimed how the big man who shot Josh was laughing as he got onto his horse and headed toward the fort. He mentioned how the man's face and nose were swollen like he had been in a fight. Travels Far went to great length to describe how he rode his horse up to Josh and sat within feet of him. He told of Josh talking to the spirits while he slept. In the morning when Josh awoke, Travels Far followed him as he struggled to rise and walk, then fell, only to rise again.

Travels Far spoke in English, then switched to tell his story in Kickapoo. As he described the determination of Josh, the other Indians looked at Josh with newfound respect, nodding and commenting on this white man's bravery. They could see the telltale signs on his face and head. The Kickapoo respected courage. Travels Far finished with the explanation that he'd intended to kill him and take his scalp. But after Josh talked to the spirits, then wouldn't quit but continued to move forward, he gained respect for the man and made the decision not to kill him. When Josh fell in the creek and passed out again, Travels Far decided to take him to their village.

Josh said, "I thank you. I want you to know that my father, who's still living back in Tennessee, came to me and told me that I couldn't quit. The blood of my ancestors ran through me and I could not disappoint them, so I kept going."

When Travels Far translated for the others, they excitedly nodded. One of the other men told Travels Far to translate to

Logan his words. "Warrior's blood flows through you, as it flows through us. Each man must, in his strength, honor his ancestors. Without them we would not be."

Logan kept eye contact with the Indian who had spoken. "What you say is true. I know my ancestors are as grateful for the Kickapoo's generosity as I am. I'll always be the friend of the Kickapoo if they'll allow it."

Around the circle there was much nodding and conversing. The pipe had made it back to Travels Far as his story ended. He stood and Josh stood alongside him. It was obvious to the Indians that this man was still experiencing much pain, but he wasn't showing it. They all stood and, one by one, approached Josh, solemnly grasped his hand, and shook it with one strong up-and-down stroke. They then dispersed to their previous duties.

Josh turned to Travels Far. "I've been here two days. Bad men would take the ranch where I work. The man who shot me works for them. I must get back to the Rocking N as soon as possible. I must leave now."

Travels Far shook his head. "Stay one more day. Your body is not yet strong enough for you to travel. Tomorrow I will give you a horse and go with you to Rocking N, for I know where it is. But for now you must rest." He motioned Josh back into the lodge.

"Did I lose my gun when I was being dragged?" Josh vaguely remembered having it when he came to by the tree.

"No." Travels Far turned to Nadie, who had been standing by the lodge listening to his story, and spoke. She went back into the lodge and brought out Josh's Colt and belt.

With relief he took it from her and tossed it over his shoulder without thinking. When it hit his shoulder, it was all he could do to keep from wincing from the pain caused by the weight of the gun belt against his sore flesh.

"Now you rest," Travels Far said again as he motioned Josh back inside the lodge.

Josh realized he was exhausted. Being up for only a couple of hours had taken much of his energy. He did need rest. There was no way he could have ridden out of here today. He just hoped he'd be able to ride tomorrow. He turned and walked back into the lodge. Nadie slipped his buckskin shirt off and gave him another bowl of the stew. He sat down, ate the stew, and lay down on the blanket. Sleep enveloped him.

PAT EXAMINED the ranch as they came down the north hillside. "If it was Mr. Nance who built those ranch buildings, he knows a thing or two about defense. Limestone walls, I'm betting close to a foot thick. Would take a cannon to penetrate them."

"Looks almost like a fort, doesn't it?" Scott replied.

"Aye, it does. Look at the field of fire. The bunkhouse can cover the ranch and barn, and the main house can lay covering fire for the barn and bunkhouse. A wily man it was who built this home."

The two men were glad to see the ranch. This was the morning of the second day of travel, and they felt themselves fortunate to have encountered no Comanches. They stopped the team in front of the house.

Juan Alvarez stepped from inside the barn with his rifle cradled in the crook of his left arm. "*Buenos dias.* How can I help you?"

"Howdy," Scott said. "We come from Camp Wilson. We've got supplies for the ranch. Josh Logan hired us. I'm Scott Penny, and this here Irishman is Pat O'Reilly."

Juan examined them for a moment, then made his decision. "Let's get the supplies unloaded. My name is Juan Alvarez. I'm glad to see some additional men here at the ranch."

The men started unloading the supplies from the wagon as Mary Louise came through the front door, followed by Bill Nance.

"I'm Bill Nance, and this is my daughter, Mary Louise. I'm glad to see you men. We've been short of help, and what with the cattle rustling and regular ranch duties, we're running pretty thin."

Scott had been filling his arms with supplies to take into the house and had his back to the house. He turned as he heard someone coming out of the house, and his eyes locked on Mary Louise. In an instant he took in her blond hair and deep blue eyes set in a smiling face. Never having difficulty finding words, Scott said, "My name is Scott, ma'am, and I'm pleased to meet you. Had I known there was such an attractive lady living here, I would've been down here knocking on your door long before now, looking for a job." He finished and smiled. His laugh wrinkles at the corners of his eyes turned up. "No offense meant, Mr. Nance."

Mary Louise colored a bit beneath her tan. "Why, you are forward, aren't you?" But her smile belied her words.

Bill Nance frowned for a moment, then smiled and said, "None taken."

Pat had stepped from the wagon, shook Juan's hand and moved to the rear of the wagon to start unloading. "I'm Pat O'Reilly, late of the Sixth Cavalry at Camp Wilson. Josh Logan and your son, Rory, and I were good friends during the war."

Scott put the supplies down, and he and Pat stepped forward to shake the hands of their new boss and his daughter.

"Speaking of Josh," Pat continued, "we have some news, as soon as we get the supplies unloaded and the horses taken care of."

"Good," Nance said. "When you're finished, meet me inside, and we'll discuss what's going on ... you also, Juan."

The supplies had been unloaded. Scott and Pat were wiping down the four horses. They had fed the horses and were about finished.

"Did you notice Mary Louise?" Scott asked.

"Aye, she's an attractive young lady."

"Attractive? Why, Pat, you are a master at understating the obvious. I don't think I've ever seen as pretty a woman as her. Those blue eyes sparkle like diamonds; and did you feel her strong handshake? She's all woman. Her blond hair looked like a field of ripe wheat in the wind, all wavy and shiny."

"Lad, you'd best get your mind off the girl and get it on the work. We've a lot to do here, and not yet have we told them about Josh. Keep your focus on the job at hand."

Scott was quiet for a moment. "You're right. I hate to admit it, but for a few minutes there I forgot about Josh. I'd best put first things first."

They finished the horses, dropped their belongings in the bunkhouse, and headed for the house. As their boots hit the veranda, Bill Nance called, "Come on in, boys."

They walked through the front door and paused for a moment to look around. The inside of the house looked pretty typical for a Texas ranch house, except for the stone floors. There was a big fireplace in the living room. Over it was a large painting of the Nance family. The family was on a rolling hill covered with the brilliant blue of bluebonnets and sprinkled with fiery orange Indian paintbrush. Mr. Nance was much younger. Next to him was a little girl of about seven years, a boy about nine or ten, and a lovely woman who must have been Mrs. Nance. She was extremely attractive, with shoulder-length blond hair. Mary Louise was a spitting image of her. The furniture in the room was older, but it appeared to be handmade by a craftsman. The room reflected a woman's touch.

"'Tis a striking painting, Mr. Nance," Pat said. "Your family was lovely."

Bill walked into the living room and looked up at the painting. "Thank you, Pat. Those were happy days. The painting was done by a young French woman who had moved to Texas. Her name was Eugenie Lavender. She was born in Paris, France. I just happened by their wagon when they were traveling. They had a little Indian problem going on, so I helped them. She was grateful and offered to paint our family. Eugenie and my wife became good friends." Bill looked at the painting for a moment longer, then turned and headed for the office. "You boys come on into the office and have a seat. Juan and Mary Louise are already here." Nance led them into his office and sat behind a large desk. "Now give me the message from Josh, and tell me why he's not with you."

Pat looked at Scott, and Scott nodded for him to go ahead and explain what had happened. Pat told them everything. He told them about his sister coming into town and Bull insulting her and how Josh had beat Bull to a bloody pulp, then posted him out of town. He explained Josh's meeting with Ruffcarn, how Ruffcarn offered Josh a job, and how livid Ruffcarn was after Josh turned him down and all but called him a thief. He told them that Scott had mentioned there were some good men in Brownwood, and Josh had authorized him to hire three with Mr. Nance's approval.

"That'll be fine if they're good men. I'd like to have cattlemen who can fight. But I don't want gunmen working here. Is that clear, Scott?"

"Yes, sir. That's exactly what Josh said you'd say. I know these boys, and they ride for the brand. They aren't scared of a fight, and they're all good with a gun, but they're mainly good hands. None of 'em are gunhands, though they may have killed in the past in self-defense."

"Good, that's settled. You can leave in the morning. Juan, why don't you go along. Better two men than one riding this country."

"*Si, Señor*, I'll be glad to."

"Now, Pat, why isn't Josh here?"

"Aye, Mr. Nance, we come now to the difficult part." Pat then told the story about Josh to Bill, Juan, and Mary Louise. "And that's all we know," Pat finished.

Nance pulled out his pipe and tobacco. He loaded the pipe,

struck a match, and lit the pipe by moving the match around the surface of the tobacco until it was burning evenly. He inhaled deeply, held it for a moment, and blew the smoke out. "What's you boys' gut feelings? Do you think the Indian took him to torture and kill or to try to heal him?"

This time Scott answered. "I've got to tell you, Mr. Nance, I've seen a lot of folks killed by Indians. This just doesn't look right to me. I think if the Indian, whatever kind he was, was going to kill Josh, he would have killed him right there and scalped him. Josh must have been covered with prickly pear thorns. I don't think the Indian would have bothered with him in that condition if he wasn't trying to save him. But that's just my thinkin'. I've been wrong before, but I hope I'm not this time."

"Do you agree, Pat?"

"Aye, it's the best theory I could come up with. I've fought the red man throughout the West, and with Josh in this condition, if he wasn't going to help him, I think he would have killed him right there or scalped him and left him to die."

"Well, I hope you're right. But even so, with his being shot, then dragged by his horse, he'd have to be a tough man to survive."

Pat looked Mr. Nance in the eye. "I've seen tough men in my lifetime, but never a man like Josh Logan. If there's anyone who can survive that kind of abuse, he'll be that man."

They heard the hoofbeats of a horse entering the ranch yard. Everyone got up to look. It was the roan that Josh had been riding. They all walked outside. The roan moved toward Juan as soon as he saw him. Juan reached out, took the reins with one hand, and spoke softly to the roan while rubbing his neck with the other hand. They all saw the blood on the saddle and withers of the horse.

Scott stated the obvious. "At least his horse made it back. Look, Josh's Winchester is still in the boot, and his saddlebags are here. I'm bettin' Josh will be back, though I don't know when or what kind of shape he'll be in. If it's okay, I'll just take his things over to the bunkhouse for when he gets back."

"You could be right, Scott," Mr. Nance said. "Go ahead and put his things in the bunkhouse. We'll hope for the best. In the meantime, we need to get you and Juan to Brownwood to get those other men hired. If Bull did this, then Ruffcarn knows, and he won't be long in acting."

"Mr. Nance, if it's alright with you and Juan, we could leave today. That'll put us into Brownwood tonight, and if those boys are looking for a job, then we could be back by tomorrow noon."

"Scott, that's fine with me. Juan, what do you think?"

"I'm ready, *Señor*. I'll get the *caballos* ready and we'll be on our way."

Nance nodded. "Mary Louise, would you run into the house and ask Teresa to fix up a grub sack for Juan and Scott?"

"Yes, Papa," Mary Louise said as she turned for the house.

In less than thirty minutes, the two men were mounted on fresh horses. Mary Louise came out of the house with the grub sacks and handed one to Juan. "Teresa included a couple of pieces of pecan pie. I hope you like it," she said as she handed Scott's to him and gave him a heart-melting smile.

"I'm sure I will, ma'am. I love pecan pie. Now you take good care of yourself. I'll be back tomorrow," he said as he tipped his hat and gave her a big grin.

"*Adios,*" Juan said as he waved. He and Scott rode out of the ranch at a trot.

17

Fianna turned to Mrs. Diehl. "I'm terribly worried about Josh."

"I understand, dear. But we can do nothing here but pray for his safety. I have confidence that he'll be fine."

The two women were sitting at the table, drinking tea. "Would you care for more tea, Mrs. Diehl?" Fianna asked as she lifted the teapot from the table.

"Why, yes, my dear, that would be nice."

Fianna started pouring the tea. "Look, Ruffcarn and his ruffians are leaving."

Ruffcarn had walked out of the King 7 Saloon with Wesley Pierce. They were followed by Grizzard Bankes, Bull, and the rest of the Circle W crew. The hands mounted up and waited as Pierce and Ruffcarn talked for a few moments; then Ruffcarn turned to his horse and stepped into the saddle. He turned south, leading his crew past the Shamrock Saloon on the right and Tiny's stable on the left.

"What do you suppose Ruffcarn and Pierce were talking about?" Fianna asked.

"Nothing good, dear, I can assure you. I don't know much

about either man, but I do know men. Those two are as rotten as they come. But of the two, I'd say Pierce is the most dangerous."

"Really? He's a very handsome man ... in a scary sort of way."

"Handsome is only skin deep, my dear. You watch that man. I feel he's evil. I've nothing to base it on except my intuition. But I'm right most of the time."

Fianna's thoughts drifted back to Josh Logan. *Josh is a strikingly handsome man, even with the scar across his forehead. It emphasizes his strong, lean features. But he's also kind, considerate, and protective of me. How can I be having these feelings about a man whom I've known for only a few days?* She faintly shook her head, as if to clear it. "Mrs. Diehl, might I be of help to you and Mr. Diehl? I'm not one to sit and do nothing."

Mrs. Diehl smiled at her and patted her hand. "Fianna, your help would be appreciated, my dear. But you're under no obligation to do anything. By the way, I'd be much more comfortable if you'd call me Victoria."

"Thank you, Victoria, I'd love to."

"Good, that's settled. My goodness, it's almost ten o'clock. Let's clear this tea service and get to work. It'll be dinnertime soon, and I must get it prepared. We can't let Tiny go hungry."

The women stood, cleared the table, and moved into the kitchen.

As she helped Victoria, Fianna thought about her aunt Kathleen O'Reilly. Fianna had been only four years old when she was taken by Pat to live with Aunt Kathleen. She vaguely remembered her parents, brothers, and sister. Her conversations with Pat had helped keep them alive for her. It had been a hard time.

Her parents had come over from Ireland in 1840 to start a new life in the land of the free. She'd been born five years later. From what Pat said, they were a happy family. Fortunately, her mother and father had been frugal with the money they had from their business in Ireland, and they arrived in the new country with substantial funds. Even so, her father and two older brothers worked at the docks, loading and unloading ships. Pat spoke of his father's dream to move the family west and start a farm.

When she was four years old, the dream came crashing down around them. That was the 1849 cholera epidemic in New York City. Her parents, two older brothers, and her sister died with that horrible sickness. Pat, who at the time was seventeen years old, with the money his family had saved, took Fianna to live with Aunt Kathleen in South Hadley, Massachusetts. With her guidance, Pat invested their parents' savings and saw the money grow.

Growing up in Aunt Kathleen's home was a wonderful experience. She was a happy woman, even though she never married. She did have a fiery temper that was reserved for those other than her family. She had started as a seamstress when she moved to South Hadley. She was so adept at her work that her business grew until she opened a dress shop in South Hadley. Fianna helped out as a young child, then worked there as she grew older and more responsible.

Pat also lived for a year with Aunt Kathleen. During that time he worked on the South Hadley Canal that detoured around the Great Falls on the Connecticut River. He was proud of his job on the canal, always telling anyone who would listen that it was the first canal for boats in the United States. Fianna remembered sadly the day Aunt Kathleen and Pat sat down with her to tell her Pat had joined the army. He was only eighteen. It broke her young heart that he was leaving, but her aunt explained that he was a man and had a right to make his own decisions.

"Don't you think, dear?"

"What? Oh, I'm sorry, Victoria, I was lost in my own thoughts. What did you say?"

"I was just saying that it's so fortunate that your brother was getting out of the army now. Isn't it funny how things have a way of working out?"

Fianna heard horses and looked out the kitchen window. She watched as a cavalry patrol was leaving the fort. "Yes, it really is. I know Pat wants to go to California, but he's so responsible. He would never leave a good friend's family in trouble. I'm sure he'll be a great help to them. After all his years in the army, he is an exceptionally capable man."

Victoria watched the ten-man patrol trot south past Tiny's blacksmith shop. "I'm sure he will be missed in the army, but Bill Nance needs capable help at his ranch or I'm afraid he might lose it to Ruffcarn."

They both heard the door to the store open and close, then they heard Mr. Diehl say, "What do you want here?"

By the tone of his voice, Fianna knew the person who entered the store wasn't a welcome customer. She stepped out of the kitchen and walked to the entryway into the store with Mrs. Diehl. She saw Wesley Pierce standing at the store counter, examining the candy on display.

"Thought I'd be neighborly and give you some business," Pierce replied, his lips lifting at the corners of his mouth into a semblance of a smile.

Diehl walked over behind the counter and said, "Make your choice, then get out."

Pierce had looked up at Diehl and was about to reply when Fianna appeared. He turned to her, and his smile broadened. "Well, hello, miss. I saw you come in on the stage, but I haven't had the pleasure of your acquaintance. Wesley Pierce at your service. Mrs. Diehl."

Victoria gave a sharp nod and Fianna simply said, "My name is Fianna O'Reilly."

"I must say, your arriving in Camp Wilson has certainly brightened a dull town. You must let me show you around sometime."

"No, thank you, Mr. Pierce. I'm particular about the men I associate with."

"I don't know what you heard," Pierce said as he looked at Victoria, then slowly turned his head to Diehl. He looked back at

Fianna. "I assure you that I'm a gentleman and merely desire the company of a lovely lady."

Fianna felt a shiver run down her spine when she looked into his eyes. His eyes looked dead and frightening.

"Maybe we'll meet later, when we're in a more agreeable setting." He turned back to Diehl and said, "Licorice, and make it quick." He tossed a nickel onto the counter.

Diehl picked up the licorice and put it into a sack. Without a word, he handed it to Pierce. Pierce turned, doffed his hat to the ladies, and strode out of the store.

"Mr. Diehl, don't antagonize that man. He's dangerous."

"Mrs. Diehl, I don't like him, and I don't want him in this store. Furthermore, I have a feeling the only reason he came over here is to see Fianna."

"Whatever your feelings, we run a store, and most people are welcome. Just remember that, please."

Diehl nodded and repositioned the .44 Colt in his belt. "You're right, my dear. But like I said, I don't like the man. By the way, Fianna, I'd say you handled yourself very well."

"Thank you, sir. I must admit to being a little frightened of him. I don't think I've ever seen anyone with eyes that cold, and he's dressed in black. What a sinister combination."

"He's a killer if I've ever seen one," Diehl said as he turned back to the shelves.

Victoria and Fianna moved back into the kitchen and continued to prepare dinner. "When they have time, the officers sometimes come over for dinner. They're all such gentlemen, even though they are Yankees." Victoria realized what she said the moment the words left her mouth. "Oh, I'm sorry, my dear; I meant no offense to you."

Fianna smiled and placed her hand on Victoria's arm. "No offense taken. The war was so hard on everyone. I can't imagine what it must have been like here."

Victoria patted Fianna's hand. "Yes, it was hard. So many

friends died, and some went to the North. It created a lot of hard feelings. It's a wonder Mr. Diehl and Mr. Nance remained friends. But they had been through so much together, a bond formed that couldn't be broken. Fortunately they both were too old to go to war this time."

Fianna thought about Pat. *It was good he wasn't here today. I love the way he's protective of me, but if he had been here today, Pierce might have killed him.* She felt sure Pierce had killed men, and she feared what might have happened to Pat. She knew her brother had killed men during the war, but that was war. Pierce was so cold and confident.

Her thoughts drifted back to South Hadley. She had grown to a woman there. She felt fortunate and thankful for her brother and aunt. They had taken care of her so well. Pat had insisted that she attend Mount Holyoke Seminary, and Aunt Kathleen supported him. Her grades had been superior, and she had graduated with honors. Now she was in the Wild West. She couldn't believe she was here. It was so exciting—frightening at times, but raw and exciting. Life was lived to the fullest here.

It had been so hard leaving Aunt Kathleen. She was growing older and would be alone. They had talked about her joining Fianna and Pat in California. Aunt Kathleen had an adventuresome spirit, and Fianna sincerely hoped she would come to live with them. She had been so strong when Fianna left, insisting that this was an opportunity for Fianna to learn and grow in the western country. She did miss her sweet aunt, though she was finding that she loved the wildness of this land and couldn't wait to begin making a home for her and her brother—and maybe someone else. *Oh, I hope Josh is alive and well.*

"Let's get the food on the table, missy; the men will be arriving soon," Victoria said as she picked up the bowl of mashed potatoes and headed for the dining room.

~

PIERCE WALKED BACK to the King 7. To all outward appearances he was unruffled and calm. Inside, he was seething. He was going to enjoy killing that old man. He'd put up with him since starting his saloon. It was obvious that Diehl thought him lower than dirt. He knew his time would come, and it was going to be a pleasure. He entered the King 7, it was empty except for Bartholf, and walked back to his table. "Give me a whiskey, Bartholf, and bring the bottle. Make it the good stuff."

"Everything okay, boss?" Bartholf asked.

"Not by a long shot. I'm tired of these high-and-mighty Texans. It's going to be a pleasure to put lead into that old man across the street. I've had a gut full of him and his ranger buddy, Nance."

Bartholf said nothing. He brought the glass and whiskey bottle over to the table, set them down, and turned to walk back to the bar.

"Why don't you sit down and take a load off."

Bartholf turned back, pulled out a chair, and lowered his massive body into the chair. "What's up, boss?"

Pierce poured a shot of whiskey, drank it, and poured another. "How do you like it here?"

"It's fine with me. Little hot in the summer, but I've got more liking for the heat than that bone-chilling Minnesota cold. That's the reason I left the logging trade up there for New Orleans. Cold just don't suit me. I'd like to be down in those islands off Florida. Now that would be the life. But that takes money."

"You know we're going to have a lot of money, don't you?"

"Well, boss, that would be mighty nice. But I wasn't real sure that I was included in the big money."

"Bartholf, you're the only man I have felt I could trust. You know, you're definitely included in the money. I'm thinking about a sixty-forty split between you and me."

"What about Ruffcarn?"

"I've been thinking more and more about what you said, and I think you hit the nail on the head. When we get the gold, Ruffcarn will be more of a liability than an asset. So we'll just have to figure out a way for him to conveniently disappear."

"That shouldn't be hard, boss. There's a lot of ways for a man to die in this country. He don't worry me. The only one in that bunch who concerns me is Grizzard Bankes. He's supposed to be real good with that gun on his hip, and he strikes me as a real curly wolf. If he backs Ruffcarn, we could have a problem."

Pierce showed his teeth in what was supposed to be a smile. "I'll take care of Bankes. I don't think he's anywhere as good as he thinks he is. We'll pay off the rest of Ruffcarn's hands, and they'll never be the wiser. They work for a wage, and that's all they expect."

"You really think that soldier boy was telling the truth? He could have been lying."

"He was telling the truth. We also took his map. Not that he was any great shakes as a cartographer ..."

"What's a cartographer, boss?"

Pierce took a sip from his whiskey glass. "Mapmaker. As I was saying, his map isn't that great, but I think I've got it figured pretty close where that gold has to be. As far as his telling the truth, I checked with our contact. He confirmed that a gold shipment from New Mexico Territory was lost somewhere in west central Texas. All the men were thought to be killed, but the army never found any sign of the soldier boys or the two wagons of gold."

"You think it's close around here?" Bartholf's eyes gleamed with avarice as Pierce talked about the gold.

"It's not close. It lies on Nance's land. I haven't looked, and I've forbidden Ruffcarn from looking. I want to wait until we own the ranch. Then there will be no chance of anyone seeing us with the gold. It'll take a few months to get it all out and over to Fort Worth, where I have a buyer who will buy all we find. Once that's done, we'll sell the ranch, and you'll be on your way to the Caribbean to live like a gentleman for the rest of your life."

"Boss, you're a genius. The time you spent getting an education weren't wasted. Why, those addled-headed fools at Georgia Military Institute would be plumb jealous."

Pierce threw back his head and laughed. He loved praise, and the picture in his mind of his fellow GMI students being jealous pleased him immensely. "Get a glass, Bartholf, and we'll drink to our good fortune."

Pierce's mind wandered to Logan. *I hope Bull is right, and Logan is really dead.*

18

S cott Penny and Juan Alvarez topped the ridge south of the ranch the next day at noon. Their trip to Brownwood had been a complete success. Accompanying them were the new hands Jack Swindell, Byron Whistal, and Jimmy Leads. Scott had found the three of them at the Happy Jack Saloon, and it had been a fine reunion. He also found them raring to go. Their money had just about run out, and they were doing odd jobs around town—not something to a cowboy's liking. If a job couldn't be done on horseback, it couldn't be done by a cowhand. Scott explained they were looking for hands for the Rocking N, and about Josh being bushwhacked. They were ready to sign up immediately.

Juan pointed to the ranch yard. "That does not look good, *amigo*." There were six men on horses, talking to Bill Nance. Pat and the other two hands were standing at his side.

"Let's join the party," Scott said as he slipped the leather thong off his Colt. The others followed suit. *If Bull Westin is down there, this time I'm gonna kill him.*

They rode down the hill at a gallop and pulled up in a cloud of dust behind Nance. "Howdy, Mr. Nance," Scott said. "Here we are back from Brownwood and loaded for bear."

"*Si, Señor* Bill, it's our pleasure to be here," Juan Alvarez said.

"Well, boys, I'm glad you made it back. Mr. Ruffcarn here was just explaining how it would be to my benefit to sell the ranch to him. Isn't that right, Mr. Ruffcarn?"

Ruffcarn had trouble hiding his look of dismay at the arrival of the additional men, all with their belt guns handy. He looked at Bull on his left and Grizzard Bankes on his right. Bankes hadn't moved from his relaxed position, with his right arm hanging loosely over his Colt. Ruffcarn regained his composure. "Mr. Nance, as I said, with the loss of much of your herd, you would be smart to take advantage of my offer. I find it extremely fair under the circumstances."

"Mr. Ruffcarn, how long did it take for you to ride over here?"

"About six hours, I imagine. Why do you ask?"

"By the time you get back, you'll have wasted a total of twelve hours. It's a shame to see that much time wasted."

"Now look, Nance. I've made you an honest offer. If you're smart, you'll take it."

"And if I don't?"

"You'll be making a big mistake. You've got your daughter to think about."

Nance's face clouded with anger. "You just stepped over the line, mister. You mention my daughter again, and you won't make it back to your ranch. In fact, get down off that horse. I'll give you a chance to beat an old man to the draw. Age has slowed me some, so you just might make it."

Ruffcarn's eyes grew large. "I didn't come here to fight you, Nance. I—"

"No, you came here to steal my ranch just like you're stealing my cattle. So why don't we just go ahead and settle this between the two of us."

Ruffcarn was holding the reins in his right hand, and his gun was on his right hip. "I have no desire for gunplay here, Nance. We can settle our differences peaceably. I meant no threat to your daughter. If you don't want to sell, that's your choice, but I want you to know that I'm no rustler. I only wanted to make you an honest offer."

"Get off my property, Ruffcarn. If I catch you or any of your men on my land, I'll assume you're here to rustle my cattle, and I'll hang you from the nearest tree."

Scott spoke up as he angled toward Bull. "Mr. Nance, just so you know, I'm choosing Bull and choosing him now. He's a no-good, yellow back-shooter, and it's time he was stopped."

Bull lifted both hands into the air. "I'm not going to gunfight you, Penny. I've heard about your reputation down south, and it just wouldn't be fair."

Scott gave a harsh laugh. "You mean like it was fair for you to bushwhack Josh? Bull, I'm tired of talking. If you don't draw, I'll shoot you where you sit."

"*Señor* Scott, maybe this isn't the time. *Señorita* Nance and Teresa are in the house. We don't want any stray bullets finding the wrong person."

Realizing he would be endangering the ladies, Scott took a deep breath and slowly relaxed. "Alright, Juan, I reckon you're right," Scott replied. "Bull, it's your lucky day. But I swear, the next time I see you, you'd better be ready."

"Now git, Ruffcarn, and take your rowdies with you," Nance said.

"This is the last chance you'll have, Nance," Ruffcarn said. He and his crew turned their horses north and galloped out of the ranch yard.

Nance turned to the new arrivals. "You boys showed up at the right time. I thought for sure we were in for it until you came over the hill. Sweetest thing I've seen in a while."

"Mr. Nance," Scott said, "we're pleased it turned out so well. But it's a crying shame Bull got away again. He's been all-fired lucky someone hasn't killed him by now. He's a real problem. Bull's about one of the best shots I've seen with a Sharps. I'd feel a whole lot more comfortable if he'd been taken out of here over his saddle."

Mary Louise walked out onto the veranda with a rifle in her hand. "Papa, you had me worried when you started getting mad. I know what you're like when you get mad. I just knew we'd have a gunfight right here in the front yard. And you, Mr. 'I'm choosing Bull' Penny. What do you think would have happened if you'd drawn that gun? I swear, you men are all alike. It seems you're always itching for a fight." She turned, tossed her blond hair, and marched back into the house.

"Whew. Mr. Nance, you've got a real firebrand for a daughter," Scott said, but he was grinning from ear to ear. "She's quite a lady."

"You're right, son. It'll take a real man to tame her," Nance said. "Now who are these folks a-riding with you?"

"Mr. Nance, this tall drink of water is Jack Swindell, the feller wearing the sombrero is Byron Whistal, and the young feller on the buckskin is Jimmy Leads," Scott said. "Jimmy may look a mite young, but he started working cattle when he was fifteen and you won't find a better hand. He also knows his way around a Colt."

"Juan, did you or Scott tell these men what they'd be paid?"

"No, *Señor,* we told them they'd be paid a fair wage by a fair man, and that was good enough for them."

"Then a fair wage it'll be—fifty a month. I know that's above average, but this is a dangerous place to work. So welcome, boys. These three with me are Pat O'Reilly, Frank Milman, and Leander Stanton. Leander here prefers Lee and I wouldn't tease him about his name. That would be terribly unprofitable. Isn't that right, Lee?"

Lee took off his hat and wiped the brim. "I just don't like Leander. You know that, Mr. Nance."

"Alright, why don't you boys unload your gear in the

bunkhouse and take care of your horses. When that's done, come on in. I think Teresa probably has dinner ready."

The men unloaded their gear, gave the horses a good rubdown, tossed some corn into the bins, and went to the house.

Teresa and Mary Louise had the biscuits, steaks, and beans on the table. Nance introduced the new men to Mary Louise and Teresa. "Howdy, ma'am," was heard around the table.

Teresa asked, "*Señor* Nance, have you heard anything about *Señor* Logan?"

"Not a word nor sign, Teresa. I think I'll send some of the boys out in the morning to scout around. Now that we have some additional hands, we can spare a few and still keep the ranch protected. But we have no idea how bad he's hurt or even if he's alive."

"I feel so bad, Papa," Mary Louise said. "I flew off the handle at you and him when he told us about Rory. I blamed you both. But I know it was no one's fault. It was just the war."

"Honey, Josh understood. He didn't blame you, and I know he held no grudge. Pat, were you at the Battle of Cedar Creek with Josh and Rory?"

"Aye, that I was, Mr. Nance. 'Twas a fearsome battle. Many men died on both sides that day."

"Were you there when my son died?"

"It's a fact. A brave man, he was. If he hadn't intervened, Josh himself would have died. We three were good friends. It wasn't often noncoms and officers became friends. But your son and Josh were special men. We hit it off right at the first. It's my honor to have been able to call your son my friend."

"Thank you, Pat," Nance said. "Now let's put this food away so that we can get to work. We've a lot to do if we're going to find those rustled cattle and save this ranch."

Scott looked over at Mary Nance sitting across the table. His heart went out to her. He knew she must be hurting bad, having just recently found out about the death of her brother. She looked up and saw the concern in Scott's eyes—a soft smile spread across her lips. It was returned by Scott.

Scott turned to look at Nance. "What's the plan, Mr. Nance?"

"In the morning, we'll get three men riding north looking for Josh. Teresa, pack them up enough supplies for four days. Juan, pick yourself two men, and while you're looking for Josh, keep an eye open for those rustled cattle. If you see any of the Ruffcarn crew, treat them as rustlers. I expect them to make a move soon."

"*Si, Señor*, that's understood. Pat, why don't you, Scott, Lee, and Jimmy stay here at the ranch. I'll take Jack and Frank with me. If it's possible, we'll find *Señor* Josh."

"Good," Nance said. "We need to get Josh back. That horse of his is getting restless. He needs to get the edge run off him."

"That gray horse is quite a horse," Pat said. "Josh rode him throughout the war. Chancy can run like the wind, and I'll be promising you, that horse likes a fight. If you look him over, you'll see he's got war wounds himself. Josh spoke of taking him out to the Colorado Territory and starting a horse ranch, breeding him with some of the mustangs."

"Why Colorado, Pat?" Nance asked. "There's plenty of good ranching country around here."

"Well, Mr. Nance, it's like this. Josh spoke of it many times around the campfire. It's an uncle he has who traveled all over the western country. This uncle, he found a place in a Colorado valley with water and grass. He bought it. He came back to the Logan home-place and filled the heads of the family with the West and with this valley. Josh told us the whole family was infected. Josh also said that the Logan clan had always had the wanderlust. The war kept them from making the move. But after the war, Josh and his older brother, Callum, left for the Colorado Territory. Only they split up in Nashville; Josh headed here to fulfill his promise to Rory, and Callum headed straight for the Territory."

"I see," Bill Nance said. "He came this far out of his way to bring us the news of Rory."

"Aye, he did. He made a promise to a good friend."

"Thank you for telling us, Mr. O'Reilly," Mary Louise said.

Everyone was finished with dinner. "Okay, boys, let's get to work," Nance said as he stood.

All of the men stood, thanked Teresa and Mary Louise, and headed for the door. Scott hung back. "Miss Nance, it's sure good to see you again. I must admit your cooking is mighty fine."

"Why must you admit it, Mr. Penny? Did you have different expectations?" Mary Louise asked innocently.

"No, ma'am. I just meant that it was mighty good. I thank you, very much, and I look forward to speaking with you again, but I'd better get moving." Scott hastily retreated, unsure of what had just happened. He had a glib tongue and could verbally fence with anyone, man or woman. But he found this woman flustered him easily, a new feeling for him.

"You'd best watch yourself, lad," Pat said as Scott came down off the porch. "It's my thought that lassie may have her cap set for you."

Scott grinned. "I'm such a good catch. What with me owning my horse and saddle, this here belt gun, and rifle. Why, any woman of good sense could see a great future with me."

"I'm only telling you what these old eyes see. That pretty lass is making plans, and those plans include you," Pat said, then chuckled. "Aye, you're in big trouble."

Jimmy had overheard Pat's comment. "She sure was eyeballing you, Scott. Though I can't imagine why, what with such a good-looking gent like me around."

Scott turned his head to reply and stopped. Over the top of the north ridge he could make out a group of riders. "Pat, looks like we have more company coming. Let's head back to the house. Jimmy, let the boys know in the bunkhouse—get ready for Indians."

19

J osh woke early. He had slept all night, and as his eyes opened, he came instantly awake a trait of self-preservation he had developed over the years. He looked around, surveying his surroundings. Travels Far lay sleeping with his wife on the other side of the wickiup. It was dark still. He listened; the camp was quiet. He lay there for a moment assessing his injuries. His head had stopped hurting. He gently felt the bullet wound; it was still sore to the touch. His face, arms, and chest were sore and tingly, but even before he moved, he realized that much of the pain had dissipated. He sat up—no dizziness. That was good.

As soon as Josh moved, Travels Far slipped out of his bed and stood, motioning for Josh to get dressed and follow him outside. Travels Far stepped outside as Josh was pulling on his buckskin shirt and slipping into his moccasins. He strapped his gun belt on over his buckskin shirt and followed the Indian. Out of the corner of his eye, he could see Nadie getting up.

"How do you feel?" Travels Far asked.

"I feel good," Josh said. He realized that he did feel good. His left leg was still sore, but it was feeling much better. He hated to lose his boot. Those boots had been with him through the war, only needed new soles and heels occasionally. Now he was without boots, and they weren't cheap.

He could breathe more comfortably. His right side still hurt when he took a deep breath, but he didn't think a rib was broken. The biggest problem now was his hands. They were still swollen, and his palms had been cut up something fierce. It would take a while for them to heal, and he needed them to be in a lot better shape than they were now—to draw a gun.

"Good, we'll eat, then take you to Rocking N."

"I'm forever in your debt."

Nadie was already building a fire outside the wickiup. Josh didn't know what she had planned, but he sure knew he was hungry. The rest of the village was starting to stir. The night guards had moved in and were going into their huts to get a little rest before they started the day. The Kickapoo lived with the constant danger of attack from the Comanches.

What I'd give for a cup of coffee, but I'm mighty happy just to be alive. If Travels Far hadn't found me, I probably would have died out there. I'd never have gotten all those prickly pear thorns out, especially in my back and neck. They'd surely be infected now. Infections could kill a man as dead as any bullet in this country. If he didn't die, he could lose an arm or a leg from infection. *Whatever salve Nadie used worked mighty fine.*

They ate a breakfast of venison and mesquite bean bread that Nadie called *pinole*. The venison was delicious, the bread a little bitter, but still satisfying. Travels Far had spoken to one of the younger men, and by the time they had finished eating, there were eight horses waiting. Josh was surprised at the number. "Why take this many men?" Josh asked Travels Far.

"Comanches. We ride long ways. Never know where Comanches might be."

Daylight was breaking over the prairie. The light of the morning sun began to wash across the deep green of the pecan trees.

"We go," Travels Far said. He and the other braves leaped onto their horses. Josh moved a bit slower. He stepped into the iron stirrup and swung himself into the saddle. *I'm mighty thankful for my own saddle.* He could feel the wooden saddle beneath the buffalo hide. The hide made it acceptable. It beat riding bareback.

Three of Travels Far's men were armed with bows and arrows, the other three with muzzleloaders laid across their saddles in front of them. Josh had his Colt, but he wasn't too sure of his ability to shoot it with his hands swollen and torn like they were. The riders stayed to the trees, venturing onto the open plains only when it was necessary, and after taking time to scan the surrounding territory. They crossed a creek that ran almost due south, then paralleled it for several hours, following ridgelines, taking care not to silhouette themselves.

The country was beautiful, even in the Texas summer heat. The rain had brightened the bunch grasses. Calico bush with its thick foliage and brilliant flowers of red, yellow, and orange dotted the prairie, sometimes growing as high as a horse's back. As pretty as the land was, on this bright summer day, the heat was oppressive. They rode without talking, the Indians' bodies gleaming as sweat flowed from every pore. Josh missed his hat. He'd had that hat for most of the war. He could sure use it now to protect his head from the heat. A hat was at the top of his list when he could find a mercantile.

A short time after noon, they passed between two mountains that rose out of the plains. "Must be careful," Travels Far said. "This is where Comanches travel often."

Josh didn't have to be told twice. He wanted no more to do with the Comanches if he could help it. He felt exposed without his Winchester. He had come to depend on that rifle. He hoped the roan had made it back to the ranch with his rifle intact. To lose it would be a tremendous loss. He had his Colt, but only the ammunition in his belt. That wouldn't last long if they had to fight.

The long ride was beginning to tell on his weakened body. With the loss of blood, it would take him at least a week or more to get back all of his strength. His head nodded momentarily, and he jerked himself back erect. He must not appear weak among these men.

Travels Far missed nothing. He saw Josh as his head dropped to his chest; then his body jerked erect. "We stop now," he said.

They were to the east of the twin peaks and again in wooded country. The oak and mesquite trees would shelter them. Josh stepped down to the ground and almost collapsed. He held onto the saddle until he could regain some feeling in his legs; then he moved near where Travels Far was sitting and sat down, leaning back against an oak tree. "Warm day," Josh said.

Travels Far smiled for the first time. "Many days this warm here. You get used to it." The smile vanished from his face as he stood and pointed. "Much dust. It looks like many riders headed north. They not Indian. They ride hard in open. Looks like they come from your ranch."

Forgetting the pain, Josh quickly rose to his feet. "Travels Far, we must be going. If that was Ruffcarn and his crew, there could have been a fight. I've got to get there and help."

"We go," Travels Far said and jumped onto his horse.

The other braves followed suit as Josh stiffly swung back into the saddle.

~

THEY CRESTED the ridge north of the ranch and halted. "Let me ride in ahead of you," Josh said. "They might be a little jumpy if we go barreling into the ranch."

Josh pulled out ahead, and with Travels Far and the other braves following, they rode down to the ranch. Josh saw Pat and Scott turn and head back to the ranch house; then Bill and Juan stepped out onto the veranda.

Josh and the Kickapoo rode into the ranch yard. Josh swung his leg over the saddle, stepped to the ground, and leaned against the horse for a moment.

Pat ran out to Josh. "Welcome back, laddie! 'Tis wondrous to see you alive."

Josh grinned at Pat as the men shook hands. "I'm mighty glad to be seen alive myself."

He straightened and motioned, his arm swinging in a wide arc. "These are my friends. If it weren't for them, I wouldn't be standing before you today."

Travels Far translated Josh's words to the Kickapoo braves. There was much nodding and gesturing.

Josh pointed to Travels Far. "This is Travels Far. He saved my life. He found me and brought me to the Kickapoo camp. His wife nursed me. You should've seen me—I looked like a pincushion. I had prickly pear thorns everywhere except my legs. I owe him much. He speaks good English, and he told me who shot me. I'll tell you all about it later. But, now, we're all tired. We need rest and food."

Travels Far again translated for the other braves. Turning to Josh, he said, "Food, yes; rest, no. We will start back to our village. We like better to rest in the forest."

Josh turned to Nance. "Mr. Nance, we need to feed them well, and if you don't mind them cutting out four or five head of cattle, I'd sure appreciate it."

"Absolutely. Travels Far, thank you for what you've done. We're your friends if you'll allow it. You'll always be welcome here. If you'd like to cut out five head of cattle and take them back to your village, I'd like that."

"We will do that. We will remember you. We may come again."

"Good," Nance said. "Get down from your horses and come in and eat before you go."

Travels Far jumped down from his horse, said something to the other braves, and they followed suit. They stood by their horses, continuing to hold the reins.

Nance waved to the cowhands. "We can take your horses and feed and water them while you eat so they'll be a little fresher."

Travels Far explained Nance's statement to his men, and there was much head shaking and raised voices as they discussed releasing their horses to these white men.

Josh stepped to Travels Far's side. "Your horses will be safe. We owe you much. We'd like to show you that. Let us feed and water them so that you'll have strong horses for your ride back to the village."

Travels Far translated again, and the men reluctantly agreed.

Nance turned to Juan. "Pick a couple of men and take these horses to water, rub them down, and feed them well."

"*Sí, Señor.* Lee, Jimmy, grab some horses and let's take care of them for our friends." Juan, Lee, and Jimmy walked over and took the reins from the Indians. The horses, unused to the white man's smell, fidgeted some, but went with them to the water trough.

"Now come inside, let's get something to eat," Bill Nance said.

"No inside. We eat here." Travels Far indicated the wide veranda.

"Fine," Nance said. "Teresa ..."

Teresa came through the door with big plates of steak and beans. "I heard you talking, *Señor.* We have plenty for everyone. I'm also making up food bags for them to take with them."

"Teresa, you're always ahead of me. *Muchas gracias.*"

"I'm a woman, *Señor.* It's my nature to be ahead of you."

Teresa, along with Mary Louise, was handing out plates to each of the Indians, who had moved up to the veranda and were sitting cross-legged, with their backs against the cool stone wall.

Scott turned to Josh, his eyes twinkling. "You can thank Pat we didn't cut loose. He recognized you as you were coming down the Hill."

"Aye," Pat said, "no man sits a horse like you."

"Thanks, Pat. I'd have been sorely disappointed if you folks had opened up on us." Josh laughed and said, "I've been shot at enough to last me for a while."

Bill Nance looked Josh over and said, "You do look like you've been beat to here and gone. Why don't you come over here and sit down in the rocker."

Josh smiled. "I reckon that'll feel mighty good." He eased his battered frame into the rocking chair. "There were a few moments I figured I was a goner for good. It feels mighty fine to just sit in a chair. What was the dust we saw? It looked like it came from the ranch."

"Ruffcarn paid us a visit. Seems he thought he could buy this ranch. You'd think he would've figgered out by now that ain't gonna happen."

The Kickapoo were watching the hands as they watered and fed the horses. When the men started to take the saddles off to give the horses a rubdown, the Indians jumped to their feet.

Travels Far said to Josh, "No take saddles from horses. Not good. We need them ready to leave when we are ready."

"They're just taking them off to give the horses a good rubdown."

Travels Far's voice rose slightly. "No take saddles off."

Josh yelled over to the cowhands, "Leave the saddles on. Just make sure they get fed and watered." He turned back to Travels Far. "The saddles will be left on. We didn't mean to concern you."

Travels Far nodded and spoke to the other men. They talked for a moment, then sat back down and finished eating. When they were finishing, Teresa came back out with a plate stacked high with her apricot fried pies. She took the used plates and handed the big plate of pies to Travels Far. He picked one up and took a bite, then broke into a big grin. Speaking to the other Kickapoo around a mouthful of pie, he passed the plate around. The pies disappeared quickly, the Indians smiling and belching.

When they were finished, Travels Far stood, along with the other braves. "Food good. Always good to eat beef. Pie was good. But now we must leave."

The cowboys brought up the horses with extra bags of grain. Teresa and Mary Louise came out of the house and handed each Indian a food bag.

"Take five head of our cattle back to your village with you," Nance told Travels Far. "And anytime you need some beef for your village, cut out what you need. We're in your debt." He offered his hand to Travels Far.

"We may never be friends, Bill Nance, but we will not be your enemy," Travels Far said as he shook Nance's hand.

Josh had moved out of the rocker when Travels Far and his men stepped to their horses. He walked up to Travels Far and placed his hand on his shoulder. "I've said this before, but I want you to know that I'm in your debt and that of your village. I thank you, Nadie, and all of your men and your village for saving my life. If you ever need help, let me know. After we've settled this problem with Ruffcarn, I'll be going west to the Colorado mountains. If you are ever there, know I'll be your friend there also. Thank you." Josh shook the hand of Travels Far.

"You are good man. Strong. You make good friend, and I feel a bad enemy. May you have good life." With that, Travels Far turned, leaped into his saddle, and led his braves out of the yard at a gallop, whooping and brandishing their weapons until they were over the north ridge.

"I'm glad they're our friends," Scott said as he watched them gallop out of the ranch. "I sure wouldn't want to meet any of them if they weren't."

"Aye, laddie, that would be no fun," Pat said. "Now, Josh boy, tell us all about your little adventure."

Teresa and Mary Louise had watched the departure of Travels Far and his Kickapoo from the veranda. Teresa marched down into the yard and took Josh by the arm. "*Señor* Pat, can't you see the condition *Señor* Logan is in? He needs a bath; then he needs a bed. If you want to talk to him then ... maybe."

Bill Nance chuckled and said, "Don't mess with her, Pat. When she sets her mind to something, it gets done. Josh, go on with Teresa. You look a sight, boy. I'd say you're a mighty lucky man."

"Reckon I am, Bill. They say the Lord looks after children and fools. I'm too old to be a child, so I guess I know where that puts me. But I'll admit that I'm thankful to be here. I will say, this will result in something mighty bad for the *hombre* who did this." Thinking about the shooter, Josh could feel the tingling in his scalp that started just before anger turned to rage. He'd recognized the sensation as a youth, and, since then, he accepted it as a warning and worked hard to tamp down the anger when he recognized it. He became a different man when the rage took him, and he didn't much like that man. He took a couple of deep breaths and felt it subside.

He had to admit, Josh thought, he was getting almighty tired of people interfering with his plans. He wanted to help the Nance family, for they were Rory's folks, but it seemed every turn he took, something or someone else was trying to keep him from making it to Colorado.

Teresa and Josh turned to the house. Josh heard a whinny from the barn. "Teresa, I've got to go see Chancy before I go to the house. I haven't seen that horse in days, and it sounds like he's been missing me," Josh said as he turned back to the barn.

Teresa placed her hands on her substantial hips. "*Señor*

Logan, you need to be in bed. But make it quick, and I'll get your bathwater ready."

"Yes, ma'am," Josh said, a grin slipping across his face.

There he was; that horse had saved his life on several occasions. He stood there, tossing his head up and down, his black mane flying. "You miss me, Chancy?" The big Morgan stretched his neck as far out as he could to get to Josh. Josh walked up and started stroking Chancy's long nose with one hand while he patted his neck with the other. "Yeah, I've missed you, too. Give me a little time to rest up, and we'll be on our way to Colorado. Can you wait a little longer?" The horse rubbed his head against Josh's arm. "I'll see you tomorrow, boy, and you'll get a chance to stretch those long legs."

Josh turned and started for the house. He stumbled and almost went down, but Scott on one side and Pat on the other caught him. "'Tis a bit worn out you are, laddie, and, I might add, you look like you've been dragged through a keyhole. I'm thinking Teresa was dead-on. Get cleaned up and get some rest. We'll be talking about your adventure later. We have some information for you, too."

The two men helped Josh up the veranda steps and into the house.

"Bring him back here," Teresa called.

They took him to the room where his bath was ready. "Now shoo; go make yourself useful. There's plenty to do on this ranch," Teresa said as she ushered the two men from the room.

Josh saw a chair and dropped into it. He was worn to a frazzle. His body ached all over, and he was dead tired. The blood loss was taking its toll.

"Now, *Señor* Josh, you need to get clean. I have a hot bath here for you. The bath will help you feel much better. Do you think you can get yourself undressed and into the tub?"

"Yes, Teresa, I think I can," Josh said. He was almost too tired to talk. All he really wanted was to put his battered body to bed.

"Good, get your clothes off and toss them out the door. I'll get them clean for you. I've laid out some clean clothes on the dresser for you. They're yours, taken from the horse that returned. Soap, washcloth, and towel are right there next to the tub. When you're ready, call me and I'll show you where you're sleeping tonight."

Josh just nodded. Teresa looked at him with concern and then walked out of the room. Josh stood and slipped the buckskin shirt over his head. He slid the moccasins from his feet, pulled off his pants, opened the door just wide enough, and dropped the pants and shirt outside on the floor. He walked back to the tub and turned to get in. There was a mirror on the dresser. The mirror told a gruesome story. He could see his old wounds: the bullet wound in his left leg, the saber scar on his right side, and the other saber scar across his forehead. He fingered the healing bullet wound on the right side of his head. He grinned. *I'll have to start parting my hair on the right side.* He could see the swelling in his left knee was going down. In fact, it was feeling much better. But his upper body looked like what the buzzards would eat. He was swollen all over, with red blotches everywhere on his legs, arms, and chest; he knew his back looked the same way. His face looked like he'd stuck his head in a hornet's nest, but, he had to admit, he felt better than he had yesterday. The only thing that still worried him was his hands. They were no longer raw, but the palms were covered with scabs from the dried blood, and they were still swollen.

Josh eased down into the tub. The wounds on his body stung and burned from the hot water, but it also felt good. He almost fell asleep. Gingerly he washed his body, careful not to dislodge any of the scabs. Clean, he stepped out of the tub. He dried off, slipped his clothes on, and slid the moccasins back on his feet. *I'm for sure gonna need some new boots. I hate that, too. I really liked those cavalry boots.* He was exhausted. He could hardly put one foot in front of the other.

He opened the door and found Teresa sitting in a chair next to the door.

"First, I must see to your hands. Please sit." She had pulled up another chair and had bandages and a can of salve sitting on the side table. Teresa spread the salve over his injured hands and wrapped them with bandages.

"That feels mighty good."

"It's a mixture that my mother used. It'll quickly heal your hands."

Josh caught himself as his head fell to his chest. "I reckon I'm a little tired."

"Come, I'll show you where you'll be sleeping," she said as she took him by the arm. "Do you think you can make it up the stairs?" Teresa asked, her concern showing in her eyes and around the corners of her mouth.

"Sure I can," Josh said. "With a little help from you."

She smiled and helped him up the stairs to his bedroom. The door was open and the bed turned back. "This was our little Rory's room. He was always such a good boy. He looked out for his sister all the time. We'll miss him for a long time," she said sadly. "But he would like for you to be here. The few letters we received, he always spoke of you." She guided him over to the bed, bent down and slipped his moccasins off.

Josh slipped his legs under the sheet, looked outside and noticed it was twilight. He could hear a bobwhite's call in the broomweeds outside the window. A mockingbird sang its stolen notes. "Rory was my best friend, Teresa. We'll all miss him." He could barely keep his eyes open. "He loved you like his mother." He looked up into her face and saw the tears in her eyes, then his eyelids drifted shut, and he was sound asleep.

～

TERESA TIPTOED from the room and quietly closed the door. Descending, she saw Bill Nance standing at the foot of the stairs. "He'll not awaken until tomorrow morning, *Señor Nance*. He is hurt and tired, and I think he is a very good man."

"I hope he heals quickly. We need to find those cattle, and I want him along when we do. And, yes, Teresa, I do believe you're right. He is a good man. But did you see the look in his eyes when he talked about the bushwhacker? Josh Logan is also a dangerous man."

20

J osh woke to a knock on the door. "Come on in."

Pat opened the door. "You awake enough to talk, Major?"

"Sure, Pat, pull up a chair." Josh swung his legs out of bed and sat for a moment. He extended his left leg and then lowered his foot to the floor. Both his foot and knee felt pretty good.

"Pat, what'd I say about major? I'm no longer in the cavalry; no need to use the rank."

"Aye, but habits are hard to break. Josh, I must talk to you about something that's been weighing on me heart. You know I'm your friend, but I feel this needs a bit of discussion."

"Go ahead, Pat. We've always been straight with each other."

Pat looked at the floor for a moment, then locked eye contact with Josh. "I've got to ask, what are your intentions toward my wee sister, Fianna?"

Josh was momentarily speechless. He'd never expected this. "Pat, I like her, but I haven't thought much about intentions. Is there a problem?"

"Maybe, maybe not. She's young, Josh, just out from the East, and impressionable. I thank you for protecting her from the likes of Bull Westin. But I fear she's building feelings for you.

"You know our plans. Once in California, we'll be sending for our aunt Kathleen. I don't think Fianna needs to be dragged to some forsaken wilderness like the Colorado Territory to live out her life, which in that country might be short, struggling to survive. I'm just asking you to give her a chance to live a decent life."

Josh sat silent for a moment. He was stunned that his good friend would be saying this, although he had thought the same thing. Colorado would be hard. It would be no place for a young woman newly arrived from the East. "You're right, Pat. I have to admit that I like her. It could possibly go farther than that, given time. But my life will be a hard one. I'd not ask any woman to partner up with me for what I've ahead ... at least not now."

"Josh, you're my friend. I feel terrible about saying this. But I just feel it must be said."

"You've got my promise, Pat. Your sister needs to grow where she can laugh and enjoy life. That sure won't be Colorado."

"Thank you, Josh. Shall we say this will be the last word on the subject?"

The two men stood. They had known each other for many years and had formed a bond of brotherhood cast in the fire of battle. Josh put out his hand, and Pat grasped it. Without another word, Pat turned, went out the door, and closed it behind him. Josh sat down again on the bed. He'd known what Pat was saying, but put it aside each time he saw Fianna. When they had first looked into one another's eyes at the stage, something happened. *Was it just my imagination? I've too many hard times ahead to drag a woman into my life. Anyway, what woman would have a big, rawboned, scarred, ex-cavalryman like myself?* He finished getting dressed and headed downstairs.

The first person he saw was Mary Louise. "Major Logan, I

must apologize for the way I treated you when you were here last. That was unforgivable. I'm truly sorry."

"Miss Nance, it was understandable. You'd just received a terrible shock. A person can't be held responsible for what is said under those circumstances. But I do want you to know that Rory was my best friend, and I, too, miss him. Now, would it be fine with you if we got back to first names?"

"I'd like that, Josh."

Josh smiled and said, "Good. My stomach thinks my throat's cut; any chance of rounding up some grub around here?"

Teresa stuck her head out of the dining room. "*Señor* Josh, breakfast is ready. Come in and join everyone."

"Teresa, I told Mary Louise that Rory was like a brother. That means you have to call me Josh."

Teresa's smile lit up her face, and her brown eyes twinkled like agates in the sun. "Then, Josh, get in here and sit down before it's all gone."

Bill Nance and all the crew were at the table. Josh looked around; counting himself and Bill, there were ten men. He would like to have more, but ten could be divided so one group could protect the ranch while the other worked cattle or did what needed to be done away from the ranch. He knew Mary Louise and Teresa could shoot if it were needed.

There was a chair next to Scott. He stood and pulled it out. Josh started toward the chair, and Scott's brow furrowed. Josh stopped as Mary Louise walked by, smiling sweetly, and sat down. "Thank you, Scott."

"My pleasure, ma'am."

"Josh, sit here." Bill Nance, seated at the head of the table, pointed to the chair next to him. "How're you feelin'?"

"I think I'm gonna live. Actually, I'm feeling good. Head's still a little sore, but the knee is fine, and the prickly pear is gone except for the itching."

"How's your hands?" Bill asked, noting the bandages around his palms and fingers.

"Still stiff. But the salve that Teresa put on last night seems to have helped a bunch. I'm able to move my fingers now, so I'm good."

"After breakfast, I'll change the bandages and put more salve on them. But you should leave the bandages on today," Teresa said as she was putting out a platter of eggs.

Bill picked up a biscuit and passed the plate. "Good, now tell me how the Sam Hill you managed to be saved by Kickapoo. They don't like white men and can be as bad as the Comanche."

Josh told his story from the sun glinting off metal and the smoke, to their riding into the ranch. All of those at the table were spellbound and amazed that he had survived. Scott and Pat told about Bull returning to town and their tracking Josh until they lost Travels Far's trail.

After listening to Josh's story, Bill Nance said softly, "Son, I'd say you either have a guardian angel looking over your shoulder or you're just plain lucky. Now, I've a little more to add." He went on to tell of Ruffcarn's visit, his demand to buy the ranch, and how Scott called out and backed down Bull. "I think the only one we need to really watch is that Bankes character. He just sat in the saddle the whole time, cool and calm. I've done a lot of rangering in my time, and I've found those are the ones you have to watch."

Scott pitched in. "Bankes sizes up to be a tough *hombre*."

While Bill Nance was telling his story, Josh was eating: four eggs, gravy, biscuits, even bacon, which he didn't see much out here, and coffee. He finished his second cup of coffee as Bill was finishing. "Bill, I think you're right about Bankes. But now we need to find those rustled cattle. I feel certain they haven't been sold, and I don't think they've been driven far. Ruffcarn knew you didn't have the men to search for them—now you do. Let's head out today and don't come back till we find 'em. We've got ten men. If we left four here, that would give us six. That should be more than enough to handle whatever we find."

Bill nodded his agreement. "Good. I made some assignments yesterday, but you're back and you're the foreman. Pick your men, and let's move out."

"Right. Let's get moving." Josh slid his chair back from the table. "Bill, I know it's not likely, but you wouldn't have an extra hat and boots around here, would you? Lost my hat and my boot when I was dragged. It's almighty hot in this country, and I don't hanker to ride without a hat."

"Just so happens I might." Bill went into his office and returned with both of Josh's boots and his hat. "Hat's a little banged up on the right side, but Teresa cleaned it up, and it's almost good as new. Scott found both your hat and your boot on the trail. Don't know why Travels Far didn't pick them up, but here they are."

"Thanks, Bill. You have no idea how pleased I am to get these boots back," Josh said. He slid off the moccasins and pulled on his boots. He'd worn them for so long they were the shape of his feet. His left foot was still tender and sore, but he was able to get his boot on, and it felt good. His hat was another thing. There was a big crease where the bullet cut through the hat and hit his head, but that hat was still functional, and he was glad to have it.

"*Señor* Josh, your hands," Teresa said. She had brought the bandages, water, soap, and salve from the kitchen with her. She had him sit down while she removed the bandages and cleaned his hands. They were healing, but they were still stiff. Where the scabs were, the skin was tight when he flexed his fingers. She spread new salve over his palms and, this time, applied a light wrapping around his palms, leaving his fingers free.

Teresa saw the concern in his face. "They will heal perfectly. It will take a little time. But they will heal. Be sure to wear your gloves."

When she finished, Josh stood. "I hope not too long, Teresa. I feel sure I'm going to be needing them real soon. Thank you."

"*De nada.*"

Bill was on the veranda when Josh walked out of the house, slightly favoring his left leg and foot. The men were gathered around the veranda, waiting for their assignments. "Bill, are you planning on joining this party?"

"Josh, I need to get out more, and this seems like a perfect time."

"Alright, we'll take Scott, Lee, Pat, and Byron. Juan, I'd like you, Jack, Frank, and Jimmy to hang close to the ranch. We don't know Ruffcarn's plans, but we'd best be prepared, and I know how handy you are with your Sharps."

Juan smiled and said, "*Si, Señor.*"

The men went to the corral and barn to get their horses. Josh walked up to Chancy. Remembering what Teresa had said, he pulled his gloves on over his bandages. His saddle and gear had been brought out to the barn. He pulled out the Winchester. It had been cleaned.

Pat stood next to him. "I knew you always liked clean weapons."

"Thanks, Pat." He checked the loads, then set the Winchester down. He led Chancy out of his stall, smoothed the saddle blanket over his horse's back, and tossed up the saddle. Chancy's muscles quivered with anticipation. Josh reached for the cinch, slipped the latigo through the ring, and checked the cinch for debris, pinching, or caught hair before pulling it tight. This horse had taken care of him for years, and Josh believed in returning the favor.

He secured the latigo, tied his gear behind the saddle and slipped the Winchester into its scabbard. Josh swung up into the saddle and rode Chancy out of the barn. Bill and all the other men were mounted and ready to go. He looked at each man. They were riding out to find rustlers. Hopefully all would return. "Let's ride."

The big gray wanted to run. Josh let him have his head for a ways. It felt good to be in the saddle again on the horse that he loved. He could feel the muscles extending and contracting and the deep breathing of this magnificent animal. It was as if he were part of this horse. He knew Chancy felt the same exhilaration he felt. This was life. He let him run for a mile, then pulled him back to a walk.

Bill rode up next to him. "I'd say that big horse wanted to run."

"Yeah, he's been cooped up too long. Bill, Scott mentioned a place over on the Pecan. I'd like to ride over there and take a look."

"You're the foreman. Whatever you like. But we need to be keeping a sharp lookout for Comanches. They can pop up anytime, anywhere."

"I know you're right. I didn't mention it, but on the way to Camp Wilson, I ran into a scalping party. They gave me a good run. I winged one of them. He said his name was Eyes of Hawk."

Nance turned to look at Josh. "And you're still alive? That boy is one mean Injun. The Comanches stole him after they had butchered his family, when he was about three years old. He's become pure Comanche and mean as spit. It's a lucky thing your hair's not hanging on his lance."

Josh turned in the saddle to see the other boys riding loosely behind them. "I can thank the fact that I saw them from a distance first, and I had Mr. Winchester and Mr. Colt to assist me. I will say, he was mighty interested in my rifle. I figure he would like to have it for his own."

"You keep an eye out for him, son. He's a dangerous man."

"I'll do that; now I want to find those cattle. Scott, how far you reckon to this holding area on the Pecan?"

"No more than seven or eight miles. We'll be close to East

Caddo Peak when we get there. Just north of East Caddo is West Caddo. There's a pass between the two that the Comanche use mighty often. We'd best stay alert."

They rode on in silence. It was midmorning, and the temperature was rising quickly. Sweat dripped from their hair onto their collars. Josh was glad he had his hat. They walked their horses to keep the dust down as much as possible. Bunch grass grew in clusters across the plains, green from the recent rain. The horses weaved in and out of light green mesquite. Occasionally they rode through dark green oak thickets. They guided their mounts up the rocky hillsides with the ocher sandstone reflecting the heat of the sun. The sides of the hills were dotted with the ever-abundant prickly pear, with its green and purple fruit on many of the pads. On each hill they stopped before reaching the crest, then moved slowly, with their hats off, until they could just see over the ridge. They carefully surveyed the country in front of them for hostiles before crossing over the top and moving on.

It had been a long morning when they crested a hill and saw the dark green pecan and oak trees with the lighter green of the big cottonwood trees along the Pecan Bayou, as it snaked its way south.

Scott rode up next to Josh. "We came out some south of where I suspect they're holding the cattle. We could move into the trees on the Pecan, and, with this little north breeze, whip up some coffee and get some water for the horses."

"Good idea," Josh said. "A little coffee and a bite to eat will refresh us all, not to mention being under those trees and out of this sun."

They eased down the hill and into the trees. The shade felt good. The men dismounted and took their horses to the creek for water. The striking of the horses' hooves on the rocky bed of the creek was more noise than Josh wanted, but the horses needed water. After the horses drank, the men moved back into the trees. They cleared leaves from a spot and started a fire with some small dry pecan limbs. Only a small amount of smoke wafted into the trees and was quickly dissipated by the leaves as it rose to the heavens.

Scott made the coffee while they opened the food bags that Teresa had prepared for each of them. They were pleasantly surprised when each bag included two of her delicious apricot fried pies. Each man took out one and ate it with his coffee.

"Mr. Nance, I swear, I don't think I've tasted food as fine as Teresa makes. This here is like dying and goin' to heaven," Scott said.

"You're right about that. She can cook. I'd say it's a real toss-up between her and Victoria Diehl."

All the hands nodded as they finished off their coffee and pie. Josh had been up the creek, scouting for sign. He came back and squatted by the fire for a second cup of coffee. "About a hundred yards up the creek is a crossing. There's been a lot of cattle cross there. More than would naturally. I also saw some shod horse tracks. We can't be far. Get this fire put out and we'll go see what we can find."

After putting out the fire and ensuring there were no burning embers, the men mounted and slowly made their way up to the crossing.

"How far up the creek do you reckon they're holding the cattle?" Josh asked Scott.

"The bend is at least another two miles. We can cross the creek here and slip up over the ridge. If we follow that ridgeline, it'll take us right to where they are. They won't know we're anywhere around."

21

"Check your weapons," Josh said. "There's a good chance we're gonna need 'em."

The six men pulled their handguns and checked the loads. They checked their long guns, ensuring there was a round in the chamber. After all the guns had been checked, Josh and Bill led out. They rode slowly over the crossing, the horses' hooves clicking and rolling the rocks as they crossed the creek. The pecan and oak trees extended about fifty yards on each side of the creek. The land sloped from the edge of the trees up the rocky ridge. Josh and Bill eased up to the edge of the trees and stopped, scanning north and south along the ridgeline. All that was visible was rock, patches of cactus, and a few scattered mesquite trees; no movement except for a solitary jackrabbit and a few turkey buzzards sailing on the rising currents of hot air.

"Move out," Josh said softly.

The men slowly rode up the ridgeline in a column of twos. A few minutes later they stopped just before skylining themselves and peered over the top of the ridge. Still no movement. Slipping quietly over the ridge, the riders drifted down the other side and turned north.

They rode silently for a couple of miles until they heard the cattle lowing. Josh turned to Pat. "You still have your army-issue binoculars?"

Pat's lips spread in a wide grin. "Aye, the colonel said to keep them—never know when I might need them."

"Good. How about slipping up that ridge and seeing what you can find out for us."

Pat nodded, pulled his Spencer from its boot, reached into his saddlebag, and pulled out his binoculars. He made his way up the ridge, skirting loose rocks on the hillside. Pat removed his hat, laid his Spencer next to him, and stretched out on the rocky ground behind a small mesquite tree. Slowly, he eased his head above the ridge. Cattle were spread across the flat. They were backed up against the Pecan Bayou to the west. The bayou made a switchback that formed a perfect pocket for holding the cattle. Scott came slipping up beside Pat.

"How many head you reckon are down there?" Scott asked as he took off his hat and eased his eyes just above the hill.

"Looks to me about six or seven hundred head. They sure found a good place to hold those cows. They've got water, and this pocket has about the best grass I've seen around here."

"How many men you count?"

Pat continued to scan the trees with the binoculars. "So far, I've only been able to pick out four. There's one over on the east side of the herd, walking his horse around 'em. I see three more at their camp. You see them back in the trees a bit?"

Pat handed Scott the binoculars. Scott adjusted them and looked where Pat indicated. "Yep. I see 'em." He panned the binoculars up and down the creek, then around the cattle. "I recognize the boy on the horse. His name is Slim, and he's kinda new. Young fella, not a bad sort. I hate to see him here."

Pat took the binoculars back. "Aye. Laddie, I fear it will be a bad day for those rustlers."

They slipped back down the hill and delivered their news.

"Four men," Pat told Josh. "Three at their camp, almost straight back in the trees, and one young fella just over the ridge and north of us about two hundred yards. Looks like they all have rifles and are well armed."

"Thanks, Pat." Josh turned to Bill. "What do you think about us splitting up? I'll take Pat and Jack, you can take Scott and Lee. You move north up the ridge and we'll go back south a ways. Shouldn't take us more than fifteen minutes for each of us to get into position. We'll ride over the hill in thirty minutes. Make it nice and slow. If we charge, it could cause them to start shooting. I'd like to keep the shooting down as much as possible."

Bill nodded. "Sounds good to me. But you boys be ready. If they start the music, we'll play their tune. Be ready, but don't shoot unless they do."

Josh and Bill checked their pocket watches, and the two groups turned in opposite directions. Thirty minutes later they were waiting in position. Josh led Pat and Lee over the ridge. He could see Bill and his men crossing the ridge at the same time, rifles lying across their saddles, in hand and ready. The tall fellow saw Bill first. He stopped and sat watching them for a moment, then turned his horse and trotted back to the camp. Josh just kept riding toward the camp. The three men had been sitting around the campfire. Now they stood and focused on Bill. They hadn't looked toward Josh. The two groups were now within seventy-five yards of the camp. Two of the cowboys in camp had slipped the leather thongs holding their six-guns in the holsters.

When Josh was within about forty yards, one of the men turned and saw them. "Howdy, boys," Josh said. They all turned and looked his way, then back at Bill. It was obvious they were nervous and confused. Josh and Bill kept riding toward the camp. They were at the edge of the trees.

Josh heard Scott say, "Hi, Slim. You boys have any coffee?"

"Howdy, Scott," Slim replied. He was a tall, skinny kid with a face full of pimples. "Didn't expect to see you out here."

"I reckon you didn't," Scott said sadly.

Josh and Bill's riders were now around the camp. The rustlers had backed up, with their backs to the fire.

"Mr. Nance, that short, stocky feller with the black hat is Norm. I don't know the other two. They must be new," Scott said.

When Scott called the old ranger by name, the four men looked at each other, and worry clouded their faces like a summer thunderstorm.

Bill Nance leaned forward on his horse. "Which one of you boys is ramroddin' this outfit?"

Norm stepped forward. "I am, and what's it to you?" Norm carried his gun tied down and low. It was obvious he fancied himself a gunfighter.

"Well, I figure the he-boar ought to lead the way to the hanging."

"Ain't gonna be no hangin' here today," Norm said and went for his gun.

Pat put a round from his Spencer through the left-hand pocket of Norm's shirt just before the bullet from Bill Nance's .44 Colt slammed into the same pocket. Norm staggered back against one of the other rustlers, who was trying to get his gun into action. Josh shot him through the center chest with his Winchester. Smoke drifted through the pecan trees. The blast of sound silenced the birds and squirrels that had been singing and barking. Slim and the other man stood with their hands held high.

Josh sat his horse, watching the other two men. It always amazed him how quickly death could happen. A few minutes earlier these men had been sitting around the fire, talking about who knows what. Now two of them were dead. "You boys drop your guns. You want to tell us how you happened to have over seven hundred head of Rocking N cattle?"

The other rustler turned to Josh. He was an older man. Silver had started streaking his hair, and wrinkles coursed across his forehead and the corners of his eyes. "Mister, I've been a cow nurse my whole life. I was passin' through Camp Wilson. Thought I'd head over to New Mexico. I stopped in at the King 7 Saloon, and they said a Mr. Ruffcarn was hiring hands. My stake was about gone, so I figgered a couple of months here and I'd move on. Reckon I picked the wrong spread."

Bill Nance spoke up, his voice hard. "You reckon those cows carry the Circle W on 'em?"

The old cowboy turned back to Nance and shook his head. "No, sir, they sure don't."

Nance looked the man over. His boots were worn down, and his chaps had patches on them. "It's a sorry way to end up," he said. "You know what's coming."

The man rubbed his thick graying mustache. "I surely do. I'd be much obliged if you'd get on with it. I've no hankering to stand here and think about it."

The afternoon wind was freshening, caressing the green leaves on the pecan trees. The shooting had scattered a covey of bobwhite quail, and they were whistling to one another, slowly getting back together. Red flashed through the trees as a brilliant-colored cardinal flew to a welcome limb, causing a nearby fox squirrel to fuss at him for a moment. Life was returning to the creek.

"Jack, we've got plenty of good trees here. Find one and get a couple of ropes over a solid limb. I'd like to get this done and get these cattle moving back toward the ranch," Bill Nance said.

While Jack Swindell found a tree, Nance turned back to the boy and older man. "You boys do this on your own?"

The older man shook his head. "No, sir. We was told to hold these cattle here till his crew came back to rebrand 'em and sell them to the army. That's what we were doing when you rode in— just holdin' 'em."

"So Ruffcarn gave the orders?"

"He shore did. And I'll just tell you. He's dead set on gettin' your ranch."

Slim hadn't said a word after his greeting to Scott. He was barely shaving. He had a mustache he was trying to grow that was so sparse it was comical. His face was pale, but he stood his ground, his back straight and his eyes clear.

The older cowboy spoke up again. "Mr. Nance, I got a request for you. Goodness knows I have no right to ask, but it's not for me. I've been over the mountain. I've seen the bear. But this boy, why, he's just startin' life. He's a good boy. Don't cause nobody trouble and works hard for his wage. He just got in with the wrong bunch. If you could see your way clear to see he gets another chance, why, I reckon he'll never throw a loop over another man's brand. I swear that's true. If you could just let him ride, I could go to my maker a happy man."

Bill Nance had seen a number of men's necks stretched for wrongdoings. He was a hard but good man. He never stole anything from anyone and had no patience for them that had. He turned to Josh. "You think we would accomplish anything by hanging this boy?"

Josh was tired of death. He'd seen so many young men slaughtered and mutilated, dying and screaming on the battle-field. "Bill, why don't you ask him if he'd be willing to straighten out and stay away from shady characters like Ruffcarn."

Nance turned back to Slim. "Boy, I've got to tell you, I have no patience with thieves. I rangered for many a year. I don't hanker to stretch a man's neck, but I surely don't truck with rustlers. If we let you go, do you think you could give up this business and become an honest man?"

Slim looked up at Bill Nance with a glimmer of hope in his eyes. "Yes, sir. Why, I'd be out of this country before the dust could settle. I give you my solemn word on my mother's grave, I'll never again take another man's property."

Nance nodded and turned to the old cowboy. "Where's your horse?"

"Why, it's that little dun mustang. He's a fine cow pony. He's been a pleasure to ride."

"Go ahead and mount up and ride over to Jack," Nance said. He, too, wanted to get this gruesome business finished.

The older cowboy mounted up and rode over to the noose hanging from the big pecan limb. Jack rode up next to him, slid the noose over his head, and positioned it with the big hangman's knot under his left ear. He took out his piggin' string. "Reckon it's better if I tie your hands. It'll keep you from flailing around."

"Sure. I don't mind."

Jack reached up to the man's bandana to put it around his eyes.

"No need to do that, mister. I'd like to see this fine country as long as possible."

Nance rode over to him. "You got any last words?"

"Well, sir, I surely do. I've had a fine life. Never had much money, and what I had, I spent on women and liquor. But I've seen a big part of this country and I've enjoyed it. I'd also like to say I appreciate you givin' the boy a chance." He looked over at the boy still standing at the fire. "So long, Slim." With his last words, the old cowboy, without waiting for Jack to slap his horse, slammed his spurs into the sides of the little dun mustang, and it leaped forward, leaving him swinging in the air. The pecan limb groaned and swayed slightly with his sudden weight, and they all heard the audible snap as the correctly positioned hangman's knot broke his neck. He swung there for a few minutes. All the men sat silent.

"Seemed like a pretty fine guy," Scott said.

Josh took off his hat and wiped his forehead, then the sweatband. "Yeah, sometimes good guys get mixed up with bad men and just can't, or won't, find the courage to step away. Bill, what do you want to do with the bodies?"

"Let's get this man buried. I didn't even know his name." He turned to Slim. "What was his name, boy?"

Slim, unashamed of the tears coursing through the dust on his cheeks, said, "Mr. Nance, that was Rusty Felton. He was always good to me."

"Well, he did seem like a mighty fine feller. Jack, you and Lee get him down and bury him under the tree. Leave the other two where they lay. Reckon they don't deserve much else."

The men dismounted and started surveying the camp. They stripped the guns from the dead men and sacked up the cooking gear and other supplies. Saddles were tossed onto the horses, and the supplies divided among the rustlers' horses.

Nance turned to Slim. "Boy, I'm gonna turn you loose. You could just as easily have hung next to Rusty. You know that, don't you?"

"Yes, sir."

"Thanks to Rusty, you get a second chance. Don't prove me wrong, or I swear I'll hang you myself."

"No, sir, you won't be wrong. I know it's easy to say, but I've learned my lesson. I swear."

Bill Nance swung up into the saddle. "Well, how about you help us herd these cattle back near the ranch. We'll get you a meal, and you can be on your way. I'd recommend south ... maybe Brownwood way. Is that okay with you?"

"Yes, sir. Thank you, sir. I'm much obliged."

The camp had been cleaned, the fire put out, and Rusty buried. The hands were turning the cattle and moving them south. They would take them south until they reached the crossing, then cross Pecan Bayou and turn them west to the ranch. Josh eased Chancy next to Bill. "Bill, if it's okay with you, I think Pat and I will ride up to Camp Wilson. I want to check on the telegrams I sent and get the word spread about Ruffcarn. We'll be back in four or five days."

"That's fine with me, Josh. Tell Jeremiah howdy for me. I'll see you back at the ranch."

Josh called Pat back from the herd. "You want to go see your sister? I've got some business at the fort, and I want the word of Ruffcarn being a rustler spread quickly."

"Aye, Major, me lad, I'm your man. But sure it is that we won't get there today."

"What's the matter, Pat? You getting too old to spend a night camped out on the ground," Josh asked as his face broke into a grin. He turned his horse toward the creek so Chancy could get some water before they started out. Pat rode along beside him. They could hear the cowhands pushing the cows down the creek.

"It's a dirty job, dealing with rustlers," Pat said.

They were in the creek bottom, about three inches of water was still running, with deeper holes on each end—a nice crossing. The horses were drinking as Josh and Pat sat relaxed in their saddles. Josh was feeling some better. The gloves over his wrapped hands protected them from injury. He slipped them off to see how they were doing. Both hands were healing well although his right hand appeared to be healing faster than his left. "Yeah, Pat, it is. I'm glad we didn't have to hang the boy. You never know how he'll turn out, but I hope this straightens him out."

"I'm thinkin' if this doesn't turn him around, nothing will. I'll tell you, Josh, I'm tired of killing. I truly am. I've been doing this since I was a wee lad of eighteen; joined the army in Massachusetts. I'll do what I must, but it would please me to no end to never look over my rifle barrel at another man—excepting, of course, Bull Westin. I said before and I'll say it again, there's a man who deserves killing."

"I reckon that won't be too long in coming," Josh said.

Chancy's head whipped up and his ears turned to the other bank. Pat's horse did the same thing a few seconds later. The bank was too high to see over, and the two men, while talking, had heard nothing. Josh looked over at Pat as the two men slid their rifles out of the scabbards and removed the thongs from their revolvers' hammers. *I don't know if these hands will let me draw, but I know I can use this rifle.*

Without changing the tone of his voice, Josh spoke again to Pat. "Sounds like the boys are moving the cattle on down to the ranch."

"Yeah," Pat said. "Are you thinking we should go down and join them. Maybe give them a hand?"

Josh whispered, "Ready?"

Pat nodded affirmatively, and they charged up the riverbank to find Travels Far and four of his braves waiting.

Travels Far was surprised that they were armed and ready. "Josh Logan, how you know we are here?"

Josh shoved his rifle back into its scabbard. "My horse here told me."

"Ah," Travels Far said and translated to the Kickapoo braves. They nodded knowingly. "Fine horse."

"Yes," Josh said. "What brings you over here?"

"Follow Comanches. They are moving south. Maybe toward your herd."

"How many in the bunch?" Josh asked.

"Twelve. Eyes of Hawk leads."

Josh turned to Pat. "We've got to help them. We haven't heard any shooting, so we may be in time."

Pat swung his horse around to head toward the herd. "Let's go."

"Travels Far, we must save our friends. It's not your fight, but if you want to join ..."

Travels Far again spoke to his braves, and they all nodded. "That's why we here."

They rode out of the trees, leaving the concealment behind. There was no time for hiding; they must get to the herd before Bill and his men were attacked. Josh raised his rifle and fired a shot. It would alert the cowhands. Hopefully they would have time to get ready for the Comanches.

Almost immediately, other shots were fired and they could hear the whooping of the Comanches. Fortunately they weren't far. As they rode over the last rise, they could see the herd stretched out in the valley, traveling west. The herd was speeding up with the shooting taking place. Josh could see the Comanches spread out, moving down from the north. They had been forced to attack before they were ready. When Travels Far and his Kickapoo braves saw the Comanches, they let out a whoop and, leaning far over their horses' necks, raced to the fight.

Bill and his men had swung down from their horses behind boulders on the other side of the valley. The Comanches fired from their horses' backs. Their ambush broken, they pressed the attack in hope of killing the white men before the others arrived. Josh, Pat, and the Kickapoo had pulled into range and, from a gallop, began firing to drive them off.

They were getting close. Josh could see two men down, but couldn't make out who they were. Dust from the herd and the racing horses made it difficult to see. When they were within fifty yards of the Comanches, Josh jerked Chancy to a stop. Chancy had been through this before. He dug in his back feet, almost squatting to the ground with his front legs stiff, and slid for several feet. When he came to a stop, he stood stock-still, except for his heavy breathing, and gave Josh an excellent firing platform. With four shots, Josh emptied two saddles, and a third brave barely stayed on his horse. Pat was firing on his right. Two more Comanches went down. Josh saw a Comanche rise from the ground to his right. He recognized Eyes of Hawk. Josh knew he would never get a shot off before the Indian fired. He saw the smoke from the Comanche's rifle and Chancy collapsed from under him. He kicked his feet free from the stirrups and rolled as Chancy fell to the ground. Blood was seeping from his neck. *Not now. Not after all we've been through.* He brought his rifle to his shoulder, searching for Eyes of Hawk. He was gone.

Josh knelt beside Chancy. There was no movement; the horse was limp. He examined the wound. It was just a few inches in front of the saddle, maybe an inch or two deep. A chill went through Josh as he considered the possibility that the horse's neck was broken.

Travels Far raced up next to a Comanche brave. As the Comanche turned with his bow, Travels Far swung his tomahawk and smashed in his enemy's skull. The Comanche fell limp from his horse. Another of the Kickapoo braves had wounded a Comanche, and they were now on the ground fighting to the death. The Comanche brave was wounded in the side from a gunshot, but was fighting bravely. He thrust at the circling Kickapoo with his knife, the blade drawing blood from the Kickapoo's left arm, but the Comanche was slow recovering, probably from the loss of blood. The Kickapoo brave stepped in and drove the blade of his knife deep into the Comanche's chest. The two embraced in a dance of death, the Comanche's knife falling from his limp hand. The Kickapoo pushed the Comanche away, and before the Comanche brave hit the ground, the Kickapoo had scalped him. He extended his arm, with the dripping scalp high above his body, and let out a single whoop.

The remaining Comanches raced away to the east, disappearing in the thick foliage along Pecan Bayou. Josh surveyed the Kickapoo and Pat. No one was hurt. That was a miracle. The Comanches expected four easy scalps, but instead were decimated. A tribe couldn't stand those kind of losses.

∿

PAT RODE to where the Rocking N men had made a stand. "Where's Josh?"

Scott said, "I saw him go down on the other side of the herd.

Look, I see him standing, but I don't see his horse." The cattle were between the men and Josh.

"I'm hoping nothing happened to that horse. He's more important to Josh than his own life," Pat said to Scott. Pat turned and pushed through the cattle until he could see Josh and Chancy. Chancy was on his side.

As Pat rode nearer, he could see the blood flowing from the horse's neck. Josh was on his knees next to Chancy.

"It was Eyes of Hawk," Josh said. "I couldn't get on him fast enough."

Pat had seen this big man caring for Chancy all through the war, and Chancy returned the favor, running his heart out when it was necessary. Now it was over, and Josh had all of his hopes and plans tied to this animal.

Chancy moved his head. He blinked his eyes for a moment and then stood up. Blood was still coming from the neck wound.

"'Tis a miracle for sure," Pat said in awe.

Josh turned to Pat. "That blasted Indian creased my horse. Uncle Floyd talked of mustangers out west capturing horses like that. It's a terrible practice. The mustangers end up killing fifty horses for the one they get. Josh took the reins and walked Chancy around, then led the horse over to where Scott and the rest of the men were. Pat rode alongside.

The Kickapoo were busy whooping and scalping.

"'Tis a bloody business. I'm just glad they're on our side."

Josh looked over the carnage, his face grim. "You're right, Pat. Like you said earlier, I'm mighty tired of this myself. But sometimes it can't be helped. We didn't ask for it."

Bill was down with an arrow sticking through his upper thigh. Lee was dead from a bullet through his chest. Josh walked up leading Chancy and moved to where Bill lay on the ground. He kneeled next to him and examined the wound. "That looks like a pretty bad hit. Fortunately, it didn't hit an artery and didn't strike the bone."

"Yep, but it hurts like the dickens," Bill muttered, then clinched his teeth from the pain. When the spasm had passed, he said, "Scott saved my life. The Indian what shot me was about to put another arrow in me when Scott rode up. He must have emptied his six-gun into him. I sure owe that boy." Pain racked Bill again as Scott walked over, shaking his head.

Scott was standing by Bill Nance. "It's a good thing you boys fired that shot. Why, we would have been goners. Those Indians had an ambush set up that would have kilt us all. As it is, they got Lee and Mr. Nance. My big question is why you came back—and with those Kickapoo."

"They found us," Josh said. "When we came out of the creek, they were waiting. Chancy heard 'em and we were ready. Figured we were going to have to try to fight our way through a bunch of Comanches. They were a sight for sore eyes. They told us about following the Comanches, and we all figured they were heading for you. So here we are," Josh said. He sighed and looked over at Lee. "Just wish we could've been a little quicker."

Travels Far walked up to Josh, his arms and hands covered with blood. "We go."

"Was Eyes of Hawk among the dead?" Josh asked.

"No. He get away again."

Bill eased up onto one elbow. "Well, whether he's dead or not, again we are in your debt. We owe you much." He gritted his teeth for a moment with the pain. As it subsided, he relaxed and continued, "How can we repay you?"

Travels Far looked solemnly at Bill. "You good man. Need nothing now. Maybe cattle in winter when game is short." He turned to Josh, shook his hand one giant shake, and leaped on his horse. His men joined him, and they rode slowly toward the north.

Scott shook his head. "Never thought I'd be in debt to a Kickapoo."

Bill looked up at Josh. "If you'll break off the long part of that arrow, I think I can ride on to the ranch. Teresa will be able to fix me up."

Josh squatted again and grasped the arrow in his two big hands. "Mr. Nance, this is gonna hurt some."

"Do it, Josh."

Josh broke the arrow, and Nance almost passed out from the pain. "I reckon we'll ride on to the ranch with you," Josh said. "I'll get one of those rustlers' horses. Chancy was shot in the neck, and I need to get him doctored up. Also looks like you'll need some help with the cattle."

Nance shook his head. "No need. Scott's here. With Jack and Slim, we'll make it fine."

Slim spoke up. "Mr. Logan, take Rusty's dun mustang. That there horse is fast, and he's a stayer. I think Rusty would be glad you were riding him."

"Thanks for the suggestion, Slim," Josh said. "Scott, can you take Chancy back to the ranch with you and make sure he gets doctored up? I think he'll be fine as long as the wound doesn't get infected."

"Sure will, Josh," Scott said.

"Juan is one of the best horse doctors I've ever seen," Bill said. "He'll take care of your horse. When you get back, that horse will be as good as new." Bill looked around. "I don't reckon the Comanches will be back today. They got a pretty tough whipping. You and Pat head on to Camp Wilson. By the way, thanks for saving our bacon. We'd have been goners had you not come back."

"Go ahead, Josh," Scott said. "We'll take care of your horse and nurse these cattle back to the ranch. Mr. Nance here will be fine."

Slim had been watching. "Mr. Nance, don't know if this is the right time or not, but I've got to tell you and Mr. Logan something."

Bill looked up at Slim and said, "Go ahead, boy. This is as good a time as any. I'm not hankering on gettin' on that horse anyway."

"Well, sir, it's something Grizzard was talking about to one of the other boys in the bunkhouse ... I kinda overheard them. Grizzard was saying that Mr. Ruffcarn wanted your ranch."

"Nothing new about that, Slim," Bill said.

"Yes, sir, but Grizzard said that he had heard Mr. Ruffcarn and Wesley Pierce talking. They were saying there was gold on your ranch."

"Why, they're danged fools. There's no gold on this ranch. Never has been, never will be."

"Yes, sir. He, Grizzard that is, said that just before the war, there was a bunch of Yankees trying to get a wagon of gold down to the coast. He said the Comanches attacked them and killed all but two, and they managed to get away. But before the other soldiers were killed, they hid the wagon. He said that Mr. Ruffcarn and Mr. Pierce said that it's on your ranch."

Bill Nance shook his head. "I can't believe that's what this is all about. I've lived on this ranch since long before the war. That rumor went around just as the war started. But there's not a shade of truth to it as far as gold is concerned. I understand those boys were killed a long way northwest of my ranch, and it was only a wagon of supplies. But what I see as important here is that Pierce and Ruffcarn are working together. That explains why Ruffcarn spends so much time at the King 7."

Josh said, "Now that we know they're working together, that'll be to our advantage. For now, though, you need to get to the ranch and get that leg looked after."

"You're right. Slim, thanks for telling us. Now you boys give me a hand getting on this horse, and put Lee across his saddle. We'll bury him at the ranch."

Josh rubbed Chancy's nose as he switched saddles and gear with the mustang and stepped into his saddle. "See you in a couple of days. Pat, you ready to try again?"

Pat grinned and said, "I am, Major laddie. I'm aching to see my wee sister and maybe visit Mr. Starit's establishment. Just do me a favor and don't find me any more Injuns today."

Josh and Pat turned their horses to the north.

"What say, on the way to Camp Wilson, we swing by Ruffcarn's place and just see what's happening there?" Josh asked.

"You're all about trouble, aren't you, Major? But maybe a little reconnoitering will be worth our while."

22

"Come," Governor James W. Throckmorton ordered, at the knock on his door.

His aide stepped into the Texas governor's office, closing the door as he entered.

"Yes, what is it, Phillip?" the governor said, scowling at his aide. "You know I don't have much time left in this office. If I last the remainder of this month, I'll be surprised."

"I know, Governor, but I felt this might be important. When you were a ranger, did you ever come in contact with a ranger by the name of Bill Nance?"

"Yes, I did," Throckmorton replied, surprised that Phillip would be mentioning Bill Nance's name after so many years. "We served in Mexico together and, later, in the rangers. In fact, I dug a bullet out of him that he had picked up chasing Comanches. Is there a problem?"

Phillip's brow wrinkled with a frown. "Well, Governor, I've heard from two senators who were also in the rangers, someone is trying to nullify the land grant that Mr. Nance received. It encompasses the water rights along the Jim Ned Creek and Pecan Bayou. I thought you might be interested."

The governor's eyes narrowed. "Have you the name of this person?"

"Yes, Governor, it's Senator Wilson, from Beaumont, and I've heard that he's working with a businessman from New Orleans."

"Get that little weasel in my office today. If he doesn't want to come, tell him I'll have him escorted by some of my less patient friends. I'll have no one stealing the ranch of a good man like Bill Nance. I'll stop this, even if it's my last act as governor."

Phillip turned. His rapid steps echoed on the wooden floor as he started for the door.

"Oh, Phillip, one other thing. Ask Senator Hayes to join me for lunch in my office today. I think he may be able to help quash this theft quickly."

Without breaking stride, Phillip answered, "Yes, sir," as he hurried through the door, closing it behind him.

Ruffcarn slammed the door, stomped into his ranch house, and flung his hat across his desk. "Bankes, we're not going to wait for that Austin bunch to get around to awarding us that land. I want Nance and all his people off the Rocking N—now. I don't care how you do it." Ruffcarn dropped into the chair behind his desk and poured a drink into a dirty glass. "That ranch is going to be mine, and it's going to be mine now."

Bankes slid his hat to the back of his head and calmly said, "You're talking about a big job. Did you get a real good look at the house and bunkhouse? They both are made of limestone at least a foot thick. The two buildings cover each other and the barn. You toss in the second story of the house, with windows all around, and you've got a heap of trouble."

Ruffcarn shouted, "I don't care what they've got, I want them out of there!"

"Mr. Ruffcarn, two things. I'm no fool. I fight where I know I have at least an even chance of winning. You saw the new hands Nance hired. Those cowboys know how to fight, or I don't know men. Just with the hands he has now, he can defend himself forever and kill a lot of folks doing it."

"Bankes, you said two things."

Grizzard Bankes leaned back and locked his eyes on Ruffcarn. "Yes, I did. You hired my gun, and if there's killing that needs to be done, I'll do it. But I'm not your personal slave to be yelled at. If that's the way you want it, you need to find somebody else. I brook no man raising his voice to me more than once."

Ruffcarn's face turned white and there was a slight tremor in his hands. "I understand. I'm sorry I yelled. I just want those people off that ranch, and I didn't appreciate the way Nance insulted me. But you understand, you work for me."

Bankes still held Ruffcarn's gaze. "I do until I don't. Now do you still want me to run Nance off his ranch? You're going to lose a lot of men, and, don't forget, there are two women on the ranch. I don't kill women."

Ruffcarn thought for a moment. Bankes's thinly veiled threat had the effect of pouring cold water on his anger. Maybe he was right. "Not now. I'll wait a couple more days. If I don't hear something from Austin soon, it still might be necessary, but I'll cross that bridge when I get to it."

Bankes took off his hat and wiped the sweat from his face with his red bandana. "Have you run all this by Pierce?"

Ruffcarn felt the anger rising again. "Pierce isn't my keeper. I don't need his approval."

Bankes's mouth spread in a wide, insolent grin as he stood to walk out. "Just asking. He looks to me like the kind who, if he felt he was crossed, could be mighty mean."

"I can handle him. By the way, if it came to that, do you think you could take him?"

Bankes thought for a moment. "Yeah, I figger I can. It'd be

close, but I'm faster than he thinks I am. I could take him. But if that ever comes up, it's gonna cost you a lot more money."

"If it ever comes up, the money will be there. Now, why don't you send some men down to where we're holding the Nance cattle. Have them change the brands, and we'll start selling them to the army. We need to get them sold before they're found."

Bankes turned and headed for the door. "Sure thing. I'll get some men down there today."

"You can go right in, Senator," Phillip said.

Senator Edward Hayes eased the door open. "Heard there was going to be a free lunch here today. Couldn't turn that down."

Governor Throckmorton looked up from his desk and smiled. He had known Hayes for many years. They had been in the rangers together with Bill Nance. "Get on in here. We might be able to rustle something up that wouldn't upset your tender stomach."

The governor stood and walked from behind his desk to meet his friend. The two men shook hands, and the governor guided the senator over to the couch, where they both sat down. "Ed, we have a problem."

"You mean General Sheridan?" Edward Hayes asked.

"Not this time, although I think I'm going to be out of a job pretty soon. I hear, through the grapevine, that General Griffin has put in a request to Sheridan to have me kicked out of office."

"That's a shame, James," Senator Hayes said. "You've done a good job here. It's too bad you can't get the federals to send more troops to the frontier, instead of them hanging around the towns trying to control politics."

"You're right. But that isn't why I invited you up here today."

Phillip stuck his head in. "Ready for lunch, Governor?"

"Bring it on in, Phillip." The two men waited while the lunch was placed on the coffee table in front of the couch.

"Thank you, Phillip," Governor Throckmorton said as Phillip quickly withdrew from the room. "Eat up, Ed. I had that bread pudding made especially for you."

The two leaders ate their lunch in silence. As Senator Hayes was finishing, he turned to the governor. "Why did you want to see me, James?"

"You remember Bill Nance?"

"Of course I do. He'd be a hard man to forget. He started a ranch out west of Brownwood, didn't he? The Rocking N, isn't it?"

"Yes, although it's north of Brownwood about ten or twelve miles—wild country; Comanche country, actually. But that's not the point. The point is that someone is trying to void his land grant and take his ranch."

"Another carpetbagger, I presume."

"I wish it were. You know Senator Wilson from Beaumont?"

"I know that little rat," Senator Hayes said.

"He's working on behalf of someone from New Orleans. It seems this person from New Orleans has an interest in Bill's ranch. I don't know who the person is, but if we could find out, we could, if necessary, help him change his mind."

"I'm with you on this. Bill is a good man. I was disappointed that his son went over to the North in the war, but we both know families who were torn apart. Our job, now, is to get past it and rebuild what's left of this great state. We can't do it with slimy little senators like Wilson trying to take land from our citizens, especially a man like Bill Nance."

"I'm glad you feel that way. I've summoned Senator Wilson for a meeting early this afternoon. He should be here any minute. I'd like you to be here also."

"It would be my pleasure. You have my support in whatever pressure you want to bring to bear on him. Why, I just had a thought. I could challenge him to a duel. That'll scare the daylights out of him."

Governor Throckmorton threw back his head and roared. "You're so right. I expect he might soil his britches, right here in the Governor's Mansion. No, I don't think that'll be necessary. But thanks for the offer."

Phillip knocked on the door and stuck his head in. "Senator Wilson is here."

The governor moved back behind his desk. "Thank you, Phillip. You can take the dishes, and then be so kind as to show Senator Wilson in."

"Yes, sir," Phillip said. He quickly picked up the dishes and went out the door. Moments later the door opened and a nervous Senator Wilson walked in. Phillip closed the door behind him.

Governor Throckmorton watched the small, thin man standing in his office. He couldn't be over five feet six inches tall. His pale face was gaunt, with a thin pencil mustache clinging to his upper lip. His eyes blinked continuously, and a surprised look traveled across his face when he saw Senator Hayes sitting on the couch. "Come in, Wilson, and sit down." The governor indicated a straight-backed chair in front of his desk.

Wilson moved to the chair. "I thought this was a private meeting."

"You thought wrong," Governor Throckmorton said. "I invited Senator Hayes here because we both have an interest in what you're trying to do."

Wilson's head turned quickly to Senator Hayes and back to the governor. "What do you refer to, Governor?" Wilson asked.

"I refer to your trying to take the ranch of a good friend of mine and Senator Hayes. You recognize the name Bill Nance of the Rocking N ranch?"

Wilson took a white handkerchief from his breast pocket and wiped sweat from his upper lip. "I haven't the slightest idea what you're talking about."

"Wilson, don't add lying to your list of unsavory characteristics. I know all about your attempt to have Bill's land grant voided. I want it to stop now. Do you understand me?"

Governor Throckmorton watched as Wilson's face went from white to red. It was obvious the little man was angry. The governor waited for Wilson's response. He'd known and disliked this man from Beaumont for several years. Wilson had accumulated tremendous acreage around Beaumont during the war. He bought the paper from banks and foreclosed on families when they could no longer pay. The governor knew the only way this man could have been elected to the Texas Senate was political graft.

Finally, Senator Wilson composed himself. "Governor Throckmorton, we've never been on the best of terms. I've heard that you won't be in office much longer. I don't see what you think you can accomplish by attempting to belittle me. I've looked into Nance's land grant for a Jefferson County constituent, and I believe it is illegal. Therefore—"

"Stop right there," Governor Throckmorton ordered. "You're not looking into the land grant for a Texan, but for a man from New Orleans. I have two questions for you. Number one, who is the man?" The governor jabbed his right index finger at Wilson. "And number two, when are you going to stop lying to me?" He could see that Wilson was flustered now and trying to figure out how he knew about Pierce.

"I . . . I—How do you know about this? Nobody knows except me and ..."

Senator Hayes sat quietly on the couch. Governor Throckmorton continued, "Except you and who?"

Wilson had all but collapsed in the chair. "Governor, I can't tell you. This man will kill me if I do. I've taken money from him, and I no longer have it. He'll kill me."

Governor Throckmorton turned cold inside. He couldn't abide liars and cheats. "Wilson, if you don't tell me, Senator

Hayes, who's also a good friend of Bill Nance, will challenge you to a duel. Senator Hayes has never lost a duel or been wounded in one. What do you think your chances will be with him?"

Wilson glanced at Senator Hayes. Hayes gave him a slight nod and smiled. "Alright, his name is Wesley Pierce. He was a big businessman in New Orleans. I knew him from my visits there. He asked me to help him with this grant, for which he would reimburse me for my expenses. I saw nothing wrong in helping a friend."

"So where is this Wesley Pierce now?" the governor asked.

"He's moved to Camp Wilson and opened a gambling establishment."

"You mean a saloon?"

Wilson pulled his handkerchief from his pocket again and wiped his forehead. "Yes."

"Why would he move to a new town that's right up against the Comancheria?" the governor asked. "That's dangerous country. There are plenty of business opportunities in safer towns."

Wilson squirmed in the straight-backed chair. "He promised to cut me in on part of it ..."

"I'm running out of patience, Wilson. Part of what?"

"The gold."

"Gold?" Governor Throckmorton asked. He turned to Senator Hayes. "Do you know of any gold in that country?"

"Governor, there's certainly no gold in the ground out there. At least no one has found any yet. But I do remember a Yankee column from northern New Mexico. It was just before the war started and they were bringing a gold column through. They were trying to get to Galveston before the war started so they could use the port. Supposedly, they were attacked by Comanches, and every man was killed except for a sergeant and a private. Those two men finally made it to Austin, but then they disappeared. Everyone took it to be ravings of deserters who had almost died from thirst and starvation."

"Do you think it's true?" the governor asked Hayes.

"Not a word of it. If it were, Southern troops or rangers would have found it. I think it was just a couple of deserters trying to talk themselves out of prison. I never believ—"

"Pierce has a map," Wilson said.

Hayes laughed. "Do you know how many treasure maps are floating around this country?"

"Alright," the governor said, "at least we know his reason, flimsy as it may be. Wilson, here's what I want you to do. Resign your seat as senator—"

"Governor, you can't make me do that. What will happen to me?"

"Frankly, Mr. Wilson, I couldn't care less. I'm sure you'll land on your feet at someone else's expense. But let me continue. I want you to resign your senate seat, stop your attempt to invalidate Bill Nance's land grant, and contact this Pierce fellow. Tell him that Bill Nance's land grant is valid, and you can do nothing else. Your alternative is . . . " Governor Throckmorton moved his gaze from Wilson to Senator Hayes, who was still smiling, and back to Wilson. "I'm sure you understand my meaning."

"Governor, you're threatening me."

The governor's voice had grown hard. "Yes. You're absolutely right. I need your decision, now."

Wilson had lost his senate seat, but he still had his wealth. "Alright, but I fear I'm a dead man."

"I wouldn't be too concerned about that. Pierce doesn't know the *hombre* that he's tied into. Nance will eat him alive. I don't think you're going to need to be concerned about Pierce, at all. Now, Mr. Wilson, I want you out of my office. The sooner you can be out of Austin, the better. Don't make it more than two days. If you need help with your resignation, I'm sure Senator Hayes will be glad to assist you. Good day."

Wilson stood. He glanced at Hayes, turned, and walked to the door. He closed the door gently.

Senator Hayes said, "I don't like that man, but I feel a mite sorry for him. He looked like a whipped dog when he walked out that door. But I don't think there will be any further problems from him. Bill Nance's troubles here are over."

The governor sighed. "I think you're right. If I have to leave office now, I can feel good about helping an old friend."

"You going to let him know?"

"I don't think so. He's got enough trouble with the Comanches. He doesn't need to be concerned about something that's finished. You or I will have a chance, in the future, to share this with him face-to-face. Thanks for coming in, Ed. I think your being here, and your threat of a duel, swung this for us. I owe you."

"James, this was for Bill. Glad to do it. But I'd better get myself back to work. Good luck to you."

Governor Throckmorton rose and, placing his arm around Senator Hayes's shoulder, walked him to the door. "I just wonder what Bill Nance is up to now. Anyway, good luck to you, Ed."

23

The morning sun turned the western slopes golden and slowly chased the shadows from among the tall trees along the creek. Josh and Pat had finished their breakfast and were preparing to mount up. "How's your hands feeling?" Pat asked.

Josh had, only moments before, slipped his gloves on. He had taken the bandages off the night before, heated water, and soaked his hands. "Pat, they're feeling good. That salve Teresa used works wonders. I've been exercising my hands, and they're no longer tight. Couple more days they should be fine.

"This is a nice little dun," Josh said as he swung into the saddle. "But he's not Chancy—sure hope he's alright."

"You and Chancy have been together for a long time, eh?" Pat asked.

"That's for sure," Josh said. "I was a youngster when he was foaled. Why, he was up on his feet before you knew it. He wasn't bashful at all. He was investigating every corner of that stall. When Pa said I could name him, I figured to call him Chancy, and it stuck."

"I've never seen a horse that likes action as much as he does. He'll make you a strong herd when you get to Colorado."

Josh turned the little dun and walked him to the edge of the trees. The two men scoured the surrounding countryside for signs of movement, waited a few moments, and started the horses out onto the prairie. "I think he will, Pat. We get this problem with Ruffcarn and Pierce settled, you and Fianna can take the stage on to California, and Chancy can take me to Colorado."

They rode at a walk, keeping the dust to a minimum, not wanting to alert anyone to their location. The Ruffcarn ranch wasn't far ahead, and Josh wanted to look it over. The more he knew about his enemy, the better off he was. He loved being in wild country on a good horse. It breathed life into his soul. He liked West Texas. It had a harsh beauty that appealed to him.

"What do you want to do when we get to Ruffcarn's ranch?" Pat asked.

"We'll approach slowly and see if we can find a vantage point. Then I'd like to just wait and watch for a while. See what we might learn of their operation. I've a feeling this isn't a very efficient ranching outfit. Seems their main thrust is the gold, with a little rustling on the side. But let's just check it out, then head on into Camp Wilson."

Pat had been on patrols throughout the area and knew exactly where the ranch headquarters was located. "I'm thinking we need to move a little more to the east. The ranch sits near a creek that runs north and south, about fifteen miles south of the fort."

The men rode on throughout the morning. The Texas summer heat was again making its presence known. They passed small bunches of cattle scattered on the prairie and back in the brushy ravines. "The ranch house lies just over that wee hill ahead of us. I'm thinking we might circle to the north side. That way, if we need to leave in a hurry, we can head due north to the fort."

"Lead the way, Pat," Josh said.

They circled the ranch, keeping the hills between themselves and the ranch. "Interesting," Josh said. "You'd think we would have at least seen some cowhands working the cattle. They don't seem to have much interest in daily ranch work."

Pat nodded. After arriving on the north side, they still hadn't seen the ranch or any hands. "It lies just over the rise. We'd be smart to lead our horses until we can crawl up to the edge."

"Like I said, Pat, lead the way."

They dismounted and led their horses up the slope of the hill. As they neared the crest, they tied them to a couple of mesquite trees that covered the hillside, and pulled their rifles from the scabbards and their binoculars from the saddlebags. Hunched over, the two men made their way near the crest of the hill, then crawled the rest of the distance, careful to stay away from the cactus.

Upon reaching the crest, they could see the ranch house, bunkhouse, and corral clearly. Everything looked in shoddy condition. No cowhands liked to do work that didn't entail being on a horse, but a good owner or foreman would ensure that necessary work was done to keep the ranch in good shape. It wasn't being done here.

At that moment, a man walked from the bunkhouse toward the corral. Both men put their binoculars on him. "That's Bull," Pat said. "From here, this Spencer could make short work of him, a little turnabout."

"No," Josh said. "Bull will get the medicine he deserves. Let's just watch the ranch for a while and head for the fort."

They continued to watch the ranch for another hour. "Not much going on," Josh said. "I'd hate to have to defend that ranch. Bullets would go through those walls like they weren't even there. Anybody inside would be dead or wounded in no time. Reckon Ruffcarn's not concerned about defense—or he's not planning on being here for long. Pat, I think we've seen enough. Let's head on to Camp Wilson."

Pat followed Josh as he slid back down the hill. Once sufficiently below the crest, they stood and dusted themselves off. "I'm for town, Josh," Pat said. "I've built a major thirst, and not for water."

Josh laughed. "We'll get that slaked in just a few hours."

They mounted and turned their horses north. Keeping Coyle Creek to their west and Hubbard Creek to their east, they moved steadily north. They kept a sharp lookout, for this was rough country cut by many ravines, any of which could be hiding Comanches. Coyle Creek gradually turned east. They entered the trees, then found a good crossing and let the horses have a drink in the creek.

"Hot," Pat said. "California will be a welcome sight. My old eyes will be happy to rest on the ocean and feel those cool breezes. Josh, you should see the land. We'll have a *hacienda* that looks out over the ocean, with a few cattle and horses. I've been fighting now for almost twenty years, and I'm ready for a rest."

"You'll rest for a month, maybe two," Josh said. "Then you'll be out looking for some excitement. You're not ready for a rocking chair, Pat. You've too much life in you."

"We'll see, laddie. Aye, we'll see."

SEVERAL HOURS later the two men rode into Camp Wilson and past the fort. They rode up to Tiny's stables and dismounted.

Tiny walked out. "Well, as I live and breathe, the man is back from the dead. It's good to see you, Josh. Everybody around here thought you were done for. Why, when Bull came riding back into town as big as you please, we figured he had surely drilled you."

"He got too close, Tiny. Another half inch and I'd be coyote fodder. But I'm doing a lot better now."

"Aye, he looked pretty bad when he showed up to the ranch," Pat said.

"Tiny, do you think you could put our horses up overnight?" Josh asked. "We're going to pull out again in the morning and head back to the Rocking N."

"Why, sure, Josh, I'd be glad to. I'll make sure they get a good rubdown, then feed them—maybe toss in some oats."

"Thanks, Tiny." Josh turned to Pat. "How'd you like that drink now?"

"Ah, 'tis music I'm hearing. Lead on."

"You're gonna make a pretty big commotion when you walk up that street, coming back from the dead and all," Tiny said.

Josh pulled his saddlebags from where he'd hung them and slid the Winchester out of its scabbard. He turned and headed out the stable door.

Pat picked up his Spencer and joined Josh. They strolled across the street, taking their time. When they came to the Shamrock, they pushed through the door and walked inside. Cecil Starit was facing the other end of the bar, talking to the cavalrymen who were there. "What'll it be?" Cecil said as he started to turn towards them. "Why, as I live and breathe—Josh Logan! Man, I thought you were buzzard bait. Step yourself up to this bar and have a drink on the house. And how is it that you're doing, me retired First Sergeant?"

"I'm living the life, Cecil. Now give me a shot of the best Irish whiskey you have back there. It has been too long since I had a sip," Pat said.

When the cavalrymen saw who it was, they gathered around Pat, laughing, asking questions, and slapping him on the back. "Give me room, lads. I'll tell you what it is that's been happening, but let me have my drink," Pat said.

"If you've got a sarsaparilla, Cecil, that would be mighty good," Josh said.

"One sarsaparilla coming up. So, tell me, Josh, how is it that you're still alive? We all felt sure you were dead, especially after Bull came back into town. That is, all of us except Pat's sister, Fianna. She always believed you were alive."

Josh and Pat exchanged glances. Josh looked back at Cecil as he took his first drink of sarsaparilla, then set it down on the bar. "Let's just say that Bull isn't the shot he thinks he is, although he did leave me a souvenir." Josh took his hat off and turned his head so that Cecil could see the deep, hairless crease along the right side of Josh's head.

Cecil whistled. "Boyo, you are one lucky fella."

"That I am, Cecil; that I am," Josh said, then took another long drink of his sarsaparilla.

"Josh, Jeremiah said that when you came, check with him. He has a message for you from the colonel," Cecil Starit said.

Josh finished off his sarsaparilla and slung his saddlebags over his right shoulder. He picked up his Winchester and said to Pat, "You coming with me, or are you hanging around here for a while?"

"Major, laddie, I'd best be going with you. I need to see my wee sister."

Josh and Pat exited the Shamrock and turned left on the boardwalk for Diehl's Emporium and Boardinghouse.

Fianna was putting canned goods on the shelf behind the counter when they walked in. She was reaching to the top shelf from the stepladder she stood on. Her tall trim figure was stretched, emphasizing her rounded hips, slim waist, and strong shoulders. A trim ankle peeked out from under her dress. Her back was turned, and beautiful auburn hair cascaded over her slim neck. Josh felt the fullness in his chest that he'd felt when he first saw her. *What a lovely, special woman she is*, Josh thought.

"I'll be with you in just a moment," Fianna said.

Her voice strummed more strings in Josh's soul. *I've got to control myself. Remember what Pat said.* "Take your time, ma'am," Josh said.

Fianna spun around on the ladder. She dropped the carton of canned beans and almost fell. Words came in a rush. "Oh, Josh, I knew you were alive. I just knew it. Everybody said you were probably dead. But I knew you were alive." She came around the counter and rushed to him. Just before reaching him, she stopped. He had put his gear down and taken his hat off. The proud, hairless scar that ran from just above his ear and coursed down the side of his head shocked her. Then she looked over his face. Most of the swelling was gone, but it was still puffy around his cheeks. She gasped and said, "Oh, you were shot."

"I guess I'm just too ornery to kill. It's good to see you, Miss O'Reilly."

Josh could see first the startled look, then changing to puzzlement, in her lovely eyes.

Josh continued, "Look who I've brought with me." He stepped aside and Fianna saw the big smile on her brother's face for the first time.

She smiled, walked over to him, and gave him a big hug. "So, you big Irishman, you haven't been taking very good care of Josh, now have you?"

Pat laughed then said, "It's him who's been taking care of me, and a good job he's done."

The Diehls walked in, Mr. Diehl with a cup of coffee in his hand, just as Pat finished. Mr. Diehl exclaimed, "By heavens. Josh, it's good to see you alive. There were many doubted that you made it, although this young lady always believed you were alive. I'm glad to see you."

Mrs. Diehl clapped her hands. "It's wonderful to see you, Josh. Why, Fianna has been beside herself. I hope you don't mind an old lady giving you a hug." She walked over and wrapped her plump little arms around him.

"Thank you, ma'am," Josh said, a little embarrassed. "Couldn't let anything happen to me. I wanted some more of that bear sign. Yours is the best I've ever tasted."

"Then you shall get some. Fianna, would you mind giving me a hand in the kitchen, and I'll show you how to make doughnuts," Mrs. Diehl called over her shoulder, already moving toward the kitchen.

Fianna hesitated, looked toward Josh and then back at the kitchen. She flashed a brilliant smile toward Josh and followed Mrs. Diehl through the dining room and into the kitchen.

"Mr. Diehl, Pat and I will be needing a couple of rooms for the night if you've got them available. We'll be heading out again in the morning."

"Not a problem, Josh. I have a message for you. Colonel Sturgis wants to see you as soon as you get to town. He said that your telegram had been answered."

"Thank you, Mr. Diehl," Josh said. "Mind if I leave my gear with you?" He turned to Pat. "I'm going up to see the colonel, if he's still in his office. You care to come along?"

"No. I'm gonna have a cup of Mrs. Diehl's fine coffee and talk to Fianna a bit. You go ahead. Anyway, officers always talk easier with other officers."

Josh walked out the door and looked straight across to the King 7 Saloon. The doors were closed, and the bright afternoon sun made it difficult to see the interior through the windows. He turned and headed for the fort.

24

Ruffcarn's two riders returned from where the rustled cattle had been kept about an hour after Josh and Pat had left. Bankes had just walked out of the ranch house and into the yard when he saw the galloping horses race into the yard. The urgent sound of the horses emptied the bunkhouse. Jake Ruffcarn strode out of the house and up to the riders as they were dismounting.

"They're gone, Mr. Ruffcarn. Every blasted head," the taller cowboy said.

"What do you mean, gone?"

"Just that. We got there and Conway and Hawkins were shot dead by the campfire. Conway had two bullets right through his heart—looked like he tried to go for his gun. Hawkins was laid out right next to him, a bullet through the middle of his chest. There were six riders. We found where they hanged, then buried Felton. We looked all around. There was no sign of the kid."

"Gone?" Ruffcarn was beside himself. "Indians?"

"No, sir, weren't no Indians what stole those cattle. These was shod horses. Anyway, Comanches would have tortured every single one of them right there. Them Comanches don't hang folks; they cut 'em and burn 'em. These were white men for sure."

"Where'd they drive the cattle?" Ruffcarn asked. "Did you follow them?"

"We did a ways. Looks like they were driving them toward the Rocking N. Also looked like they were attacked by Indians. What was crazy was that other tracks showed that Indians were fightin' Indians right there. Why, they left several scalped Comanches. Some of the white men were hurt, too. But after the fight, they split up. Part of them drove the herd toward the ranch, and two of the shod horses headed up this way. Indian tracks went east and north. It was sure confusing."

"You think it was Nance?" Ruffcarn asked.

"I sure do. But he had a bunch of riders with him. He wouldn't leave the ranch without protection, and he had five other riders with him. So he's hired more riders."

Ruffcarn's face was the color of fresh blood. He was seething. He turned to Bankes. "What do you think, Grizzard? Do you think he's hired more men?"

Grizzard mulled the thought over for a moment. "Well, when we were there, Penny came riding up with three more riders. We know that Logan hired Penny and the soldier boy. If you figure Logan is dead, that gives them around eight or nine, counting Nance, and that old Mexican he has working for him, plus the two hands he already had. Any way you cut it, he has more men now than he had before Logan showed up—and we still don't know that Logan is dead." As he made the last statement, Bankes looked over at Bull.

Bull glared at Bankes for a moment; then he kicked at a rock and said, "He's dead."

Ruffcarn spun around and headed to the house. "Bankes, you and Bull come into the house. The rest of you get your gear and your horses saddled. We're hitting Nance and we're hitting him hard."

The hands went to the corral and started roping horses. Bankes and Bull followed Ruffcarn into the house. As Bull was closing the door, Ruffcarn kicked a chair across the room and slammed his fist down onto his desk. "I'm tired of this," he shouted. "We've waited too long. I want Nance dead, along with everyone on that ranch—everyone."

Bankes's stoic expression never changed. "You don't want to do that. You kill those women on that ranch and we'll all be marked as woman killers. There won't be a place to hide from here to Montana. And they don't just hang woman killers. They'll skin you or burn you alive."

Ruffcarn calmed down a little. The thought of being skinned alive put a damper on his enthusiasm. "We're still attacking that ranch. If we can keep from killing the women, so be it. But if they die in the process, they just shouldn't have been there."

Bull had been standing by the window, watching the men saddle the horses and get the needed supplies from the storehouse in the barn. "I'm with you, boss. I think it's way past time to kill Nance."

Bankes slowly turned his head to look at Bull with undisguised contempt. "There's the man for you, Ruffcarn. He'll do just whatever you say. But I've had it with this outfit. Count out my pay. I quit. I've never harmed a woman, and I don't plan on starting now."

Ruffcarn spun on Bankes. "You can't quit now. The fighting is just starting. I need you here to lead the hands. Bull, go on and get ready. We'll be out in a minute."

After Bull left, Ruffcarn said, "I'll double your pay. In fact, you stay and I'll cut you in as a partner. We're going to be rich."

"I know all about your gold. Personally, I think both you and Pierce are operating short of a full deck if you think you're going to find lost gold in this country. Even if there's some truth to it, I'm not killing women to get it. I've got one hundred and fifty dollars coming. Count it out, and I'll be on my way."

Ruffcarn was mad clean through. His right hand itched. He could almost feel the pressure of the revolver's grip in his hand. He took a deep breath and tried to relax. He knew Bankes would kill him before his gun ever left its holster. Ruffcarn walked over to his safe, removed the money, and tossed it on the table. "Get off my ranch and never come back."

Bankes smiled. "That's just what I intend to do. Let me give you a word of advice. Don't mess with Nance. That old ranger is tougher than you'll ever be." Bankes picked up his money and sauntered out of the house. Without saying a word to anyone, he got his gear out of the bunkhouse. He went to the corral, saddled his horse, and stepped up into the saddle.

Ruffcarn could hear Bankes through the open windows.

"You boys are bitin' off more than you can chew with this raid. If you're smart, you'll git while the gittin's good. Otherwise, you'll either be shot dead or stretching a rope. *Adios.*" Bankes walked the horse out of the corral and turned north, without another word.

Ruffcarn came out of the house as Bankes was leaving. "Bull, you're foreman now." He mounted his horse and said, "We'll camp on Pecan Bayou tonight and hit them early in the morning. Let's go." The fifteen gunfighters and cowhands rode out of the ranch, headed for the Rocking N, with Ruffcarn and Westin in the lead.

JOSH STEPPED up on the porch of the colonel's office and opened the door. The sergeant sat behind his desk with several papers in front of him. At the sight of Josh, he stood and said, "Welcome back, Major Logan. Colonel Sturgis is in his office. Just knock and go in."

"Thank you, Sergeant," Josh said.

He knocked and stepped in the door. Colonel Sturgis looked

up from his desk. He stood and walked around his desk to Josh. "Welcome back to Camp Wilson, Major. The rumor was that you were dead. I will say First Sergeant O'Reilly's sister never accepted that fact. I ran into her several times in town, and she was always asking if any of our patrols had found you. It was my sad duty to tell her no each time. She's a striking young lady."

"Yes, sir, she is," Josh said. "I was fortunate. Someone ambushed me, and if it wasn't for the Kickapoo, I'd probably be dead. But they took care of my wounds, and here I am."

Colonel Sturgis surveyed Josh's scar from Bull's shot. "That was very close, Major. You're a lucky man."

Josh smiled. "You're the second man to tell me that today, sir; and as I agreed with him, I must agree with you also. I was very fortunate. Now, Colonel, Mr. Diehl said you had a message for me."

"Yes, I do. Seems your message kicked over a bucket of red ants back at headquarters. General Sheridan personally sends his thanks and best wishes."

"Thank you," Josh said.

Sturgis continued, "Just reading between the lines, I'd say there's a colonel in New Orleans who has no future in the army, at best, and may ultimately find himself confined to prison or worse. Seems this colonel not only issued fraudulent purchase orders, but was involved in the selling of contraband, including firearms, to the South during the war."

"Have they found out who he was working with?" Josh asked.

"It seems he had a business relationship with Jake Ruffcarn and Wesley Pierce."

"So what does that mean to the Rocking N, Colonel?"

"Major Logan, it means that I would appreciate your honoring my order for five hundred head of cattle and fifty head of horses to be delivered within the month. There'll be further orders from Fort Concho, Fort Davis, and Fort Richardson. It'll be a distance to drive the cattle, but I would imagine, in these times, it'll be worth it."

"Thank you, Colonel Sturgis. This will be good news for Mr. Nance. Also, you should know that Jake Ruffcarn is a rustler. We found where he'd been hiding the rustled cattle from the Rocking N. The men holding the cattle have been dealt with. But one of them told us that they were working for Ruffcarn, and that he planned on rebranding the stock and selling it to the army. He also said that Ruffcarn and Pierce are in cahoots. They think there's gold on Mr. Nance's land. Figured to drive him off and take it over for themselves."

Colonel Sturgis pulled out a box of cigars from his desk and offered one to Josh.

"No, thanks, Colonel; don't smoke."

"Nasty habit," Sturgis said as he clipped off the ends of the cigar and lit it. "I never liked Ruffcarn nor Pierce. I've contemplated, on several occasions, putting the King 7 off-limits. Just before you arrived, I dispatched a detail to pick up Pierce and Bartholf. Since Pierce and Ruffcarn colluded to defraud the army, I believe the two of them will spend a long time in prison; and having committed treasonous acts by selling contraband to the enemy, they may both stretch a rope."

"Good," Josh said.

The two men were interrupted by a knock at the door. "Enter."

A sergeant stepped into the office. "Sir, Pierce and Bartholf were gone. No sign of them. Looked like they packed in a hurry and hightailed it out of here."

"Alright, Sergeant," Colonel Sturgis responded. "I know some of the men frequent the King 7. Someone let Pierce know. I want you to talk to those men, find out who told him, and if they know where Pierce may be. Also, I want the King 7 boarded up and placed off-limits."

"Yes, sir." The sergeant wheeled and was out the door, closing it softly.

Josh smiled. "Kinda late to be boarding up the King 7, isn't it?"

Colonel Sturgis laughed. "Yes, it is, but it'll keep the men from getting into the whiskey."

Josh stood. "Colonel, thank you for sending those messages for me. I've some business to take care of, and I'll be heading back to the ranch. Scott Penny or Juan Alvarez will be bringing up the stock. Mr. Nance took an arrow in the leg in a skirmish with the Comanches. He'll be laid up for a while."

The colonel stood and both men shook hands. "Give him my regards and tell him I look forward to doing business with him. Good luck to you."

Josh's mind was on Pierce as he walked back to the Diehls' store. He was thankful that Pierce had left. That meant at least one less gun to deal with. He didn't know him, but he knew his type and didn't like it. Good riddance that he was gone. He watched a rider coming down the street. It was Grizzard Bankes, and he was in a hurry. Josh slipped the leather thong from his Colt.

25

Bankes saw Josh and rode directly for him. Josh relaxed his muscles, knowing that no matter how sore his hands were, he might have to use them. He moved the Colt slightly, just to make sure it was loose in the holster.

Bankes pulled his horse up in front of Josh. "You'll not be needing that six-gun. I'm not being paid. I've quit."

"So what do you want?"

"I wanted to let you know that Ruffcarn is riding right now for the Rocking N. He was mad as a hornet when he found his rustled cattle rustled. Kinda funny, actually. Anyway, he wants Nance dead. In fact, he said, 'I want everybody dead,' or something along those lines. Logan, I don't harm women. He's going there to kill everyone, including Nance's daughter and his cook. So I quit."

"Thanks for letting me know," Josh said. "I've got to get back to the ranch."

"If you get started now, you might make it. Ruffcarn wanted to hit them in the morning."

"Bankes, I figured you and I might have it out. I'm glad it

turned out this way. No matter what happens, your name won't be included with that bunch. Nobody'll be after you."

"Thanks, Logan. I think I'll mosey up to Montana. Always heard that was a fine place to live. Reckon Mr. Diehl will sell me some supplies?"

"I'm sure he will. Come with me. O'Reilly and I have to get moving." Josh started for Diehl's store and Bankes followed. They entered the store together.

Jeremiah Diehl took one look at Bankes and said, "You're not welcome here."

"He is, Mr. Diehl. He's quit Ruffcarn. Bankes here brought word that Ruffcarn is on his way to attack the Rocking N. Ruffcarn plans to kill everyone. Pat and I need to start back to the ranch now. Hopefully, Tiny has four good horses. If we ride all night, we might make it in time."

"I'm going with you," Diehl said.

"No, sir. I appreciate your offer, but we need someone to stay here with the women. Pierce has disappeared. I imagine he's running for his life, but I'd like you to stay here, just in case."

"Josh, it's a hard thing you ask, but I'll do it. Now let me get you some supplies. Do you have enough ammunition?"

"Yes, sir, we're well stocked. I don't want any more weight than necessary. We'll be riding hard. Just a little food that we can eat when we stop to water the horses and we'll be fine. I'd also appreciate it if you would give Grizzard here whatever he wants and put it on my bill. I'll take care of it."

Pat had walked in from the dining room. He had their gear with him. "I heard you talking. Thought we might need this." Fianna and Mrs. Diehl were with him.

Fianna's green eyes were large. Her face was pinched from fear. "How can you make it in time?" she asked Josh.

Pat stood for a moment then moved toward the door. "I thought you were a man, Bankes, and you proved it. Good luck to you. Josh, you get the rest of the supplies, and I'll be getting the horses ready with Tiny." He turned back to Fianna. "Me wee sister, don't you worry, we'll be fine." He reached out and smothered her in a big bear hug; then he released her and was out the door.

Josh turned to Fianna. She was looking at him with concern; it had been a long time since a woman other than his mother had worried about him. He so wanted to take this lovely girl into his arms and tell her just how he felt, but he couldn't forget his conversation with Pat. The best thing for Fianna was to go to California with Pat. Colorado was no place for her.

"Miss O'Reilly," Josh said, turning back to the supplies, "we'll ride all night. Ruffcarn's not planning on attacking until morning. Mr. Diehl, would you advise Colonel Sturgis what's happening? He may be able to dispatch a column. It'll take time for them to get ready, so I doubt they'll get there in time, but they'll be able to put Ruffcarn into custody and stop this idiocy."

"I'll do that, my boy," Diehl said as he handed two sacks of supplies to Josh.

Mrs. Diehl came in carrying two sacks also. "Take these doughnuts with you. They might help keep you going tonight."

"Ah, Mrs. Diehl, I can't think of anything better. Thank you.

"Thanks again, Bankes. You ever get to Colorado, look me up." Josh nodded to everyone else and was out the door, walking quickly toward the stable.

Pat had the horses saddled and ready. Tiny was bringing out two more fine-looking horses. With two horses for each man, they would be able to travel faster. Josh tossed two of the sacks to Pat and tied two behind his saddle.

"Take care of that lighter sack, Pat. Mrs. Diehl stuffed it with bear sign."

Pat's face lit up. "I can ride like the wind with doughnuts. 'Tis a happy man I am."

Tiny looked at the sacks. "If I'd known Mrs. Diehl was giving out bear sign just for riding all night, why, dad-burn it, I'd be going with you."

Through the seriousness, the three men laughed. They knew what might be coming, and a man must find humor when he can. "I'm bettin' you'll see some bear sign at the dinner table tonight." Josh turned serious. "Thanks for the horses, Tiny. Don't know when we can get them back."

"Don't worry about it," Tiny said. "You boys just be safe and make good time. The Nances are good people. I'd hate for anything to happen to 'em."

"Let's get moving," Josh said. "We're burning daylight." He and Pat left Camp Wilson at a gallop. Long shadows were marching across the street as the sun slid slowly below the horizon.

~

WESLEY PIERCE SAT on his horse below the ridge to the west of Camp Wilson. They were in a ravine, just behind a stand of mesquite—well hidden from the town, but able to see everything that was happening. Bartholf was on the ground, looking through their supplies for something to eat. He had the extra horse tied to a mesquite. The two men were watching Josh and Pat as they raced out of town with an extra horse each.

"Those boys are in a bit of a hurry," Pierce said. "Bankes must have told 'em something that has their bowels in an uproar. My guess is that Ruffcarn, that simpleton, is up to nothing good, at least as far as Logan is concerned."

Bartholf handed Pierce a piece of jerky. "We don't have a lot, boss. We had to get out of there too fast to pick up much."

"Don't worry about it. We can get supplies from Diehl or Ruffcarn."

"Boss, are you still thinking about taking that girl? Could make things a little dicey."

Pierce ignored Bartholf's question. His mind drifted to Fianna. He would take her soon. She was a pretty girl, but she was uppity. He'd met that kind in New Orleans society, in Savannah where his folks lived, and at the dances when he attended Georgia Military Institute. They were stuck-up and sophisticated, until he got hold of them. He'd shown more than one that he knew how to handle women, and this Fianna O'Reilly, graduate of Mount Holyoke Seminary, was about to learn that her haughty ways wouldn't work with a strong man like himself. He'd teach her respect. He had what women wanted.

It was getting darker, almost time to take Fianna. He watched as Bankes came out of Diehl's store, swung into the saddle, and tied his supplies to his saddle horn. Bankes headed north out of town. Pierce had really wanted to kill Bankes. He knew he could. Bankes wasn't near as fast as he thought he was, but they might meet some other time. He could take care of him then. Pierce watched the man until he disappeared into the trees at the crossing. In one way, he hated to leave here. He knew Camp Wilson was going to grow. It was located at the confluence of the Clear Fork of the Brazos and Collins Creek—plenty of water. That was the main requirement in this country. With all the buffalo, hunters and skinners would be flocking here as soon as they heard about the new town. This would be a town of plenty— plenty of suckers to fleece.

The quarter moon was just starting to illuminate the eastern hills. If he was going to grab the girl, now was the time. Pierce turned to Bartholf. "Let's go."

Bartholf untied the little grulla mustang, climbed onto his roan and followed Pierce into town. They rode up to the Diehls' store, puffs of dust exploding quietly from under the horses' hooves.

"Wait here," Pierce said. He walked to the door. It was still unlocked. He opened the door and walked in. He'd so been looking forward to this.

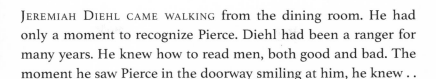

JEREMIAH DIEHL CAME WALKING from the dining room. He had only a moment to recognize Pierce. Diehl had been a ranger for many years. He knew how to read men, both good and bad. The moment he saw Pierce in the doorway smiling at him, he knew . .
.

Jeremiah had removed his apron just a few minutes earlier. His .44 Colt was where he always kept it, slipped behind his belt, butt toward his right hand. Even as he dived to his left and felt the smooth butt of his .44 in his hand, he knew—he was too slow. Everything happened so slowly, his gun was just clearing his belt, and he could see Pierce with his gun pointed at him. It was as if it just appeared in his hand. *I always knew this day would come.* He saw the smoke from Pierce's Colt and felt a smashing blow in his chest. His gun was no longer in his hand. *Who's screaming? Victoria?* He wanted to comfort her. He . . .

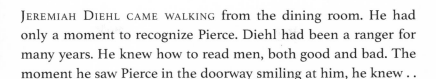

PIERCE SAW the two women come into the room just as he pulled the trigger. It felt good. He was fed up with that old ranger and his mouth. He started to put another bullet into him, but the man's wife was bending over him. He was dying, any man could see. He looked up at Fianna. "You're coming with me, Miss O'Reilly."

Fianna stepped back from him. "No, I can't. My brother—"

"Oh, yeah, you can. I don't much mind shooting women, but I won't if you come with me. If you give me any trouble, I'll put a bullet in the old woman and put her out of her misery," Pierce said, and smiled again. Nothing moved above his lips. He stepped over Jeremiah Diehl and grabbed Fianna's arm.

Mrs. Diehl jumped up and threw herself at him, clawing and kicking. He threw her off and struck her a vicious blow to the head. The blow sounded hollow, like smashing a watermelon, as the barrel of his six-gun drove into the side of her head. She fell across Mr. Diehl. They both lay in a bloody pile on the dining room floor.

"I said let's go." Again Pierce grabbed Fianna, and this time, he dragged her across the dining room into the store and out the door.

"My brother will kill you."

"He won't be the first to try. I've left a few men lying in the dirt because of their women. I don't mind adding one more. Now get on the horse," Pierce said and shoved her toward the grulla.

She hesitated. There was a commotion down the street at the Shamrock and Tiny's blacksmith. She could also hear men at the fort. Just another minute. Bartholf reached across the little grulla and grabbed Fianna by her beautiful auburn hair. She screamed as he lifted her by the hair onto the horse's back. Cecil Starit, shotgun in hand, came running out of the Shamrock. Pierce threw two quick shots at him and jumped onto his horse. Cecil dived back through the door, the bullets striking the frame. Tiny came out of the stable as Pierce, Fianna, and Bartholf raced by. His rifle leaped to his shoulder, but he held his fire as they disappeared into the darkness. They were gone.

Tiny and Cecil ran to Diehl's store. They raced through the door and found both Jeremiah and Victoria unconscious on the dining room floor.

"Tiny, run to the fort and get the surgeon," Cecil said as he examined Mrs. Diehl's head wound.

Tiny plowed through the door and headed for the fort, running as fast as he could. Cecil lifted Mrs. Diehl from across Jeremiah's body and laid her gently aside so that he could examine her husband. Blood was running from a chest wound.

Jeremiah looked so small now. Cecil took out his knife and cut Jeremiah's shirt from his body. He rolled him over. Sure enough, the bullet had gone all the way through. He took Jeremiah's shirt and stuffed it into the hole in his back. Cecil pulled the tablecloth off the dining table, wadded it up, and held it against Jeremiah's chest. He sat like that for what seemed like forever, until he heard footsteps, and the surgeon came running through the door.

The surgeon pushed Cecil aside and examined Jeremiah. He heard a faint heartbeat. "This man is still alive," the surgeon said. "Get me some water boiling. I've got to get these pieces of shirt out of his wound." He laid Mr. Diehl back on the floor and checked Mrs. Diehl. "She should be alright. It's a head wound. She'll probably have a mild concussion, but she'll be okay."

Tiny was back with several of the cavalrymen. The doctor turned to the men and said, "Get him up on the table. Gently now."

The soldiers gingerly lifted Jeremiah to the table. The doctor looked around for Cecil. "Where's my hot water?"

Cecil came in with a pan of boiled water. "She still had the stove fired up. I guess she was trying to get ready for the morning." He set it down on a stand next to the table.

The doctor opened his bag, took out some instruments, and began to work. He washed his hands and used the dish towel that Cecil had brought from the kitchen to dry them. The surgeon started digging in the chest wound with a pair of forceps. "I need another pan," he said. He picked pieces of clothing from the wound for what seemed like an hour, dropping them into the pan.

Mrs. Diehl came awake. She was a frontier woman, and though she had lost control for a moment when she saw her husband shot, now she was calm. "Is he still alive, Doctor?"

"Barely," the surgeon said. "If the bullet had been an inch to the right or left, he'd be dead. He has a fighting chance if we can get this wound clean and keep it that way."

"What can I do, Doctor?" Mrs. Diehl asked.

"Just wait till I'm done. Then you can take care of him. He could still die, but at least he has a chance. He's still alive—that means he's a fighter. He just might make it. You can thank Mr. Starit. He was able to stem the blood flow until I arrived."

"Thank you, Cecil. I don't know what I'd do without Jeremiah."

"No need for thanks, Victoria. I'm just glad the doctor arrived so quickly, thanks to Tiny."

Mrs. Diehl turned to Tiny. "Thank you, Tiny." She looked around quickly. "Where's Fianna?"

"Gone, ma'am," Tiny said. "Pierce and Bartholf took out of here with her in tow. I tried to get a shot, but it was so dark, I didn't want to take a chance of hitting her."

Mrs. Diehl shook her head. "Poor Fianna. That Wesley Pierce is an evil man. No woman is safe with that man."

THEY RACED through the moonlit night. The faint light slipped around each tree and cactus, barely providing enough light to see the trail.

Pierce and Bartholf said nothing as they rode. Bartholf held onto the grulla's reins, and Pierce led the way. They were headed for Ruffcarn's ranch. Pierce felt sure they would be safe there for a while. Ruffcarn might put up a squawk, but he could handle him. Anyway, he was going to have to eliminate Ruffcarn sometime; this just might be the time. Right now Ruffcarn didn't matter, the gold didn't matter; all that mattered was the girl. She needed a lesson on how to respect a man, and he was going to give it to her. He, at least, had time for that. With the army coming after him, it was a good thing he'd been warned. He would have to get out of Texas. He might have to leave the US. That would mean giving up the gold. He hated that. He had worked so hard to get Nance's ranch and get the gold. Sometimes he wondered if he should have done everything himself. If they hadn't gotten involved in selling cattle to the army, that was Ruffcarn's idea to make a little extra money and seem legit, the army probably wouldn't be after them now. He should have gotten rid of Ruffcarn when they left New Orleans. He had proven to be a liability.

Pierce smirked in the moonlight. It didn't matter now; he had the girl. He'd show Logan who was the best man. What a shock to see him still alive. That was another loose end left to one of Ruffcarn's hirelings. Evidently Bull Westin wasn't near as good a shot as Ruffcarn said he was. It didn't matter now. They would be at the ranch in a few hours. He needed some rest and time to plan; then he'd take care of the girl. He looked back and could see Fianna riding easily in the saddle, her long hair streaming in the wind, glistening silver in the moonlight. He smiled in anticipation.

26

Josh and Pat raced toward the Rocking N. It was dangerous riding. With the thin light of the quarter moon, a missed step or sharp ravine could see a horse or rider injured or dead, but there was no other choice. Two more guns could make the difference. The mesquite and cactus flashed by as they pushed on toward the ranch. The men were switching mounts every hour.

They had crossed Coyle Creek a few hours back and were continuing to parallel Hubbard Creek as they rode south. Now, at a walk, they wanted to water and feed the horses and let them rest a short while. The four horses were good animals, but they had a long way to go. With only two horses per man, the horses would die long before they reached the ranch if they were continuously run. Though the men needed to get there as soon as they could, they wouldn't get there at all if they killed their horses. Josh signaled Pat and they turned into the timber along Hubbard Creek. The men found an easy slope to walk the horses into the creek bed and let them drink. "Think we'll make it in time?" Pat asked.

"Pat, I don't know. It just depends when Ruffcarn attacks. If he attacks early, we won't make it. But we've got to rest these horses, or we won't make it at all."

"Aye, 'tis hard on the animals. Being the honest man that I am, I must admit that it's a tiny bit tough on these old bones."

"Don't think it has much to do with age, Pat. I'm sore myself. Why don't we get these horses back up the bank and get them on some grass for a short while. At least give them a little to eat."

After the horses finished drinking, the men led them into a small meadow under the trees. They staked the horses out on ropes and pulled some of the doughnuts from the sacks that Mrs. Diehl had given them. Pat took a bite and said, around the doughnut he was eating, "That Mrs. Diehl is a fine lady. She cooks like an angel. Seldom it is I've had the pleasure of dough-nuts this often. And I'm glad that she and Mr. Diehl are there to watch over Fianna. Don't think anything would happen to me sister in town, but it still gives a man comfort."

"I'm sure it does, Pat. With Mr. Diehl having been a ranger, you've got to be pretty confident that Fianna will be alright."

The two talked a few more minutes as the horses grazed. Then they tied up their sacks, rounded up the horses, and started off again. They walked the horses in the timber for a ways and Pat said, "I'm happy we have at least a wee bit of a moon. If we're crazy enough to race around at night, at least we've some small light to see by."

The men stopped when they reached the edge of the trees to make sure they didn't have unfriendly company waiting for them; then they rode out. The clock was ticking. What time would Ruff-carn attack the ranch? Would it be early or later? Would they be close enough to help? Josh didn't know. All they could do was keep riding.

∼

RUFFCARN and his men had camped three miles from the ranch. They were confident that surprise would tilt the battle in their favor. They broke camp as the sun was slipping over the ridge to the east. The warmth was cutting the chill of the early morning. As they swung into the saddles, Bull asked Ruffcarn, "What's your plan, Mr. Ruffcarn?"

"We'll go to the ridge north of the ranch house. I want some men behind the house and on the south ridge. As soon as we see cowhands out in the open, we'll hit 'em hard. That'll take the fight out of them; then we'll just take care of the rest."

"What about the women?"

"Bull, I don't want any witnesses who can testify against us. Do you understand?"

"Yes, sir, I surely do. But I think there are some of the boys who might get their back up at just plain killing—specially women."

Ruffcarn turned his horse so that he faced the riders. "Have I paid you men well?"

Heads nodded in the affirmative, and a few "yes, sirs" could be heard.

"You hired on to fight. Are you ready to take the Nance ranch?"

Again, he received the same response.

"There'll be a bonus in it for every one of you. But I want you to understand, I want no living witnesses. Do you understand what I'm saying?"

There was some murmuring; then one of the hands spoke up. "You saying you want everyone kilt—including the women?"

"That's what I'm saying."

The gunman turned and spit. "Well, I ain't never kilt no woman nor murdered no man, and I ain't a-startin' now, no matter how much money you pay me. Don't know if you other boys want to be known as woman killers or not. But I've got me a hankerin' to see Montana."

With that the speaker slipped the thong from his revolver and sat tall in his saddle, staring at Ruffcarn. After a few moments, he slowly turned his horse around and headed north, for Montana. Three of the other men had loosened their revolvers in their holsters while the gunman was speaking. Without saying a word, they turned their horses and followed him.

"You can't leave now," Ruffcarn shouted.

The gunmen never turned. Ruffcarn turned to Bull. "Do something."

"Mr. Ruffcarn, sir, there just ain't much to be done. That is, unless you want a shoot-out right here. We've still got more men than Nance, and we're gonna surprise him. I reckon our best move is to go ahead with your plan. You did say there was a bonus in it, didn't you?"

Ruffcarn fumed, but he saw that he had only two choices: attack or ride back to the ranch. "Yeah, Bull," he said loudly. "Everyone will get a bonus when this is finished. Let's go."

RUFFCARN'S CREW had just gotten into position when Juan stepped outside. Bull was behind a rock that was the perfect height as a rest for his .52-caliber Sharps. The other men were scattered in the hills north, south, and west of the ranch.

Bull watched as Juan stretched. The morning sun reflected off his upturned, weathered face—another hot day in Texas. Juan turned toward the barn.

Bull's shot echoed across the valley. Juan never heard it. The big 475-grain slug plowed through Juan's left arm, shattering the bone. It continued its deadly path, rupturing both lungs and destroying his heart, exiting his right side. Juan's legs folded, and he collapsed in the ranch yard. He was dead before he hit the ground. The rest of Ruffcarn's dry-gulchers opened fire. Glass broke from windows in the house and in the bunkhouse.

THE DOOR of the bunkhouse flew open, and Scott dashed out toward Juan. Bullets kicked up dust all around him. He grabbed Juan by the collar and turned back for the bunkhouse. He made one step into the bunkhouse, with Juan, when he was hit. He hit the floor, still holding Juan's collar with his right hand, blood running from the front and back of his left shoulder.

Bullets ricocheted off the outside of the house and bunkhouse. Jack Swindell dragged Scott and Juan into the bunkhouse and slammed the door. Byron Whistal and Frank Milman had grabbed their rifles and were starting to return fire. "Juan's dead," Scott said. "I know the sound of that rifle. It was Bull. If it's the last thing I do, I'm gonna take pleasure in filling his big gut with lead."

Jack ducked from the sound of a bullet crashing through the window and slamming into the opposite wall. "Let me get that arm bound up for ya. It's bleeding pretty bad."

"Git back to shooting. I'll take care of this," Scott said as he yanked a sheet off the nearest bed, tore a strip off with his teeth, and wrapped it around his back and chest with his right hand. He pulled his rifle off the table and slid to the nearest window. "Can y'all tell where the shooting is coming from?"

Byron yelled, "From the north and south slopes. Looks like they've got us in a pretty good cross fire. Just got one as he started to move down. Anybody know where the kid is?"

Scott couldn't use his rifle. His left shoulder gave him the dickens just trying to get the rifle up to where he could shoot. He pulled his revolver. "Can't do much damage with this, but I might get lucky. Jimmy Leads should be over in the ranch house. He said something about wantin' a cup of coffee. He must have gone over there no more'n ten minutes before the shooting started."

Byron ducked and fired again. "There's three men in the main house, and Mr. Nance can't hardly get around."

"He can still shoot," Frank Milman piped up. "I see firing coming from at least two sides of the house. I'm bettin' Teresa and Miss Nance are shootin', too."

Scott saw Jimmy Leads at a front window momentarily. The boy fired, and one of Ruffcarn's toughs pitched forward, kicked for a moment, and lay still. "That kid can shoot," Scott said as he fired again at the hillside.

The Sharps boomed again, and Frank ducked back from the side window, feeling the right side of his head. "That was close," he said as he brought his hand away with blood on it. "Just grazed me. I sure would like somebody to kill that feller."

Scott yelled, "Look out, here they come."

Ruffcarn's men had spread out on both the north and south slopes. They were running from rock to rock, moving down on the ranch. Byron could see a leg sticking out from behind a rock. He took careful aim and squeezed the trigger. The leg jerked out of sight, and they could hear a man screaming on the hillside. Byron grinned. "Guess he won't be running anywhere for a while."

THERE WERE five guns firing from inside the ranch house. Bull said, "Mr. Ruffcarn, we may have bitten off more than we can chew. We got the Mex, and I think that was Penny who tried to pull him in. Looked like he was hit. But we've already lost at least three men, and two more are wounded. Those folks are holed up inside those rock buildings. Only way we're gonna hit 'em is with a lucky ricochet bouncing around inside there."

Ruffcarn saw what Bull was saying. He had no idea the two buildings could be so easily defended. He was losing men, and besides killing Juan and hitting Penny, they'd done no good at all. "What about getting down there up close?" he asked Bull.

"Not a chance. They've got protection, and we'd be cut to

ribbons." As Bull finished speaking, the man next to him fell back holding his stomach, blood gushing through his fingers.

Ruffcarn pounded on the rock in front of him. "I pay these men to fight. I want them to fight!"

Bull shrank farther behind his rock, not even looking out. "I'm telling you, we can't win like this. We need to get out of here and try something else."

Bullets were singing by like angry bees. Rifles and handguns crashed from both sides. Ruffcarn started slipping back over the ridge, keeping rocks and cover between him and the houses. "Let's get out of here. Signal the men." Ruffcarn managed to get below the crest of the hill and leaped onto his horse. He spun the horse around and raced back to his ranch.

27

J osh and Pat could hear the gunfire. They had been riding all night. All four of the horses were exhausted. Josh turned to Pat. "I hate to kill these horses, Pat, but we've got to get to the ranch and help."

"Aye, you're right." With that, Pat spurred his horse. The surprised horse leaped forward. He had heart and would run until he dropped.

Josh did the same. The men raced toward the ranch. As they drew closer, the gunfire sounded like war. They came over a small swell and caught a glimpse of Ruffcarn disappearing to the northeast. The two men slowed their horses to a walk.

Josh said, "If we stay in these mesquites, we should be able to get close before they know we're anywhere around."

They unlimbered their rifles. Both Josh and Pat hung their extra handguns on the saddle horn. They walked the horses through the trees just as the remaining men on the north side came over the ridge to get to their horses.

There were only three, and one of them was Bull Westin. The men were running toward their horses. Josh and Pat maneuvered their horses out of the trees. Bull and the other men slid to a stop.

"Howdy, Bull," Josh said. "Reckon this is the way it was going to end all along. You've got a lot to answer for, and it's time to pay up."

Bull's mouth was open. Bull swung the big Sharps up and Josh's Winchester spoke. The .44-caliber bullet hit Bull just above his gun belt. He stepped back, dropped his rifle, and went for his six-gun. Pat shot one of the other gunmen with his Spencer. Before Pat could get off his second shot, Josh shot the remaining gunman through the chest, then swung the Winchester back on Bull as his revolver was clearing the holster. Josh shot him again. Bull sat down on the hillside. The six-gun slipped from his fingers. He looked at Josh. "You were dead. I saw it."

"You're just not as good as you think you are, Bull," Josh said, keeping the Winchester trained on the dying man.

Bull looked down at the blood oozing from between his fingers. "You've killed me."

"You had your chance. I told you to leave this country, but you didn't do it."

"I should've left," Bull said. He sat for another moment, then slowly fell over onto his right side, into a patch of prickly pear —dead.

Pat looked at him for a moment. "'Tis sad it's taken this long for that heathen to meet his maker."

The shooting had stopped. They could see several men to the south and east of the ranch slapping leather as they did their best to get as far as possible from the Rocking N. Josh and Pat waited for a few minutes. They didn't want to get shot out of the saddle by the Nance crew as they came riding over the ridgeline. They eased up to the ridge, where they could see several dead men behind rocks. One man was holding his shoulder and looking at them. Josh moved his rifle to cover him.

"I ain't no danger, mister. My shoulder's busted. I'm liable to bleed to death. I just need some help."

Pat looked at him for a moment and said, "Laddie, throw your rifle and pistol as far as you can." Pat watched as the gunman first pulled his six-gun with his good hand and threw it down the hill, followed by his rifle. "Now, that's a good lad. You knew there were women on this ranch, and you came here anyway. Your horse is back there over the hill. You get to it and ride out of here. That's all the help you'll be getting. If I help you, it'll be to the nearest tree. Now you go on and git. If you're still here when we come back..."

Josh and Pat rode slowly down the hill. Men were gathered in the yard. The women were just coming out of the house, running to the bunkhouse. Josh saw Scott step out of the bunkhouse as Mary Louise came up to the door. There was blood all over Scott's left shoulder. He put his good arm around her and held her close as she sobbed into his chest.

Scott watched them as they rode up. "Juan is dead. Bull killed him; you could hear the Sharps. When this wing gets better, I'm goin' after him, and I'll not stop until he's dead."

Josh stepped into the bunkhouse. Juan had been laid out on the floor. He looked peaceful. "No need," Josh said. "Bull won't be killing any more people."

"You killed him?"

"Aye, Scotty," Pat said. "Deader than a casket. Josh here put two of those .44s through his middle. He's back up on the hill, lying in a patch of prickly pear. There'll be no more worrying about the likes of him."

"That," Scott said, "is the best news I've had in a long time. I shoulda killed him when he drew down on Josh. That would've saved a lot of suffering."

"Scott," Josh said, "you can't think like that. We can 'what if' and 'should've' ourselves into an early grave. We take what life gives us and do our best. You saved my life, and I thank you."

Bill Nance came out of the house with a rifle in his left hand and a crutch under his right arm and slowly made his way across the yard.

Mary Louise left Scott's arms and ran to her father. "Papa, they killed Juan. He just walked out of the bunkhouse, and they shot him." She laid her head on his shoulder, and tears coursed down her smooth cheeks.

"I know, honey. I know. He was a good man and a good friend. We're all going to miss him." He turned to Scott. "I saw it happen. Scott, I also saw you run out and pull him in. That was a brave thing to do with all the bullets flying."

Scott looked embarrassed. "Mr. Nance, he'd a done the same for me."

Bill Nance replied, "I suspect you're right."

Scott turned to Frank and Jack. "Boys, why don't you get a grave dug where the other graves are under that big oak. Is that alright with you, Mr. Nance?"

"That's fine, son. We'll have a service for him later. A couple of you boys bring him on into the house. We'll get him cleaned up and dressed in his finest clothes and give him the burial he deserves."

Jimmy and Byron picked up Juan and carried him across to the house. "Bring him in here," Teresa said. "He could be a fierce man at times. But he loved us all." She indicated the dining room table. She had spread a big white sheet across the table for them to lay him on.

"Mr. Nance, I need to talk to you," Josh said.

Bill turned to hobble back to the ranch house. Puffs of dirt drifted up from his boots and crutch as he slowly made his way to the porch. He and Josh sat in the chairs on the porch. Scott moved to sit down.

"Scott, what are you doing?" Mary Louise asked. "Don't you know you've got a hole in your shoulder?" He wobbled a bit as he turned for the door, and she quickly put her arm around his waist to help him inside. "Let's go to the kitchen," she said. "I'll have you fixed up in no time."

Josh raised his eyebrows at Bill. "Anything going on there?"

Bill filled his pipe slowly. "I think my daughter may have found her match. I like that boy. I do hope he stays."

Pat had sat on the steps to the veranda. "I'm thinkin' you won't have any problem keeping him around."

"I've got some good news," Josh said to Bill Nance. "I sent a telegram off before I left Camp Wilson the first time. The answer had arrived when we got to town. It said that Pierce and Ruffcarn were in cahoots with some colonel in procurement. The three of them were selling guns to the Confederacy during the war. Colonel Sturgis said that his orders had been changed, and he was looking forward to you delivering five hundred head of cattle and fifty head of horses to him as soon as you can. He also said there would be orders for deliveries to Forts Concho, Davis, and Richardson. Mr. Nance, I think your troubles are over."

"That's mighty good news, Josh," Bill Nance said. "What are your plans now?"

Josh grinned. "Bill, I was headed for Colorado when I stopped here. That's where I'll be going. I'm hoping Chancy is better. He's gonna need to be in real good shape to do the work I expect of him when we get there."

The three men laughed. Bill Nance took a long draw on his pipe and relaxed back into his chair. "Josh, your horse seems to be doing much better. Juan said he's still limping on his right front leg, but he thought that would go away in a short time. You can't ride him yet, but in a few more days he should be good as new. What about you, Pat? What are your plans?"

Pat tipped his cavalry hat back. "I, too, will be leaving. Me wee sister and I will be off to California. A lovely land it is."

Bill Nance started to answer, but the pounding of horses' hooves caused him to turn as three cavalrymen, leading three horses, topped the north ridge and trotted down into the yard.

Josh noticed the sergeant take in the bullet-chipped walls and the blood still in the yard.

The sergeant addressed Pat. "First Sergeant, I have an urgent message for Major Logan from Colonel Sturgis."

"Lad, this here is Major Logan; message away."

"Major Logan, sir, the colonel says that Miss Fianna O'Reilly has been taken by Wesley Pierce and Bartholf of the King 7 Saloon. They—"

Josh and Pat were up immediately. "When did this happen, Sergeant?" Josh demanded.

"Sir, it was right after dark last night. Mr. Diehl was shot and may die. Mrs. Diehl, the poor lady, was pistol-whipped. The fort is too short-staffed to send troops out searching for the lady, due to the Indians. But the colonel says to tell the major that the sergeant and the two troopers are at his disposal, and the colonel thinks Pierce may have gone to Ruffcarn's ranch."

Josh spun toward Bill, but before he could say anything, Bill Nance said, "Take as many men and fresh horses as you need. You think you two will be able to make it? You look dead tired, and these troopers don't look much better."

"We'll sleep when this is over," Josh said. "I'd like to take Jack and Bryan with us. That'll leave you, Jimmy, Frank, and Scott."

"Don't forget Slim," Nance said. "He's still here and came in mighty handy in the fight."

"Thanks, Bill. Sergeant, are you and your men up to turning around and chasing Pierce?"

"Beggin' the major's pardon, sir, but we'll be by your side as far and as long as you want to go," the sergeant responded. "Mr. Nance, if you could spare us some horses, ours are plumb worn out."

"Consider it done, Sergeant. Take your pick and we'll return your horses when we come into Camp Wilson."

Teresa and Mary Louise appeared at the door with a tray of cups and the coffee pot. "Sergeant, you and your men step down from your horses and have some coffee. We'll bring food out in just a moment," Mary Louise said.

The sergeant and his two men unhorsed and made for the coffee. "Thank you, ma'am. That's mighty nice of you."

"*Señor* Josh, I'll have food ready for you all by the time you're ready to go."

"*Muchas gracias*, Teresa," Josh said as he and Pat ran for the corral.

28

Fianna felt relief when they rode into the ranch. Surely, someone here would help her. She only had to let them know that she was held against her will. They rode right up to the ranch house. Bartholf and Pierce stepped to the ground and tied all three horses to the hitching rail in front of the house. The moon had set, and the only light was provided by the myriad of stars across the heavens.

Pierce came back and extended a hand to help her from the horse. "Watch your step out here; it's dark."

As her foot touched the ground, the thought of running passed through her mind.

Pierce gripped her hand. "Don't think about running off. You wouldn't get far, and that would be most upsetting. I have plans for you. If you cooperate, I think you'll enjoy it." Pierce led her into the dark house.

Bartholf was lighting a lamp when they came in. He left the room, and she could hear him rummaging around in the kitchen. Soon light came from the kitchen.

"What are you going to do with me?" Fianna asked. "By now, there are men out looking for me. It's only a matter of time before they find me; then they'll kill you. People out here have no patience with men who harm women. When the owner of this ranch gets back, you'll be in big trouble."

Pierce laughed, lit a lamp, and led her to a bedroom. "You stay in here. We all need some rest." He put the lamp on the dresser, closed the door, and left the room.

She quickly scanned the spartan room. There had been no woman's touch here. A chair sat in the corner. There was no closet, only a bar attached to the wall for hanging clothes. The dresser looked like the product of an unskilled carpenter, thrown together with no drawers and no mirror. There was one window, and she walked over to it and tried to open it. It wouldn't budge. She could faintly see herself in the window, and she looked a mess. Through the thin walls, she could hear the two men talking. She heard Ruffcarn's name mentioned several times, and it sounded like they meant him harm. Could she be at Ruffcarn's ranch? She thought that the two men were friends, as much time as Ruffcarn spent at the King 7 Saloon. *Why would they be talking about killing Ruffcarn?*

Fianna sat on the bed. She knew she was in terrible trouble. Josh and her brother had left for the ranch. There was no way they could help her. The men from town wouldn't be able to leave until daylight if they planned on tracking her, and she was deathly afraid of Pierce. Her skin crawled when he looked at her. She felt like he undressed her every time his eyes passed over her. She had to find a way to escape. That would be her only salvation. Hopefully, when Ruffcarn and his men arrived, she would be set free. She lay back on the bed. Her mind had been working feverishly trying to figure out a way out of this mess, but now the fatigue gradually overcame her. Her eyelids closed and opened, then closed again.

≈

SHE HAD no idea how long she'd slept. Loud voices in the living room awakened her. Outside, the sun had been up for hours, and the house was warming up. She moved to the door and tried to open it. Fianna was surprised. They were so confident, they hadn't even locked the door. She opened it just far enough that she could see into the main house. Ruffcarn was standing in the living room and appeared to be extremely upset. "I was trying to get rid of Nance. That's why I attacked the ranch. I didn't expect it to be so well fortified."

Pierce still spoke in his low, cold voice. Fianna had to strain to hear what he was saying. "Ruffcarn, that was a stupid move. Now they'll be after you. No telling how close they are behind you."

"Don't worry, it'll be a while before they get here. We shot up the ranch pretty bad. In fact, I saw Alvarez shot dead by Bull, and we also got Penny. We've got time to get our stuff together and get out of here. We've got the map. We can head west and, on the way, look for the gold. They'll never expect us to go west."

Pierce shook his head. "I can't believe I partnered with such an idiot. Don't you know the gold is gone? There's no time to search for it. It's possible we might have the cavalry breathing down our necks from the fort. So we've got to get out of here, now."

"If you hadn't taken the girl," Ruffcarn said, "we wouldn't be worrying about any cavalry. Pierce, why can't you stay away from the women? I know you killed those women in New Orleans. You got the police after us there, and now you've gone and gotten the cavalry after us here. Maybe we ought to just split up. You go your way, and I'll go mine."

Fianna could see Pierce clearly. The man was so calm. He stood there looking at Barthol. Barthol was much bigger than Pierce, but Pierce's stance exuded a frightening, cold confidence. His face never changed expression. Pierce said, "Maybe you're right. We've had some successes, but no partnership lasts forever. I've got the money from the bar, and you've got the money from the cattle sales to the army. You want to just split it?"

She could see Ruffcarn's look of surprise. Evidently he didn't expect Pierce to agree. Ruffcarn said, "Why, sure, let's go into the office. I've got the ranch money in the desk. We'll see what the total is and split it." She watched Ruffcarn turn to go into the office.

Pierce's hand went to the back of his neck, and a slim-bladed dagger, sharp on both edges, appeared in his hand. Pierce said, "Good idea, Ruffcarn; that's agreeable to me." He took one step forward for leverage, threw his arm around Ruffcarn's throat, and drove the knife up under Ruffcarn's left ribs.

The big man struggled momentarily. Pierce turned him loose; Ruffcarn stayed on his feet for a moment. He stumbled as he turned around, but remained standing. His eyes were wide with surprise. "Why?" he asked as he fell to the floor.

Fianna watched, choking back a scream as Pierce leaned over to look the dying man in his eyes. He calmly cleaned the knife by wiping the blade on Ruffcarn's shirt front. Fianna could see a smile of pleasure on his face, his lips parted, showing perfect teeth. Pierce spoke almost in a whisper; she had to strain to hear him. "Because I could."

For some reason, Pierce looked up directly at Fianna and said, "Good afternoon, missy. Did you have a nice rest?"

She could feel the hairs on the back of her neck tingle; a cold chill ran down her spine. She watched Pierce as he straightened up and slipped the knife back into the scabbard behind his neck. "I've been letting you rest. You looked tired last night."

The fact that he was speaking in such a familiar voice, as if he and she had been friends for years, was frightening. Only moments before he'd drained the life from his partner. Now he walked toward her. She saw all the details. He hadn't shaved, and there was dark, black stubble all over his face. His hair was smoothed back on his head, and his black eyes glinted like flint.

He moved closer. The pupils of his eyes, little pinpoints, almost disappeared in the blackness. The afternoon sun shone through the main room windows, betraying the dust on the few pieces of furniture, but doing nothing to dispel the chill she felt. His black pants were dusty, as were the normally brightly polished boots. He looked the part he lived—a slimy, deadly killer who preyed on women for recreation.

He reached her, pushed the bedroom door wide open, and strode in. She backed up until her thighs touched the foot of the bed. She tried to move to the side, to get away from the bed, but he stopped her. His smile was hungry. He leaned forward to kiss her, and she turned her head in disgust. She saw his smile vanish. *I can't be here, I just can't.* She felt his left hand reach behind her head and grasp a handful of hair. He jerked her head around so that she was face-to-face with him, then brought his head a little closer, and his lips touched hers. Her brother's words leaped into her mind: *You're never whipped until you quit.*

She opened her mouth against Pierce and he pressed closer. She felt his lips move between hers and she jerked forward. Her lovely white teeth sank deep into his bottom lip. She tasted the sickly sweet of his blood and clenched her teeth tighter. He screamed into her mouth, but she wouldn't let go. He jerked away from her and left part of his lip in her mouth. Fianna doubled up her little fist and hit him with a roundhouse right that landed squarely on his mouth and nose. He yelped, and as he stepped back, his right boot heel caught on the dresser leg. He sprawled on the floor. She spit his lip onto his chest.

The bedroom door was open, and she made a dash for the front door. She had blood on her face and down the front of her dress, and her auburn hair was awry. She could hear Pierce getting to his feet. She grasped the front door handle, yanked hard, and ran into the front yard—right into Pat's horse.

Pat jumped to the ground and she flung herself into his arms, sobbing against his chest. She was safe.

She heard Pierce slide to a halt as he came out the front door. She turned and saw him standing there like a statue, blood running from his nose and butchered lower lip. Four rifles were pointed at his chest. He stood motionless. Fianna followed Pierce's gaze as he stared toward the bunkhouse. At the bunkhouse, two troopers were holding the three remaining gunmen who had returned to the ranch with Ruffcarn.

Pat pushed her to arm's length and looked her over. "Are you hurt?"

"No, Pat." She looked up at her brother. "I'm so glad you're here. I don't know what would have happened if you hadn't arrived when you did."

Pat looked at Pierce with disgust. "Did this piece of trash do this to you?"

"Yes. He shot Mr. Diehl and struck Mrs. Diehl with his pistol. For all I know, they're both dead."

"No, ma'am," the sergeant said. "Mrs. Diehl was up with a sore head, and Mr. Diehl, according to the doc, has a fighting chance."

"Oh, that's such good news. Thank you, Sergeant." Fianna turned her head and saw Josh.

29

J osh hadn't spoken. Now he slid his rifle back into the scabbard and stepped down from the saddle. He looked Fianna over, examining her carefully. There was blood on her face and down the front of her dress. "I'm glad you're safe."

Josh turned his gaze toward Pierce. With the loss of part of Pierce's lower lip, his bottom teeth were exposed in a gruesome, lopsided grin. Blood ran from the wound, down his chin, and onto his white shirt.

Josh looked back at Fianna, putting together what had happened. His scalp began to tingle, but he ignored the warning. He took a step toward Pierce. Pierce's hand moved to the back of his neck.

"He has a knife behind his neck!" Fianna screamed.

Josh leaped toward Pierce and grabbed his wrist. Pierce's wrist disappeared in the grasp of Josh's big hand. He twisted and Pierce went to his knees. The calm demeanor of the killer crumbled. Josh watched with loathing as the man groaned in his grip. He reached behind Pierce's neck, pulled the knife from its scabbard, and released him.

Pierce struggled back to his feet. Josh watched as Fianna, covered with Pierce's blood, walked over to him. "You're an evil man," she said. "I heard Ruffcarn say that you had killed other women in New Orleans. I have the feeling that you'll never kill anyone else." She slapped Pierce. It sounded like a gunshot in the quiet yard. Fianna looked up at Josh and said, "He killed Ruffcarn just before you rode up. He's a snake."

Pat watched intently, his eyes narrowed. "How does it feel, laddie? You like treating women rough? The last man I heard of hurting a woman was burned to death by the town. Would that suit your fancy?"

Pierce didn't look anything like the cool gambler everyone was used to seeing. His eyes darted from left to right, like a cornered ferret looking for escape. Sweat was pouring down his face and into the wound where his lip used to be. He looked up at Josh, and with a quiver in his voice said, "If you let me go, I can tell you where there's a wagon of gold. You'll be rich."

Josh laughed, a cold humorless laugh. "Pierce, you and Ruffcarn went through all of this subterfuge and killing. Before you meet your maker, I want you to know this. There is no gold. They were supply wagons. And your map isn't even accurate. The attack happened west of Camp Wilson, not at the Rocking N." Josh shook his head. "All this killing was for nothing."

Pierce looked up at him and said, "It's there. I know it is. The soldier who gave me the map assured me it was there. We even had it checked and was told a wagon loaded with gold was lost out west of the Rocking N."

Josh said, "So why did that fellow tell you?"

"He owed me money, and he gave me the map to settle up."

"And why would he do that? Were you beating him?"

Pierce looked at Pat, then nervously scanned the rest of the men. "My men were. I told you, he owed me mone—"

"Don't you know that men will tell you anything if they're being tortured? You and Ruffcarn were fools."

"But I confirmed it."

"With your army partner? By the way, he's been arrested and will probably be facing charges for treason. The army released that information in hope of drawing Southern troops out west to look for gold that wasn't there."

Pierce stood silent with his head down, blood still dripping from his mouth where his lip used to be.

Pat said, "I've been inside, Josh. There's no sign of Bartholf, though the back kitchen door was open. No telling how long he's been gone. Ruffcarn is dead. What do you want to do with him?"

Josh's eyes caught Fianna's. She'd been focused intently on him. The feeling that coursed through his heart almost left him weak. How could he leave her? He said, "Pat, forget about Bartholf. The man will die out here without a horse, and we're taking all the horses. Let Eyes of Hawk take care of him.

"Drag Ruffcarn's body outside and burn the buildings. This has been an evil place from the beginning. Let it burn to the ground." He turned to Pierce. "Where's the map?"

Pierce took it out of his pocket and handed it to Josh.

Josh tossed the map to Pat. "Burn that, too. Good men have died because of it. We'll stop it here."

"Aye," Pat said. He pulled Ruffcarn out of the house and tossed the map through the front door.

"Sergeant, would you take all these men over to that big live oak by the barn? See if you can find some extra ropes in the barn. We're going to need them."

"Yes, sir. You planning on hanging them all, Major?"

"That I am, Sergeant," Josh said, indicating the gunmen. "These men attacked a ranch where there were women, and they made no effort to ensure those women's safety. All they deserve is a strong rope."

The gunmen looked at each other. The big one said, "Look, mister, we were just following orders."

Josh turned cold eyes on the three and said, "Now you can

follow your boss to hell. Jack, you and Bryan see if you can find some coal oil. Get all the animals out of the barn. We're gonna burn this place to the ground."

Jack and Bryan rode over to the barn and started emptying it of stock. They came walking out with a couple of cans of coal oil and began dousing the barn. It wouldn't take much. The lumber in the rickety buildings had been dried by the Texas wind and would burn like kindling.

"What about me?" Pierce asked.

"Oh, I haven't forgotten you, Pierce," Josh said. "If I were a Comanche, I'd skin you alive and enjoy every minute. But I'm not, so the best I can do is hang you along with the other trash. Now git over to that mesquite tree."

Pierce stumbled, his confident air gone. All Josh saw now was a small frightened man. Pierce's head swiveled like an owl as if looking for a nonexistent rescue. The three other men were already in their saddles, with nooses around their necks.

Josh turned to Fianna. "You probably don't want to watch this."

She looked up at him, her eyes glistening, and said, "I've learned this is a hard country. I'm part of it now. Men like this can't be allowed to live and do again what they've done to others. I'll watch."

Josh nodded. *She keeps surprising me.* He walked over to the tree. "You men have anything to say?"

The three sat stoically. They had refused blindfolds. The men looked at Josh and shook their heads.

"Sergeant, will there be a problem if you and your men are involved in this?" Josh asked.

"This is the frontier, Major, sir. I can promise there will be no repercussions from the army."

"Good. Get on with it, then."

The sergeant nodded and the troopers slapped the rumps of the three horses. The horses leaped from under the men and left them dangling from the ropes. The oak limb bent with the weight of the men as they swung beneath its protective shade. Josh's men were somber.

This is a dirty business. Anger rose in Josh as he thought that all of this had been caused by two men with no scruples. He turned to Pierce and said, "Get on the horse."

Pierce stepped back from the stirrups. He was visibly shaking and tears were welling in his eyes. "Please, I have money in New Orleans. You can have it all. There's money in my saddlebags; I don't want any of it. Please, I don't want to die."

Josh grabbed him by the arm and thrust him toward the saddle. He said, "Now you know how those poor women felt when you killed them. If you don't get on the horse, I'll put you there."

Pierce grasped the saddle horn. His foot missed the stirrup the first time; then he managed to get his boot in and pulled himself into the saddle. Pat had mounted his horse and rode him up beside Pierce. "This is more merciful than you deserve," he said as he slipped the rope over Pierce's head and tightened it around his neck.

"Any last words?" Josh asked.

"Please, I don—" Pierce said as Pat slapped the horse's rump with his reins.

The horse jumped out from under Pierce, and the man who had killed so many people and ravaged so many women hung from the end of the rope, his life quickly leaving his body.

"Leave them hanging," Josh said. "Hang Ruffcarn up here too. Sergeant, find something to write on; I want a sign around Pierce's neck. I want it to read, 'This man was a woman killer and these men rode with him.'"

"Yes, sir," the sergeant said. He turned to one of the troopers. "You heard the major. Make it quick."

Josh had forgotten Fianna as he carried out his gruesome duty. He turned to look for her and saw her standing by the front of the house, the back of her hand pressed to her mouth. Tears coursed down her cheeks, making little trails in the dust. He walked over to her and put his arm around her. "I'm sorry you had to be here for this dirty business, but we couldn't let these men go. Any one of them, especially Pierce and Ruffcarn, wouldn't hesitate to do it again."

She looked up at him, her green eyes large as they swam in her tears. "You're right. It's just hard to see men die, even bad ones."

He held her for a few more moments. She leaned against his side, putting her head on his shoulder. The warmth of her body against his felt natural. *I've got to talk to Pat.* He pulled away from her and said, "We still have some work to do before we can leave."

The men had taken the rifles and handguns out of the house and bunkhouse. Jack said, "Josh, we're ready to burn this place anytime."

"Light it off; the sooner we get it burned, the sooner we're out of here."

Jack turned and waved to the men who held the torches. They tossed them into the ranch house, the bunkhouse, and the barn. The dry buildings lit up like the kindling that they were. Flames licked up their walls, sending dark smoke up to the heavens. The heat was intense. Fianna and Josh backed into the middle of the yard and watched them burn. It didn't last long. Within a short time there was nothing but smoldering ashes.

Josh looked at Fianna. "Are you rested enough? I'd like to start back for the ranch. We need to let them know what's happened."

"I'm fine, Josh. I'm not a hothouse flower."

"I'm beginning to figure that out," Josh said. He walked over to the sergeant and his troopers. He shook each man's hand, then said, "Sergeant, I want to thank you and your men. You've been of great assistance. If it's alright with you, I'd like for you to take all the firearms back to the fort. Since Ruffcarn spent all his time rustling Mr. Nance's stock, we'll take the horses back to the Rocking N."

"Major, sir," the sergeant said, "it's been a pleasure and an honor riding with you. We'll take care of these weapons, and I couldn't think of a more deserving man than Mr. Nance. If you're back in Camp Wilson, we'd be obliged if you'd have a drink with us."

"I'd like that, Sergeant." Josh watched the troopers as they rode out of the yard with the weapons tied onto their extra mounts. It had been a long day, and the day wasn't over yet. Pat was with Fianna, talking. Jack and Byron were rounding up the horses they had let out of the corral before they burned the barn. He walked over to Pat and said, "Well, Pat, are you ready to take your sister to the ranch?"

"Aye, Major, I think we both are ready to be on our way. There are no sweet memories here."

"I'm anxious to meet the Nances," Fianna said, "and to get away from here." She looked at the big live oak, where five men swung in the wind.

They saddled a horse for Fianna and trotted out of the yard. The loose horses followed them, and Jack and Bryan brought up the rear, riding drag to watch for stragglers. They topped the hill south of the burned-out ranch.

Josh took one last look back. The oak tree bore its morbid fruit with dignity, its dark green leaves fluttering in the afternoon breeze. The buildings were leveled; only part of the corral still stood. It was a forlorn place. Maybe the hanging men would deter others from doing the same thing. He turned forward in the saddle. Fianna was looking up at him. He could see the questions in her eyes. When they camped tonight, he would have to talk to Pat.

30

The sun was slipping behind the western bluffs when they drove the horses into the deepening shade of pecan and oak trees along Pecan Bayou. They found a protected camping spot on the creek. There was brush along the outer border of the trees and a small open park next to the creek. Josh took Fianna's hands to help her dismount. He could see the fatigue lines around her mouth, but she was still game.

"If you'll get some wood and the supplies, I'll get some coffee started," Fianna said; then she smiled like a beacon in the darkening woods.

Josh smiled back into that beautifully strong face, with the faint line of freckles running across her nose. "I'll do it, but we must be careful. Get the boys to dig a pit, bank up around it, and keep the fire small. That'll prevent the glow from escaping. We're deep in Comanche country. I don't want your lovely hair hanging on some brave's lance."

"Oh, I didn't think of that. I wouldn't want that either. I think jerky and hardtack would be delicious tonight."

Josh grinned and said, "You can eat that if you like, but

Teresa, the cook at the ranch, sent some food with us. You're welcome to join us."

Fianna laughed a soft, lilting laugh. "Why, thank you, sir. I'd love to."

Josh grew somber as he looked around, realizing that this was the same place where he had camped with Scott and Bull for the first time. This was where it all had started. It seemed like months ago, but had only been a couple of weeks. Had all of this happened so fast? How could he even think about taking this lovely young woman with him to the Colorado Territory? He'd known her for less than two weeks.

He'd killed so many men in such a short time. Granted, each had deserved to die, but so many? When he'd made the promise to Rory, he had no idea what it would entail.

Like his pa always said, "A man can't control his consequences; he can only control his decisions." Pa was a rock.

Josh looked forward to the time that Ma and Pa would be with him and Callum and his remaining brothers and sister—and Fianna?

The other men had dismounted and were going about the duties of getting the campsite set up, the horses down to the creek for water, and the saddle horses rubbed down. There was plenty of grass. Jack and Bryan strung ropes among the trees to form a corral. They could hear the comforting cropping of the horses as they enjoyed the fresh grass.

Fianna walked along the creek for a short distance and found some wild onions. She washed them off in the creek, then handed them out to the men to go with the food that Teresa had prepared. Pat had an extra bag with him that Teresa had sent along for Fianna. The men pulled up logs to sit on. All of them were experienced Indian fighters.

Josh watched Fianna around the men. She was confident and friendly. She'd endeared herself to these tough cowboys. They knew what she had been through and marveled at her quick recovery. They respected her for it.

"Jack," Josh said, "how about you taking the first watch. We'll do two-hour shifts. Bryan, take the second, and I'll take the third. I'd like for us to be on the way again by daylight."

"Sure thing, boss," Jack said. He picked up his rifle and moved out into the trees.

Bryan nodded to Josh and continued to drink his coffee.

Josh turned to Pat. "Feel like checking the horses with me?"

"Aye, I need to stretch my legs."

Josh looked at Fianna across the embers of the fire. "We'll be back in a few minutes." He held her eyes for a moment. *Is she aware what this conversation could mean to both of us?*

The two men walked over to the temporary corral where the horses were contentedly eating. Josh could just see Pat in the faint moonlight. "Pat, you're my best friend. We've been through things together that most men will never know nor understand. Last thing I want to do is throw a hitch into your plans—but I love Fianna."

Pat's expression didn't change. "Aye, I know. Do you think I'm blind? Why do you think I talked to you about her going to California? I could see what was happening between Fianna and you when we were at the Diehls'."

Josh shook his head. "I had no idea you knew. I didn't even know then. How could you know?"

"I've got eyes. I could see how you two responded to each other. But, Josh, she's still young. She needs to go with me to California."

Josh's heart sank. He couldn't ask Fianna to go against her brother's wishes. Pat was a friend he didn't want to lose, but he didn't want to lose Fianna either. Josh scuffed his boot in the leaves and said, "Pat, when you first talked to me, I was willing to accept your decision. I didn't like it, but I was willing to do what you wanted. But did you see how she handled Pierce? She stood there and watched those hangings. She didn't have to, but she did it because she felt she needed to. Look how fast she's recovered. Why, she rode here like a trooper, even after all she's been through. Pat, she's a strong woman. She's what the West needs. She's who I need to build a life with—but I don't want to do it without your blessing."

Pat just stood there thinking. "I don't know that I want her stuck on a ranch in the middle of nowhere. She's been to school. That girl needs to use the smarts that are in her head, not disappear on some Colorado ranch. She needs to go to California."

"Pat, I don't know what's in store for her in California. I know that she'll never find another man who will love her and take care of her like I will; and all that education is great. She'll be able to teach our kids, so they'll grow up with knowledge of the world in their heads, not just ranching and tracking that I'll be able to teach them. The two of us will grow strong, responsible citizens who will help grow this land. She's strong, and she can do it."

Pat said, "Laddie, I know of no other man I would like to be my Fianna's husband, but I'm still concerned about her and the Colorado Territory. You'd still be in Indian country. Why, you'd have to cross the Comancheria just to get there. Who knows what might happen."

"Anything could happen on the stage to California. Life is hard, Pat; we both know that. But it's that hardness that makes us stronger. I'm asking for your sister's hand in marriage, and I promise you I'll always take care of Fianna."

"Who's taking care of me?" Fianna asked as she stepped out of the shadows. "Are the two of you talking about me? Don't you think if you're going to talk about me, I should be present?"

"Ah, me wee sister, this is between Josh and me; don't you fret yourself. Now why don't you move back to the camp, and we'll be acoming in a wee little while."

Fianna stomped her foot in the leaves and said, "Patrick Devane O'Reilly, don't you 'wee sister' me. I'm twenty-two years old and fully capable of making my own decisions." She turned to Josh. "And you, Mr. Major Logan, sir, if you have feelings for me, it is me you should be talking to, not my *wee* brother." With that, Fianna Caitlin O'Reilly turned sharply around, tossing her long flowing red hair, and marched back to the camp.

The two men looked at each other sheepishly. "I have no problem telling she's your sister," Josh said to Pat.

"Aye, she is, and you'd have your hands full with her," Pat said.

Josh smiled, though it was too dark now for Pat to see, and said, "I wouldn't mind that kind of trouble at all."

"Let me think on it, Josh. As you say, she's a strong woman."

"Pat, I just had a great idea. You could come with us. It's a big country out there. Why, we could have adjoining ranches." Josh chuckled and said, "At least we wouldn't have to worry about our neighbor rustling our stock."

"You're right on that, laddie. I thank you for the invitation, but I still need to think on it. I'm growing a mite tired of fighting and killing. Those hangings today took a lot out of me. They all deserved it, but I'm just getting tired. Speaking of tired, we've been up for two days. I think I could sleep for a week." With that, Pat turned and walked back to the camp.

Josh waited for a few moments, thinking about their conversation. He wanted Fianna with him. He needed to convince Pat, and now, it seemed, he needed to also convince Fianna. Josh realized that he was exhausted. He needed sleep. He walked back to the camp. Pat, Fianna, and Bryan were already asleep. He spread his ground sheet, slipped his Colt out of his holster, and laid the Winchester next to him, then he lay down.

～

"Boss, boss—"

Josh opened his eyes and Bryan was standing over him.

"Alright, thanks," Josh said. "Everything quiet?"

"Yeah, so far nothing's stirring. The horses are quiet. You were sleeping real sound."

"Yeah," Josh said. "Glad you weren't a Comanche; we'd all be dead. Hopefully, that's the last time I sleep that sound unless I'm in a bed."

Josh slipped his revolver back into its holster and picked up the Winchester. He walked around the horses, talking to them to keep them calm. They weren't like those jumpy longhorns, but it always helped to talk to them. Several of the horses came over to him and he rubbed their noses. He waited a few minutes more and moved out to the edge of the trees. The quarter moon was still up, casting some light across the prairie. He loved this time of day. All was quiet. An occasional owl hooted back in the trees. He could hear an armadillo rooting among the leaves for any beetles or ants it could find. The stars looked so close he could touch them. Even though the moon was still up, the Milky Way was visible in the otherwise dark sky. Two coyotes serenaded the countryside with their mournful howls.

He found a comfortable spot against an ancient oak and sat slightly outside the line of trees that paralleled the creek. This gave him a wide view of the prairie. He'd been on watch for two hours when the stars started to fade. While it was still dark on the ground, he moved back into the trees so he wouldn't be visible when it became lighter. He heard someone up in the camp. As dawn progressed, the few clouds turned from a ghostly gray to deep purple and then to a bright golden hue as the sun rose above the hills, chasing the shadows from the valley.

He could hear voices back at camp and caught an occasional whiff of coffee. Footsteps warned him of someone approaching from the camp. It was Fianna. She handed him a cup of coffee, and their hands touched. He felt the warmth of her long fingers as she held her hand under his for a few moments. He looked down into those emerald green eyes. "Fianna."

She smiled into his eyes and placed her hand on his cheek. "I know."

Josh was about to mention building a fire to her when he detected movement out of the corner of his left eye. He slowly turned his head and saw five Comanches riding single file just inside the tree line toward them. He pushed Fianna behind the tree. The Indians hadn't seen them yet, but they would at any moment. Josh recognized Eyes of Hawk in the lead. Before they saw him, Josh stepped out into the edge of the trees, directly in their path. The movement gave his position away. The Indians saw him immediately, but didn't stop. When they were about fifteen feet from him, they pulled their horses up.

Eyes of Hawk looked down at Josh. "We meet again, Josh Logan."

Josh turned slightly so that he could bring the Winchester to bear quicker and said, "Yes, and this time we aren't shooting at each other."

Eyes of Hawk said, "Not yet."

One of the other Indians said something to Eyes of Hawk, who turned and looked deeper into the forest of trees. Josh heard the click of a hammer being eared back behind him. "You are not alone," Eyes of Hawk said.

"No, my friends are with me."

"You have many horses with you," Eyes of Hawk said. Now it was light enough to make out the horses back in the trees. "And I smell food."

Alright, Josh thought, *this may be crazy, but I'm going to try it.* He spoke loudly to ensure that his men would hear him as he said, "We have a little, but we would share it with our friends."

Eyes of Hawk nodded. He swung his leg over his horse and jumped down. He said something to the Indians with him, turned to Josh and said, "We will eat."

The Indians led their horses back to the camp and tied them to the trees. Fianna handed each a cup of coffee. They drank it greedily and nodded their appreciation. They could hardly take their eyes off her. She was taller than they were, and they were fascinated by her red hair. After they had finished the coffee, she passed out what remained of Teresa's dinner. The Indians ate silently. When they were finished, Eyes of Hawk stood and looked at Josh. "How is your horse?"

Josh held Eyes of Hawk's eyes and said, "He's fine. He was only creased."

"I was not aiming at your horse."

Josh smiled. "I know."

"We go," Eyes of Hawk said. He turned and motioned to the other braves.

They all walked to their horses and jumped on. Eyes of Hawk looked down at Josh. "You are brave man. Your spirit is strong. Where are you living?"

Josh said, "For now at the Nance ranch. You know it?"

"The old ranger."

"Yes, but I'll be leaving soon. I would ask something of you."

Eyes of Hawk nodded.

"Twice we've been in battle. Men have died. I don't seek battle, nor does the old ranger. But we will fight. This you know."

Again Eyes of Hawk nodded.

"I would ask that we fight no more. I can live with you, or I can die with you. I prefer to live, as does the old ranger."

Eyes of Hawk spoke slowly. "You speak true words, for we have met in battle. Our women mourn the death of their men. We want no more mourning. I choose to live with you." Eyes of Hawk extended his arm and Josh took it, grasping his arm just above the wrist, as did Eyes of Hawk. They held the grip for a moment; then Eyes of Hawk turned his horse and continued in the direction they had originally been going. The other Comanches followed him, never looking at any of the white men.

Pat walked up and said, "Now, laddie, that was a brassy play. I could've spit when you brought those savages into our camp. I knew we were in for it. Just goes to show, you never know what a Comanche is going to do."

"Didn't know what else to do. If we started shooting, there would've been dead on both sides. Now we might have a reprieve for us and the ranch. Speaking of the ranch, why don't we break this camp and get on over to the Rocking N. I'm ready for a little less action."

They broke camp, took the horses to water, and crossed the creek. It was only a few hours to the ranch.

THEY CAME over the north ridge with the horses. Everything looked normal as they rode into the yard. Mr. Nance came hobbling out of the ranch house. Slim was saddling a horse, while Frank and Jimmy waited on horseback. "How about you boys take these animals off our hands?" Josh said.

Slim gave one final tug on the cinch and swung up into the saddle. The three hands herded the horses into the corral. "Good to see you back," Frank said as they took the horses.

Josh swung down from his horse and walked over to help Fianna down. "Thanks, Frank; it's good to be back."

"Mr. Nance, this is Miss Fianna Caitlin O'Reilly. She's Pat's sister, but don't hold that against her." It felt good to joke, Josh thought. The war was over and everyone could relax. Bill Nance and Fianna spoke for a few minutes.

Mary Louise came through the front door, her smiling face lighting up when she saw Fianna, for they didn't see many women at the ranch, especially women her age. "Why, you must be exhausted; come in, and we'll get some water drawn. I know you'd love a bath," Mary Louise said.

Fianna smiled and then said, "That would be so nice."

The girls went into the house, leaving the men standing around in the yard. Scott had stepped out of the bunkhouse. His arm was in a sling, but he looked none the worse for wear. "Howdy, boys, glad you made it back," he said. "I'm just sorry I wasn't able to go with you. Where did you find Miss Fianna? Did you get Ruffcarn? I see you brought back some of Ruffcarn's horses. How'd that happen?"

"Slow down, Scott," Josh said. "We'll tell everyone what happened after we get these horses taken care of."

"Aye, laddie. I think it's a story you'll be enjoying," Pat said as he led his horse to the barn.

The men unsaddled the horses and led them over to the water trough. "How's it been around here?" Josh asked.

Scott said, "Quiet as a church mouse. Why, it's been so quiet you'd think there weren't even any Indians around."

Josh walked over to Chancy. The horse was straining at the stall door to reach him. "How you doing, boy?" Josh asked. He checked the bullet wound in the horse's neck. "Looks like this is healing real good. What did you put on him?"

"Juan had a concoction that he made up personal like," Scott said. "He really took good care of your horse, Josh. He was a good man."

Josh nodded and rubbed Chancy's neck. "Yeah, I'm just sorry we couldn't have gotten here quicker."

After they had finished taking care of the horses, Josh, Pat, and Scott headed for the house. Bill had gone back up onto the porch and was sitting in a rocking chair. "Come on into the house and tell us what happened," Bill said. The men waited as he stood and limped into the house ahead of them. "Let's go into the office."

Teresa came into the office right behind them, carrying cups and the coffee pot on a tray. "Welcome back, *Señor* Josh, *Señor* Pat. It's good to see you safe."

Both men took off their hats. "Thanks, Teresa," Josh said.

"Aye, *señora*, tis good to be back and taste some of your delicious coffee," Pat said.

Teresa smiled and left the room. The men sat down, took a sip of coffee, and waited while Bill fired up his pipe. "Alright, now tell me all about it."

Josh proceeded to tell him about what had happened at Ruffcarn's ranch. He left out nothing.

Bill listened quietly until they were finished. He took a couple more draws on his pipe, then said, "Boys, I appreciate what you've done. Josh, I know you just planned on stopping here long enough to tell us about Rory. I appreciate you staying. I don't mind admitting, I don't think I could've done it without you. I imagine you're planning on heading out soon."

Josh said, "Yes, sir. You've got the wagon we brought down from Tiny's, or at least Scott and Pat did. If it's alright with you, we'll get a good night's rest and take off in the morning. We can take Tiny's wagon and horses back to him. I think Fianna might prefer the wagon after all the horseback riding she's done the past couple of days." Josh turned to Pat. "Is that alright with you, Pat?"

"Aye, 'tis fine with me. I could use a good night's sleep and a couple of Teresa's meals."

Bill said, "That'll be fine with me, though I hate to see you go. By the way, Colonel Sturgis led a patrol through here yesterday afternoon. He brought the message that Jeremiah is out of the woods, and Mrs. Diehl is doing just fine."

"That's good to hear. I know Fianna will be glad to get that news," Josh said.

"Also, Slim is staying on as a hand. I think that boy will make a fine man."

"I couldn't agree with you more," Josh said. "He just got mixed up with the wrong crowd."

Bill turned to Scott. "You think you could hang around and ramrod this place for me?"

"Why, Mr. Nance, I'd be happy to. I've been thinking about settling down. This would be a good place to sit a spell."

Josh turned in his chair to look at Scott. "I thought you were headed to Colorado to do some prospecting? I was planning on offering you a job out there. I could use a good hand."

Bill chuckled, then said, "I think Scott might have found something, or someone, of interest around here."

Scott cleared his throat. His face turned red. "Mr. Nance, I don't—I mean—"

"Relax, Scott," Bill said. "I may be old and shot through with a Comanche arrow, but I'm not blind."

Everyone laughed. Josh said, "This is a first. Since I met him over on Pecan Bayou, I don't think I've seen Scott speechless."

"Why's everyone laughing?" Mary Louise said as the two lovely young women swept into the room.

All the men stood and smiled. Josh couldn't take his eyes off Fianna.

Bill looked at Mary Louise, his eyes twinkling, and said, "I've just offered Scott the foreman position. Seems he found a reason to stay and work with us."

Mary Louise looked quickly at her father. "Good, you need a good foreman." She took Fianna by the arm, flashed a brilliant smile at Scott, and the two beautiful women left the room with a flourish.

EVERYONE WAS GATHERED in the ranch yard. The wagon was hitched up and the horses were anxious to be on their way. The women were saying their goodbyes. Bill shook Josh's hand. "I can't ever repay you for what you and Pat have done."

"Glad to help," Josh said. "If you're ever in Colorado, you'll be welcome at the ranch. It'll be southwest of Colorado City. There's a wide, green valley among the mountains with plenty of water and grass."

"Maybe," Bill said. "Pat, thanks for your help. You and Josh were good friends with Rory, and I appreciate you helping us. I know Rory would be pleased."

"He was a good man, Mr. Nance," Pat said. "I was there when Josh promised Rory to tell you. It's pleased I am to have been able to meet you and your lovely daughter and help a mite."

"We'd best be on our way," Josh said. "We're burning daylight. Teresa, thanks for the good meals. Mary Louise, I'm sure you'll keep your new foreman in line. Scott, though I know you'll be staying here, there will always be a place at our table for you. Mr. Nance, thanks for the horses."

Josh climbed up into the wagon, took the reins, and off they went. He raised his hat and waved. "*Adios.*" They headed north to Camp Wilson. Chancy was tied to the back of the wagon, along with three excellent horses that Bill Nance had insisted they take. "We left early; we should arrive in Camp Wilson tomorrow. Probably no later than noon. What do you think, Pat?"

"Aye, I'm thinking you're right."

"Pat, have you had a chance to think on what we talked about?"

Fianna looked at Josh, then back to her brother. Pat continued to ride in silence. Finally he said, "I've thought on it quite a bit, Josh. I have many concerns. Colorado is a new and wild territory. You'll have plenty of dangers out there. Here you've got the Comanche to contend with. But in the territory there's Ute, Cheyenne, Shoshone, and Arapaho. That's just to name a few. It's no tame land you're going to."

Josh contemplated what Pat had said. "All you say is true, Pat, but the fact is, as a new land—every man, and every woman—" Josh looked at Fianna "—has a chance. It's not yet a state. There will be growth and, for the right people, great opportunity."

Josh could feel Fianna fidgeting next to him on the wagon seat. He chanced a side glance at her. He could tell she had something to say and was about to say it.

"Pat, Josh," Fianna said, "as I told you the other night, if you have something to say about me—*say it to me.*"

Josh looked over at his best friend. "Pat?"

Fianna reached over and yanked the reins out of Josh's hands and pulled the horses to an abrupt halt. "*I said talk to me.*" She was looking back and forth between Pat and Josh. Her brilliant green eyes flashed. Her lovely lips were pursed. It was obvious to Josh that now was the time.

Josh looked at Pat. Pat sighed and said, "I'm thinking Colorado might be a good thing." He grinned at Josh.

Josh turned to Fianna. She was looking at him. Her eyes were wide with anticipation. He took the reins from her hands and tied them around the brake; then he grasped her hands in his. "Fianna," Josh said, "I don't have much more than danger to offer you. But I believe that the two of us can build a life in Colorado that we'll be proud of."

Fianna continued to look into his eyes. "What are you asking me, Major Joshua Matthew Logan?"

"Fianna Caitlin O'Reilly, will you come west with me? Will you be my wife?"

Josh looked at her beautiful face, those lovely emerald eyes, and waited for her answer.

"It took you long enough," she said softly. "Yes. I could think of nothing that would make me happier."

Josh took her in his arms for the first time, there on the wagon seat. He'd never known such contentment and excitement together. She pushed herself back a little to softly press her lips to his.

Pat waited for a few seconds. "Uh-hum," he said, clearing his throat.

The two of them parted, smiled at each other, and grinned at Pat.

"Well, I'm thinking that seals it," Pat said. "We'd best find us a preacher man when we get to Camp Wilson."

31

It was noon of the following day when the happy couple and Pat rode up to Tiny Bakton's Blacksmith and Livery. Tiny walked out to greet them as Josh helped Fianna out of the wagon. Josh asked, "How's Jeremiah and Mrs. Diehl doing?"

"I'm telling you," Tiny said, "that's one tough old ranger. He's already up and moving around—still weak. But that doesn't stop him from sitting out in front of their store to see what's goin' on. Mrs. Diehl was cooking the next day. She hasn't missed a meal. Why, I think she's as tough, or tougher, than Mr. Diehl. Now, your turn. How's the Rocking N?"

Pat stepped down from his horse, put both hands on his kidneys, and leaned back. "It's sure the truth; I'm getting too old for all this riding. Tiny, 'tis all done. Bull and Pierce and Ruffcarn have met their maker, and I'm sure they're not too happy. The ranch is safe. I'm sorry to say that Juan and Lee are dead. Scott received a wee little wound in the shoulder, but he's fine."

"Miss Fianna," Tiny said, "I'm surely glad to see you safe. The whole town was mighty worried about you. Mrs. Diehl will be as happy as a bee in a flower to see you."

Fianna turned a radiant smile on Tiny. "Why, thank you, Tiny. I must hurry and see her." She smiled at Josh and rushed toward the Diehls' store.

"Let's get these horses taken care of," Josh said.

The three men led the horses into the stable. Tiny looked Chancy over, examining the wound's entry and exit. "Look's like your horse is healing well, Josh," Tiny said. "You two go on up. I'll make sure these animals get a good rubdown, feed, and water."

"Thanks, Tiny," Josh said.

Pat and Josh grabbed their saddlebags and rifles and started up the street. Cecil stepped out of the Shamrock Saloon. "Glad to see Fianna is alright. I imagine you boys took care of Ruffcarn and Pierce."

"Aye," Pat said. "We left them both swinging from a big oak tree. Bull died of lead poisoning administered by Josh. We never saw hide nor hair of Bartholf. Looks like he got away. Why don't you join us for lunch at Mrs. Diehl's and we'll tell you all about it. Then I'll come back down for a taste of Irish."

Jeremiah Diehl was sitting in a rocker in the dining room when Pat and Josh entered. "Sorry about not protecting Fianna," Diehl said. "Pierce was just too quick for me."

Pat walked over and shook Jeremiah's hand. "'Tis not much more that you could've done. You're a lucky man, and Mr. Pierce came out the loser when he tangled with me wee sister. She can be quite a handful." Pat glanced over at Josh as he said the last words.

Mrs. Diehl walked into the room beaming. "Josh, I'm so happy for you and Fianna. It just so happens that among his other talents, Mr. Diehl is a minister. He'll be able to fix you two up before you head west. I'm just so glad for you. Fianna, it is lunchtime; would you mind being a dear and help me get this table ready? I'm sure we'll have a crowd, all wanting to hear the news."

It looked like the whole town had turned out. Even Colonel Sturgis, who had just returned from patrol, was there. Everyone sat around the long table with anticipation of hearing the tale of Pierce and Ruffcarn and Bull. Josh and Pat took turns in the telling. Pat told of how Pierce had looked with a sizable portion of his bottom lip gone. They told of the death of Juan Alvarez and Lee Stanton. Colonel Sturgis pitched in that he'd seen Mr. Nance, and he was getting around well, considering the arrow wound in his leg. Fianna couldn't resist telling about the romance between Scott and Mary Louise. There was laughter and appreciation around the table when Pat told the story about Josh inviting Eyes of Hawk and his braves into their camp. When they were about finished, Josh said to Fianna, "We'll need to leave soon. When would you like to get married?"

Fianna smiled, then said, "There's no time like the present, good sir."

"Wait a minute," Mrs. Diehl said. "No woman wants to come right off the trail and get married. Fianna, come with me. Gentlemen, help yourselves to the coffee. It'll take us a while. Mr. Diehl, if you're feeling like it, I would suggest you get your good book ready."

"Pat, I'd consider it an honor if you'd stand up with me," Josh said.

"My honor, Major laddie. 'Tis a blessed day."

Mr. Diehl started giving orders. "Men, get this table cleared off and moved. Josh, go get washed up. You can't get married looking like a saddle bum. I'm not going to be able to stand, so you men bring that rocker over here."

Everyone jumped to, even Colonel Sturgis. When they had everything moved, the colonel turned to Josh. "Major, I have a blouse that's too big for me. I'd consider it an honor if you'd wear it for your marriage."

"I'm no longer in the army, Colonel," Josh said.

"That's not a problem. You served your country with honor. No one would object to you wearing the uniform." Colonel Sturgis hurried back to his quarters.

Josh cleaned up as best he could. The scar across his forehead was fading, but the scar along the side of his head was livid. He looked at himself in the windowpane and wondered what such a beautiful woman could see in him. Through the window, he saw Colonel Sturgis returning with the jacket and a hat.

Colonel Sturgis came in and handed Josh the hat. "I noticed yours. I have a couple of extras. Figured you could use a new one."

Josh tried the hat on. It was just a fit. "I can surely use a new one. I'm much obliged, Colonel."

He had just slipped on and buttoned the jacket when Fianna came into the dining room. She had cleaned up and changed to a lovely soft yellow dress that accentuated the curves of her young body. Her auburn hair cascaded down over her bare shoulders like a waterfall in an evening sunset, but it was her face Josh couldn't take his eyes from. Framed by the red of her hair, her emerald green eyes were lit with happiness. Her full red lips were spread in a smile only for him, exposing perfect white teeth. *I'm the luckiest man in the world.* He looked around the room. Everyone was awestruck by Fianna. Pat offered her his arm and escorted her through the men in the dining room, to Josh.

The ceremony went quickly. Josh could remember only those deep emerald pools and being prompted by Mr. Diehl to say, "Yes."

He heard Fianna whisper, "Yes."

Mr. Diehl said, "I now pronounce you man and wife."

Josh looked down at Mr. Diehl, and Pat said, "Aye, you can kiss her now, laddie."

There were chuckles around the room as Josh bent his head and kissed his wife for the first time. Pat came up and kissed his sister and congratulated Josh. The other men in the room took their turn congratulating the newlyweds. Fianna and Mrs. Diehl were laughing, and everyone was enjoying the wedding. Josh said to Mr. Diehl, "Thank you for all you've done. But we do need to start for Colorado—"

Mrs. Diehl heard him and interrupted, "Josh Logan, what do you mean? It's the middle of the afternoon. You can spend the night here and leave early in the morning—when everyone is rested."

That brought a chuckle from the room.

Josh laughed and smiled at Fianna. "Mrs. Diehl, you didn't let me finish. I was about to say, we do need to start for Colorado, but that will wait till morning. Today we'll enjoy the company of friends, and as you said—get a good rest before we leave."

That brought another round of laughter. The celebration continued through the afternoon. Mrs. Diehl had fixed a massive plate of doughnuts, and Tiny was enjoying himself immensely, as was everyone else.

Josh slipped the jacket off and handed it back to Sturgis. "Thanks, Colonel. I appreciate the loan."

"I couldn't have done it for a better man. You've rid us of vermin we don't need here. Good luck to you."

"Thanks, and good luck to you also." Josh caught Fianna's eye across the room. She was laughing and thoroughly enjoying herself. She was a vision. This was her day. "I need to check on Chancy. I'll be right back, and we can move the party upstairs if that's alright with you?"

"Why, husband, you're a bit forward, aren't you?" Fianna said with laughing eyes. "Yes, go check on your Chancy. I'll be waiting."

"Would you like me to go with you?" Tiny asked around a doughnut.

"No, Tiny," Josh said. "I wouldn't want to be the one to get between you and bear sign." That brought a huge laugh from everyone. "I just want to check on Chancy, and I'll be right back."

Josh stepped outside Diehls' Emporium and Boardinghouse, turned right, and headed to the stable. His boots rang hollow on the boardwalk before he cut across the street. He noticed the stable doors were closed. *I thought Tiny kept the stable open except at night.* He put the momentary concern aside. *Tiny probably closed it for the wedding.* Josh opened the smaller door and stepped into the stable. With the doors closed, it was dark inside. He stood for a moment, waiting for his eyes to adjust.

He felt like a mule kicked him in his left jaw. Dazed, he staggered to his right and fell into the hay pile.

Bartholf reached down, dragged him up, and yanked his Colt out of the holster. "You won't be needing this, soldier boy." He tossed the gun across the stable. "Where's the map?"

Josh's eyes were becoming accustomed to the dim light. He could make out Bartholf clearly. "Are you crazy? You had a chance to be safe—to be gone. Now you're back for that stupid map?" Josh shook his head. "We burned the map in the house—it's gone. And, Bartholf, there never was any gold."

Bartholf stared at Josh. "No map? You burned the map?" He let out a sound like an animal in pain and swung at Josh again.

Only this time Josh wasn't there. He slipped under Bartholf's left jab and planted a quick right hook to Bartholf's floating ribs. It was like he was hitting a wall. Bartholf didn't even wince. Bartholf kicked out and caught Josh backing up. Josh went sprawling onto the floor of the stable. Bartholf was on him cat-fast. He kicked at Josh and caught him a glancing blow in the ribs. Josh rolled again, and as Bartholf aimed a kick at the side of his head, Josh grabbed his boot and twisted hard, throwing Bartholf to the ground. Josh leaped to his feet. Bartholf was on his feet in an instant. He moved in, grinning.

Josh hit him with a straight right jab to the mouth, splitting his lip. Bartholf spit blood and continued to grin, blood showing on his teeth. He feinted with a left jab. Josh fell for it. He dodged to his right, directly into Bartholf's uppercut. It caught him in the solar plexus. He doubled over, backpedaling quickly, trying to get air into his paralyzed lungs and to stay away from Bartholf.

Bartholf moved in again. Josh had barely caught his wind when Bartholf hit him with a straight left jab that caught him above the right eye. The skin split, and blood gushed into his eye. The blow had rocked him back on his heels. He lost his balance and fell through the door into the street. He scrambled back to his feet as Bartholf came through the now open door. Josh stepped in close, feinted with his right, and kicked Bartholf on top of his left kneecap.

They were in the street now. Bartholf went down into the dirt. He held his knee for a moment, then slowly got up. Josh was breathing heavily, but was feeling good. He could feel the adrenaline coursing through his body, and his scalp was starting to tingle. Josh knew rage was taking over, and he didn't care. This was the animal that had pulled his wife onto the horse by her hair.

Bartholf was more cautious now. He threw a left jab, and Josh tossed it off. Sure enough, Bartholf came in with a high right cross. Josh went in under it with a left cross. He put all of his weight behind the punch and slammed Bartholf directly over the liver. The bigger man stopped and folded over from the pain. Josh stepped in and hit him with a right, a left, and a right to the face, smashing his lip and cutting his eye; then he straightened Bartholf with an uppercut to the chin. Bartholf fell back against the hitching rail in front of the King 7. The hitching rail gave way, and he sprawled on the boardwalk.

The liver punch had hurt Bartholf. Josh could see his eyes widen in concern with the realization that he might have met his match. He lay on the boardwalk for a moment, recovering, then pushed himself up to his full height and swung his arms, stretching his back muscles. He glanced away from Josh, then charged. His shirt was torn, and the bulging biceps pushed through the rents in his shirt. Josh tried to move back, but Bartholf came on too fast and managed to get his arms locked around him. The pain in his back was intense as Bartholf squeezed. Josh hit Bartholf a left and right in the face, but Bartholf continued to increase the pressure. In desperation, Josh cupped both hands and slammed them over Bartholf's ears. The instant increase in pressure burst Bartholf's left eardrum. Bartholf dropped Josh as blood erupted from his left ear. He grabbed for his ear, and Josh hit him with another hard hook to his liver. Bartholf went to his knees. He looked up in time to see Josh's big left fist coming straight for his jaw. The sound of the collision between Josh's fist and Bartholf's jaw rivaled the crack of a musket. Bartholf's lower jaw was askew, and he was on his knees with his head lolling from side to side. Josh started to move in again when Pat grabbed him. He turned on Pat with his left hand cocked.

"It's me, Josh," Pat said. "It's over. You beat him. You beat him good."

Josh looked at Pat as if he didn't know him. "Do you know what this animal did to Fianna?"

He felt the rage slowly fading. He looked down at Bartholf and then at his fists. His hands were bloody and bruised. He took a deep breath. His body ached all over. Josh looked around him, realizing for the first time that a crowd had formed. He found Colonel Sturgis. He slowly walked over to the colonel. "Sir, could you take care of this man? He was with Pierce when he shot Mr. Diehl and kidnapped Fianna."

"He'll be dealt with, Major Logan. I must say this has been the best fight that I've ever seen. I'm glad to have known you."

Logan nodded. He was tired. His arms felt like stumps, and his hands were starting to ache. He staggered forward a step and felt someone take his arm and guide him toward the Diehls'

Emporium and Boardinghouse. He looked down through his blood-covered eye and saw his lovely Fianna.

She looked up at him with those emerald green eyes that he loved and said, "You know, Josh, we could stay for two days—before we leave for Colorado."

Suddenly, he felt his fatigue slip away. "Why, Mrs. Logan, I think that's a wonderful idea."

EPILOGUE

I t was another hot day in West Texas. The wind scattered a fine dust over the landscape, but the coyote didn't notice. She was panting from exertion. The pack rat she was chasing had run into his hole, and the hole went deep into the ground. Her pups had not eaten, and she needed to feed them. The pack rat wouldn't be much of a meal, but it would be something, at least until she could kill something bigger.

She had been digging quite a while when she felt a vibration in the ground. She came up out of the ravine to see what was happening. There, across the prairie, was a sight she seldom saw. It was a wagon with several horses, one a big gray, and three humans. The coyote's curiosity got the better of her, and she trotted toward the wagon. She sat on her haunches, licked her front leg for a moment, and watched the redheaded woman point at her. The coyote sat there and scratched behind her right ear as the wagon slowly passed by.

The coyote lost interest and trotted back to her quest. She could hear the wagon slowly moving northwest. The pack rat had tunneled even deeper into the sand. As the coyote dug, her foot hit a rock. The pack rat must be under the rock. She increased her digging, dirt flying out behind her for six feet. The rock was heavier than most rocks, smooth and hard to move. Her foot kept slipping off the rock. Still, she continued to dig. Her pups depended on her. She could smell the pack rat. It wasn't far. She became more frantic. The sun was setting, and she must get back to her pups. She managed to get one foot behind the rock and pulled with all of her might. The pack rat came dashing out as the rock fell and rolled down into the ravine. She had to jump to get out of the way as other rocks followed, but she was ready for the pack rat. She grabbed him and shook him until she knew he was dead; then, with the satisfaction of knowing that she had food for her pups, she trotted proudly out of the ravine and turned toward her den. She had a ways to go and wanted to get there quickly. The setting sun felt good on her back as she trotted away to feed her pups.

The angle of the ravine allowed the setting sun's rays to glint off the rocks she had exposed. They were in the bottom of the ravine, their heavy weight already beginning to force them deeper into the soft sand. They were rectangular in shape and gold in color.

Author's Note

Thank you for reading *Logan's Word*. I hope you enjoyed it.

If you'd like to continue the Logan Family adventure, check out the sequel, *The Savage Valley*. It is available in both ebook and paperback on Amazon.

I would love to hear your comments. You can reach me at don@donaldlrobertson.com, or fill out the contact form at the website below.

Join our readers' group to receive advance notices of new releases, or excerpts from new stories by signing up at:

www.donaldlrobertson.com

You have my word that your information will remain private and will not be shared.

Thanks again, and as Roy and Dale used to sing:

"Happy trails to you, until we meet again."

BOOKS
Logan Family Series

LOGAN'S WORD

THE SAVAGE VALLEY

CALLUM'S MISSION

FORGOTTEN SEASON

SOUL OF A MOUNTAIN MAN

Clay Barlow - Texas Ranger Justice Series

FORTY-FOUR CALIBER JUSTICE

LAW AND JUSTICE

LONESOME JUSTICE

NOVELLAS AND SHORT STORIES

RUSTLERS IN THE SAGE

THE OLD RANGER

BECAUSE OF A DOG

Made in United States
Orlando, FL
26 April 2022

17188440R00171